Clearly, Jonah never knew that he'd swept her off her feet six years ago,

when she'd been a timid, mousy twenty-one-year-old.

Then he'd shown up here in Big Bend Country, as tall and good-looking, as virile and sexy, as she remembered.

And this time around, he looked at her and smiled at her the way he had in her dreams.

Of course, his smile would fade if she told him the truth, revealed her true identity.

Still, whether or not she did had nothing to do with his opinion of her and everything to do with what was best for little Joey.

Her orphaned nephew. *His* nephew, unbeknownst to him....

Dear Reader,

Welcome to Special Edition…where each month we publish six novels celebrating love and life, with a special romance blended in.

You'll revel in *Baby Love* by Victoria Pade, our touching THAT'S MY BABY! title and another installment in her ongoing A RANCHING FAMILY saga. In this emotional tale, a rugged rancher becomes an instant daddy—and solicits the help of Elk Creek's favorite nurse to give him lessons on bringing up baby.

And there's much more engaging romance on the way! Bestselling author Christine Rimmer continues her CONVENIENTLY YOURS miniseries with her thirtieth novel, about an enamored duo who masquerade as newlyweds—and brand-new parents—in *Married by Accident*. And you won't want to miss *Just the Three of Us,* Jennifer Mikels's tender love story about a high-society lady and a blue-collar bachelor who are passionately bound together for the sake of an adorable little boy. Then an estranged tycoon returns to the family fold and discovers unexpected love in *The Secret Millionaire* by Patricia Thayer— the first book in her WITH THESE RINGS series, which crosses into Silhouette Romance in September with *Her Surprise Family.*

Rounding off the month, Lois Faye Dyer will sweep you off your feet with a heartwarming reunion romance that results in a surprise pregnancy, in *The Only Cowboy for Caitlin.* And in *Child Most Wanted* by veteran author Carole Halston, a fiercely protective heroine hides her true identity to safeguard her nephew, but she never counted on losing her heart to the man who could claim her beloved boy as his own.

I hope you enjoy these books, and each and every novel to come!

Sincerely,

Karen Taylor Richman
Senior Editor

Please address questions and book requests to:
Silhouette Reader Service
U.S.: 3010 Walden Ave., P.O. Box 1325, Buffalo, NY 14269
Canadian: P.O. Box 609, Fort Erie, Ont. L2A 5X3

CAROLE HALSTON

CHILD MOST WANTED

Published by Silhouette Books
America's Publisher of Contemporary Romance

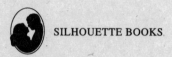 SILHOUETTE BOOKS

ISBN 0-373-24254-9

CHILD MOST WANTED

Copyright © 1999 by Carole Halston

Look us up on-line at: http://www.romance.net

Printed in U.S.A.

Books by Carole Halston

Silhouette Special Edition

Keys to Daniel's House #8
Collision Course #41
The Marriage Bonus #86
Summer Course in Love #115
A Hard Bargain #139
*Something Lost,
    Something Gained* #163
A Common Heritage #211
The Black Knight #223
Almost Heaven #253
Surprise Offense #291
Matched Pair #328
Honeymoon for One #356
The Baby Trap #388
High Bid #423
Intensive Care #461
Compromising Positions #500
Ben's Touch #543
Unfinished Business #567
Courage to Love #642
Yours, Mine and...Ours #682
The Pride of St. Charles Avenue #800
More Than He Bargained For #829
Bachelor Dad #915
A Self-Made Man #950
The Wrong Man...the Right Time #1089
Mrs. Right #1125
I Take This Man—Again! #1222
Child Most Wanted #1254

Silhouette Romance

Stand-In Bride #62
Love Legacy #83
Undercover Girl #152
Sunset in Paradise #208

Silhouette Books

To Mother with Love 1992
"Neighborly Affair"

CAROLE HALSTON

lives with her husband, Monty, in a rural area on the north shore of Lake Pontchartrain, near New Orleans. They are camping enthusiasts and tow their twenty-six-foot travel trailer to beautiful spots all over the United States.

Fans can write Carole at P.O. Box 1095, Madisonville, LA 70447. For a free autographed bookmark, send a self-addressed, stamped business-size envelope. Visit Carole's web site by accessing the Harlequin Enterprises site (http://www.romance.net), where she is listed as a Harlequin/Silhouette author.

Chapter One

"A kid?" Jonah Rhodes was taken aback. "You're telling me this Molly Jones is a single mother?"

That bit of information pretty much clinched his gut instinct: he was wasting his time here in Amarillo, Texas. When the police in his hometown back in Georgia had passed along the tip, he'd been skeptical that it would lead him to the Gulley sisters. In truth, Jonah's zeal for tracking down the fugitive pair and bringing them to justice had died during the past six years. But since he'd been headed to southwest Texas, anyway, he'd detoured the extra miles out of a sense of brotherly duty.

"Old Mr. Griffen wasn't sure which of the two gals was the birth mother," explained Betty Willie, the informant. Her dyed red hair, framing a plump face, looked unnaturally bright even in the dim lighting of her over-furnished apartment. "Molly, the older gal, took care of the little tike. He kept on living with her after the younger gal, Lynette, wasn't around anymore. Old Mr. Griffen figured Lynette must have taken off with the boyfriend who always picked her up on a motorcycle.'' Betty heaved a sigh as Jonah shifted restlessly on the sofa. ''I wish Mr. Griffen hadn't up and died of a heart attack last week. You coulda got his story firsthand. And he coulda shared in the ten-thousand-dollar reward,'' she added on a hopeful note.

The greedy glint in her hazel eyes stirred disgust in Jonah. He reminded himself that he'd originally offered the reward six years ago, intending to capitalize on the greed that led one human being to betray another for monetary gain. At the time he'd acted out of the bitter rage that had consumed him when his sixteen-year-old brother, Joel Rhodes, was violently killed and the person responsible, Joel's juvenile-delinquent girlfriend, Karen Gulley, fled from the law and escaped any punishment. The way Jonah saw it, Karen might as well have pulled the trigger of the policeman's gun that fired the fatal bullet. Joel had been a good kid before he got mixed up with her.

The older sister, Susan Gulley, who'd skipped town with her bad-egg sibling, shared the blame. She'd refused to cooperate when Jonah had sought her out just a month prior to the tragic episode that had ended in Joel's death and the eventual disintegration of the Rhodes family. Jonah remembered begging the pretty young blond woman to do everything in her power to break up the teenage couple. He'd been wasting his breath. Susan had defended Karen and made excuses for her.

''The ages are right.'' Betty Willie broke into Jonah's grim thoughts. ''Three years ago when old Mr. Griffen saw that cable TV program about rewards for missing persons that hadn't ever been collected, he placed Molly Jones in her early or mid-twenties. And she was blond with blue eyes. He guessed Lynette Jones to be eighteen or nineteen. Her hair was black instead of brown, but you can't tell about the real color of women's hair.'' Betty raised a dimpled hand and patted her overly bright auburn locks.

''Why didn't Mr. Griffen contact the Georgia police himself after he saw the TV program three years ago?'' asked Jonah. Dozens of other people all over the United States had. By then Jonah was married to Darleen and busy making fortunes for his investment clients and himself. He'd put his family tragedy behind him, had even forgotten about the reward, which amounted to a bounty on the heads of the two runaway sisters.

Betty was answering his question. ''The old fellow was too softhearted. Several times when he was carrying in groceries, the older gal, Molly, took the time to stop and help him. So he didn't want to get her in any trouble. He didn't even mention his suspicions to the neighbors until after she and the little boy moved out a month or so after the TV show. Nobody paid any attention to the poor old guy.''

Until Betty Willie had come along several years later, heard Mr. Griffen's story and acted on it.

''Jones could be an alias,'' she said.

''Yes, along with Smith and any number of other common names. I've checked, and there's no phone listing for a Molly Jones or an M. Jones in Amarillo. No Lynette or L. Jones. Nor do the police have any knowledge of them.''

''You could hire a private investigator.''

''If there were more reason to believe these two women really are the Gulley sisters, I could hire a private investigator,'' Jonah agreed. His glance fell on a partially completed sweepstakes entry form that lay on the coffee table atop the litter of advertisements for magazines and other merchandise that had accompanied the form.

Betty followed his gaze and heaved another disappointed sigh, apparently reading his thoughts—that his odds of following up her tip and locating the Gulley sisters were about the same as her odds of winning the sweepstakes prize of ten million dollars emblazoned on the entry form.

"You lost all interest when I mentioned there'd been a little boy about two or three years old," she commented, rising to her feet as Jonah stood up, preparing to leave.

He nodded. "The time scenario makes it unlikely there would have been a child that age."

During their first nine months as fugitives, one of the two sisters would have had to get pregnant and carry the baby to term. Based on his very brief acquaintance with Susan, the older girl, he couldn't quite picture her as the type to sleep around. If anything, he would have guessed she was a virgin. And Karen, hard-boiled at sixteen, wasn't the type to be an unwed mother. She would have taken the easy way out and gotten an abortion.

No, Jonah didn't believe this Molly and Lynette Jones were the Gulley sisters, and, frankly, he was relieved rather than disappointed as he strode toward his brand-new pickup truck out in the parking lot of the apartment complex. A divorced man now, Jonah was starting out a new life by taking off six months to a year and doing some long-overdue traveling around the U.S.A. The last thing he wanted was to reopen the unhappiest chapter of his past.

Minutes later Jonah was headed due south on I-27, his destination Big Bend National Park. As far as he was concerned, the search for the Gulley sisters was officially ended.

"Can I help you find a particular book?" inquired a petite brunette woman. The name tag pinned on her brown park ranger's uniform identified her as Heidi Sykes.

"Thanks, but I'm just browsing," Jonah replied, smiling his appreciation for her helpfulness.

He'd arrived at the park yesterday in the early afternoon and set up camp in the Basin camping area. This morning he'd risen early and gone hiking. Having gotten his exercise, he'd decided to visit the main Visitors' Center at Panther's Junction during the afternoon. After inspecting the interesting exhibits, which included a topographical model of the huge park situated in a bend of the Rio Grande, he'd wandered into the gift/bookshop and was fast collecting a whole stack of informative books and guides to purchase.

With no TV, there would be plenty of time to read up on the history of the area and the flora and fauna. Jonah would probably spend a couple of weeks here in Big Bend country before he moved on. It would take every bit that long—and perhaps longer—to explore the park, which encompassed over seven hundred thousand acres of rugged Chihuahua Desert wilderness.

Vast was certainly the key word to describe the landscape with its rocky mountain ranges and valleys and plains stretching as far as the eye could see. *Awesome* kept coming to mind, too. The congestion of downtown Atlanta seemed far, far away in another world entirely. Jonah didn't miss the hustle and bustle one bit, although, admittedly, it felt strange having leisure time on his hands.

"Hi, Roger. Welcome back. How was your vacation?"

Jonah couldn't help overhearing Heidi's voice, since she was standing only a few feet away.

"It was a nice change of pace," came a man's reply. "I visited my folks up in Michigan."

"You saw the flyer I put on your desk about the bingo fund-raiser tomorrow night in Study Butte?"

Roger chuckled. "I saw it, and I read your note." He sounded sheepish.

"I knew you wouldn't want to miss it when you learned that Molly Jones would be there."

"You got that right. She's calling the numbers?"

Jonah had been trying to tune out the conversation. Suddenly he was eavesdropping against his will, smothering a curse. Why couldn't these two have had this chat out of his earshot?

"Yep. Which means she'll be in plain sight for you to gaze at her like a sick calf. Why don't you ask her out, for Pete's sake? She's single."

"Because I haven't worked up enough nerve. I get tongue-tied when I talk to her. She's so…fine."

"You men always fall for the pretty blue-eyed blondes," Heidi accused.

No denial was forthcoming from Roger. "Well, I've got to go check out the Glenn Springs Road and make sure it hasn't washed out," he said. "See you around, Heidi."

Jonah turned his head and got a look at Roger. He was a well-built sandy-haired man in his late twenties who might have come straight off a Michigan farm to don his brown park uniform.

This blue-eyed blond woman named Molly Jones undoubtedly wasn't the same Molly Jones who'd been living in Amarillo three years ago. There were probably several dozen women with the same name and the same general description residing in the state of Texas. Even if she turned out to be the Molly Jones who'd helped old Mr. Griffen with his grocery sacks, that didn't increase the odds that she was Susan Gulley, originally from Columbus, Georgia.

Still, Jonah knew damn well he would have to satisfy himself that he hadn't stumbled upon the Gulley sisters' whereabouts. The easiest way to do that would be to go to the bingo fund-raiser himself and get a look at the park ranger Roger's heartthrob.

The very fact that she was calling the numbers for the bingo game made him that much more skeptical she would turn out to be Susan Gulley in disguise. Susan had struck him as far too shy to be comfortable standing in front of a group of people. Also, while she was certainly a pretty girl, Jonah couldn't imagine her having the kind of effect on Roger that would make the park ranger tongue-tied in her presence.

After tomorrow night Jonah intended to turn a deaf ear if he happened to hear the name Molly Jones again, in Texas or elsewhere.

The drive to Study Butte, a former mining community, was roughly fifty miles along two-lane highways, most of that distance within the park itself. Mindful of the forty-five miles per hour speed limit, Jonah allowed plenty of time. With virtually no traffic, he settled back, his resentment of being on a wild-goose chase fading as he gazed out at the wilderness scenery and watched the rugged mountain ranges turn shades of delicate violet that deepened to purple as night fell.

Following Heidi's directions, Jonah easily located the community center in Study Butte, population less than a hundred people. It had been named after a miner named Will Study, who pronounced his surname Stewdy, hence the odd pronunciation.

The community center building was a plain one-story cement-block structure painted the tan color of adobe. Some talented artist had used the outside walls as a canvas and created a mural depicting the colorful and lawless era of the past when Mexican banditos and fierce warring Indians roamed freely in Big Bend country. The figures on horseback seemed so lifelike that Jonah made a mental note to come back during the daylight with his camera.

The parking lot wasn't paved. Jonah's hiking boots kicked up little clouds of red dust as he walked from his pickup to the building. Other arrivals spoke to him with casual friendliness. Jonah couldn't help noticing that Western garb was the chosen style. Men and women wore cowboy boots and tooled-leather belts with ornate silver buckles. Stetson hats were apparently as common down here in southwest Texas as baseball caps were back in rural and small-town Georgia.

Thanks to Heidi, Jonah understood the setup when he entered. A woman and a man, seated behind a table just inside the door, were distributing bingo cards and accepting money. A poster-size sign stated what Heidi had explained—there was no charge, since public gambling wasn't legal in the state of Texas. However, a five-dollar per card donation to the school fund would be much appreciated. Jonah handed over a twenty and took four cards.

A quick glance around told him that, not surprisingly, none of the women present resembled Susan Gulley. For all he knew, Molly Jones might not be among them yet, but Jonah felt positive she wouldn't resemble Susan when she stepped up on the platform at one end of the room, where a microphone on a stand had been positioned near a wire cage with ping-pong-size numbered balls.

A concessions counter was located along an adjacent wall. Long tables surrounded by folding chairs took up the rest of the space. Jonah made his way to a table in the center that had an unoccupied chair facing the platform. Once he'd sat down, he soon began chatting with two outgoing local people who seemed to be real characters—a man named Casey, who owned and ran a gas station in Study Butte, and a real estate agent named

Flora. Both were retirement age, probably in their late sixties, but it was obvious that neither of them had any thoughts of retiring because they thrived on their work.

That's what he wanted to find, Jonah reflected, a means of livelihood that he could enjoy. While he was traveling around the country, he intended to be on the lookout for a good business opportunity, preferably in a small-town setting. Jonah had tolerated big-city life, but he hadn't liked it.

"Guess it's time to get the show on the road," Casey said.

"Doesn't Molly look pretty in that red dress?" Flora commented, her tone fondly approving. Like Casey, she was gazing toward the platform.

The din of voices had quieted and people were arranging their bingo cards with an air of expectation. Jonah looked toward the platform, too, with mild curiosity that swiftly turned to disbelief. He blinked and stared at the woman standing before the microphone. Her shoulder-length tawny hair was streaked with golden blond. She wore a short red dress and red Western boots, a white Stetson set at a saucy angle on the back of her head.

Pretty didn't quite describe her. She was a knockout.

More to the point, Jonah was almost certain she was Susan Gulley.

"Is everybody feeling lucky tonight?" she drawled into the microphone. Her amplified voice sent shivers down Jonah's spine, shivers of male pleasure. When a dozen people called out friendly responses, she smiled a dazzling smile that speeded up his pulse. "We have some great prizes just waiting to be claimed."

"Is one of the prizes a kiss, Molly?" called out the man who had been working at the door.

"Shame on you, Charlie. You're making me blush,"

she chided him. ''Without any further ado, why don't we get started? Watch those cards closely, folks.''

Jonah could have cared less about watching his cards. He didn't take his eyes off her while she manually rotated the cage, plucked out a ball that had popped into a cuplike receptacle, then read out the number. ''B-4.''

Doubt had set in. Despite the resemblance, this vibrant, self-assured woman couldn't be the shy, demure Susan Gulley he remembered well from that one meeting six years ago. She'd blushed whenever their eyes had met. The voice was different, too. Molly Jones sounded more Texan than Southern.

She's not Susan, Jonah told himself, relaxing.

Afterward he would seek Molly Jones out and introduce himself and ask her whether she had relatives in Georgia. A grin tugged at Jonah's lips as he admitted he was glad to have a good excuse to talk to Molly Jones. Now it was easy to understand why the park ranger from Michigan, Roger, was bowled over. Jonah was in pretty much the same state.

''You have B-4,'' Flora said to him, reaching out a beringed hand to tap one of his cards.

''Thanks, Flora.'' Jonah obligingly placed a cardboard disk in the square she'd indicated.

He tended his cards in a lackadaisical manner as Molly proceeded in her role of numbers caller, her gaze roving over the faces of the crowd. Jonah was amused by his own eagerness for her to make eye contact with him. Had he ever been this attracted to a woman on sight before?

Certainly not to Susan Gulley, although he'd found her pretty and appealing before he'd brought up the subject of Karen Gulley. At that point any man-woman interaction had died.

Molly had finally zeroed in on the people at Jonah's table. Casey and Flora both waved at her. Her smile grew warm as her gaze lingered on them. Jonah silently urged her to look at him. Finally she did. His smile automatically broadened, while hers froze on her lips. For the space of a few seconds she stared at him as though she'd seen a ghost. Then she quickly recovered her poise.

Jonah was jolted by her reaction. Maybe he was wrong. Maybe she was Susan Gulley, and she'd recognized him.

For Molly, spotting Jonah Rhodes among the crowd was like the awful reverse of waking up from a nightmare and being relieved and grateful that the nightmare wasn't real. One moment she was feeling safe and happy. The next moment her worst fear had come true.

The Rhodes family had tracked her down. Had they learned of Joey's existence and put two and two together?

Panic seized Molly. It was all she could do to stand there on the platform and go through the motions of calling the bingo numbers when frantic instinct told her to rush home to her condo and grab her nephew up in her arms, buckle him into her automobile and drive as fast as she dared for parts unknown.

A vision of the precious five-year-old boy helped restore sanity. Thirty minutes ago when she'd left him, dressed in his new Batman pajamas, he'd been proudly holding out a plate of cookies to Manuel, his teenage sitter whom he greatly admired. Earlier in the afternoon Molly and Joey had made the cookies together.

I'm not running away this time, Molly resolved. I'll stand my ground and fight.

Her immediate challenge was to get through the next two hours. That is, if Jonah Rhodes were patient enough to sit through the fund-raiser. The prospect of his creating a scene before her friends and neighbors set off fresh waves of panic that Molly had to subdue as she mechanically went through the motions of calling the numbers.

"Bingo!" called a woman's voice.

The winner was Heidi Sykes, who worked for the park service. After she'd read off her numbers to verify them, she came up to the stage to claim her prize, a gift certificate for a gas fill-up at Casey Doyle's gas station in Study Butte.

"Hey, Heidi, now don't run out of gas getting your tank plumb empty," Casey called out to her.

His joking remark brought laughter and prompted other facetious comments. Molly welcomed the diversion of attention away from her and risked a glance at Jonah Rhodes. He was looking intently at her, the smile gone from his face.

It dawned on her suddenly that he had been smiling when she first saw him. A friendly male smile. She couldn't imagine that Jonah Rhodes would feel in the least friendly toward her, whether or not he knew about Joey. Could this man possibly be a stranger with an amazing resemblance to the handsome older brother of Joel Rhodes?

Please, God, Molly prayed.

Bolstered by cautious hope, she spoke into the microphone and settled the crowd down. As she resumed calling out numbers for the next round of bingo, Molly kept a watch on the man and grew more optimistic. He must be a stranger. If he were Jonah, his expression would be hard and accusing. Vengeful. Instead he had a thoughtful, puzzled air.

The next person to call out "Bingo!" was Ellie Sommerfield, the wife of a rancher. The fact that two women in a row had been winners brought loud joking complaints from some of the local men.

"Hey, maybe it's ladies' night, guys," Molly quipped into the microphone. She'd relaxed enough that her smile felt more natural on her lips. She allowed herself a bold glance at the Jonah Rhodes look-alike. Whatever had been bothering him, he'd evidently put it out of his mind.

He grinned back at her, his eyes sending admiring male signals. Molly's heart did a little flip-flop and her pulse quickened. Whoever he was, he affected her the same way Jonah had six years ago on that one occasion she'd talked to him. He'd bought her a cup of coffee at a café in her hometown. His hometown, too, although he had relocated to Atlanta.

At that time Molly had been terribly shy. Her name hadn't been Molly then, of course. It had been necessary to take on a different identity to protect Joey, necessary to become a different person altogether, a person she liked a whole lot better than her old timid self. Six years ago she would never have had the confidence to stand on a stage in front of a hundred people.

A new thought flashed into Molly's head. Had she changed so much outwardly that people who'd known her back in Georgia, including Jonah Rhodes, might not recognize her now?

Maybe the man sitting out there was Jonah, and he'd gotten that puzzled air from trying to figure out why she seemed familiar.

One way or another, she would find out who he was later on. Because before he left tonight, he would try to meet her. Intuition told her that.

Molly quieted the hubbub and turned the crank of the cage, aware that her fear and nervousness were mixed with anticipation.

As things turned out, it wasn't necessary to wait until the fund-raiser was over to end the mystery. After Molly had called a long series of numbers, Flora Holmburg exclaimed in her throaty voice, ''You've got bingo on two cards, dear boy!'' She was addressing the man who'd become the focal point of Molly's attention.

''So I do,'' he said with slight surprise.

Molly seized the opportunity fate had given her. After he'd read out the numbers and she'd verified them, she followed the same format she'd used with the previous two winners. ''Congratulations to—'' She broke off, adding apologetically, ''I'm sorry, but I don't believe I know you personally.''

If he didn't readily volunteer his name, Molly would drop the matter right there. Down here in Big Bend country, people's names, along with all the other facts about themselves were their own business. It was a hangover from more lawless days.

He rose to his feet. Molly held her breath with the awful suspense, panic flaring up inside her. What was he going to do? What was he going to say? *I think you do know me very well.*

''I'd sure like to correct that,'' he said, and grinned at the male chuckles. ''I'm Jonah Rhodes, originally from Columbus, Georgia.'' His voice was as deep and attractive as Molly remembered it being.

She clasped the microphone stand, needing to hang on to something for support. Everything hinged on her acting ability. The slightest hint of recognition would be her undoing. ''Hi, Jonah. You can come and get your prize. It's a good one, too. Four coupons for a Texas-size mug of coffee and a big slice of homemade pie at the Cactus Café. Yum-yum. Right, folks?''

Jonah was making his way to the platform, threading a path between tables. *Just look at him as a good-looking guy who's a stranger*, Molly said to herself.

It was easy advice to follow. Molly came up with all pluses and no minuses as she took in the details of Jonah's appearance. Neatly trimmed dark brown hair. Brown eyes.

Clean-cut, strong facial features. Height about six foot two. Broad shoulders. Rangy, muscular build. Jeans and denim shirt. Plain leather belt and hiking boots.

He'd reached the platform.

"Here you are." Molly stepped to the edge and held out an envelope containing the coupons. He accepted it with his left hand, which was bare of a wedding ring.

"Thanks, Molly," he said without any hesitation in speaking her alias.

"You're welcome," she answered. "Enjoy your coffee and pie."

Almost euphoric with her relief, Molly offered up a prayer of thanks as she returned to her station in front of the microphone. She would deal later with her other emotions, including the absurd sense of hurt that she'd deceived Jonah Rhodes so easily.

Obviously she hadn't made the same kind of indelible impression on him six years ago that he'd made on her.

Chapter Two

"We'll take a fifteen-minute break," Molly announced at the midway point. "Snacks and soft drinks will be on sale at the concessions counter. So stretch your legs, folks."

Jonah sprang to his feet. He was thirsty, but he would pass on buying a soft drink. The urge to talk to Molly Jones was much stronger.

Apparently he wasn't the only person in the room with the same urge. By the time he'd made his way through the milling bodies and gotten within ten yards of her, she was surrounded by a cluster of men and women, among them Roger, the park ranger. Jonah had spotted him earlier, wearing a fancy Western shirt.

Damn. Sharp frustration welled up inside Jonah.

After hanging around for ten minutes, he reconciled himself to waiting until later to get Molly aside. By hook or by crook he was going to talk to her privately before he left here tonight.

The crowd at the concessions counter had thinned out. Jonah bought a soft drink and was downing it when Flora joined him. Suppressing his disgruntlement, he made conversation with the real estate agent, inquiring where her office was located.

"It's in the Mexican Village, between Study Butte and Terlingua on Highway 170," she replied. "So is the Cactus Café. So is Clementine's Closet, the dress shop Molly manages."

Jonah perked up as he digested the scrap of valuable information Flora had dropped. Now he knew where to find Molly after tonight. "I've seen ads for the Mexican Village in some of the tourist publications," he recalled.

"It's the closest thing to a shopping mall you'll find down here in Big Bend country. Drop in and say hi to me, too," she said with a knowing smile.

"I'll do that," Jonah answered, grinning. He didn't pretend not to understand what she meant—that when he visited the Mexican Village for whatever reason, he would definitely be looking Molly Jones up at her place of employment.

When he'd won his prize earlier tonight, Jonah had stuck the envelope in a back pocket of his jeans, figuring he would keep one of the coupons for free coffee and pie at the Cactus Café, on the chance he might use it, and give the others away to people at his table. Now he would keep at least two of the coupons. They gave him the perfect excuse to take Molly on a coffee break.

Not that he needed an excuse.

"It's time to win some more great prizes. Folks, please find your chairs." Molly's amplified voice filled the room, creating the pleasurable shivers down Jonah's spine.

As he accompanied Flora back to their table, he reflected that he hadn't been surprised to learn this gorgeous woman with an uncanny resemblance to Susan Gulley held down a management job. It was more reason to doubt Molly was Susan in disguise. When he'd met Susan six years ago, at the age of twenty-one, she'd been employed as a checkout person at a major discount store. Jonah remembered her being rather apologetic about her job and telling him that she was taking night courses toward a college degree in business.

He remembered himself feeling sorry for her because she hadn't been fortunate enough to have parents to send her to college. According to Joel, the father had abandoned his family early on, and the mother had drunk herself to death. Susan and Karen had been raised in foster homes as wards of the state. It wasn't the best kind of childhood, granted, but Jonah's sympathy hadn't extended to being willing to see his brother's life ruined.

Sympathy had died altogether when Joel was gunned down and it was too late to save him from Karen Gulley's destructive influence.

Jonah shook off the bad memory, returning to the present and the male enjoyment of feasting his eyes on Molly Jones in her red dress and red Western boots and white Stetson hat, an outfit he couldn't imagine that Susan Gulley would ever wear.

"Good night, folks. A big thank-you from all of us parents for making this fund-raiser for the school a success." Molly blew a kiss and turned away from the microphone.

For just a moment the earlier panic rose up inside her. Keep your cool, Molly, she ordered herself, taking in a deep calming breath. With any luck, Jonah Rhodes would be heading for the exit. Outside he would get into his automobile and drive off into the night and soon forget about her. If so, she would have escaped this close call.

"Great job, Molly." Charlie Pendergast had stepped up on the platform.

"Thanks, Charlie."

He went over to unplug the microphone cord. "The cleanup committee will take over from here," he said.

"I can stay a few minutes and help out."

"We have plenty of hands. You've already done your part."

Molly glanced over her shoulder and saw Jonah's dark head and broad shoulders disappearing through the door. Sure enough, he was leaving without talking to her.

She eased out a breath. "In that case, I'll go home and pay my sitter."

It took Molly another five minutes to make her exit by the time she paused to accept compliments from the half-dozen or so local people who were busily stacking folding chairs and sweeping the floor and bagging up garbage.

Emerging from the building, she saw that the parking lot had nearly emptied. Her dark green sports utility vehicle stood alone. She had started toward it before she noticed a man sitting on the rear bumper of a pickup truck. He stood up.

Jonah Rhodes.

He hadn't left, after all.

"Hi," he said. "I was hoping you would come out sooner or later."

Molly had stopped in her tracks. She pressed a fisted hand against her pounding heart. "It's not a good idea to sneak up on people in this part of the country. You could get yourself shot."

"Sorry. I didn't mean to give you a scare."

"Apology accepted. Was there something I could do for you?" she asked politely. Her legs were strong enough to propel her forward again. She started walking toward her car.

"Satisfy my curiosity, for one thing," he replied, moving so that her path would bring her abreast of him.

"What would you like to know?"

"You weren't by chance living in Amarillo, Texas, about three years ago, were you?"

Oh, God, had he tracked her and Lynette to Amarillo? If so, he must know about Joey.

Molly found her voice. "I would have said it was by choice rather than chance, but, yes, I lived in Amarillo before moving here to Big Bend country. Why?"

He fell into step with her. "I was there a few days ago, interviewing a woman named Betty Willie who claimed she had information about two sisters originally from Columbus, Susan and Karen Gulley. She described two young women who had previously been tenants in her apartment building. Their names were Molly Jones and Lynette Jones."

Molly's knees had turned to jelly, but by some miracle they didn't buckle under her. She kept walking at the same pace. "Are you a private detective?"

"No, just someone with a good reason to track down the Gulley sisters. They were involved in a family tragedy." His tone was grim, striking new fear in Molly's heart.

"I don't recall a Betty Willie in my apartment building in Amarillo," she said.

"There's no reason you should. She'd only heard about you from her neighbor, an old man you may remember, Ed Griffen. He died recently."

"I'm sorry to hear that. Yes, I do remember him, but we never had an actual conversation. I can't imagine how he concluded I was a native of Georgia."

"Bear with me, and I'll fill you in as briefly as possible."

They reached her car just as he was finishing his

sketchy explanation. Molly was grateful now that she'd had to park so far from the building when she arrived earlier tonight. The yellow rays of light from the outside fixtures barely reached this far. She would have preferred total darkness, but the sky overhead was brilliant with a million stars.

"So after watching this TV program, Mr. Griffen got it into his head that I was one of these fugitive sisters? How bizarre." Molly hadn't seen the TV program or even heard about it. How frightening to be so oblivious to danger.

"What's really bizarre is that you actually do look a lot like the older sister, Susan. I take it you don't have relatives in Georgia."

"None that I know about. But then I have a rather bare family tree."

"Frankly, I'm glad you're not Susan Gulley," he said. "Because I'd sure like to see you again."

There was no doubting his sincerity. She'd managed to fool him.

"I'm afraid I don't have time for a social life, not while my son is small." Molly opened the door of her automobile. He stood out of the way as she swung the door wide. Then he moved closer and grasped her elbow to help her up into the seat, his touch strong and warm and male.

"Is that a tactful way of telling me to get lost?" he asked.

"It's partly that, as well as being truthful with you." The bluntness was necessary to combat her own complicated regrets.

"Ouch. I guess I'm more out of practice in the dating game than I realized." His tone was rueful, but Molly could sense that he was smarting with her rejection.

She started up the engine, quelling the impulse to

soothe his injured feelings. "Goodbye," she said. "Enjoy your stay in Big Bend country."

"Thanks." He closed the door of her automobile and turned to walk away with long strides without bidding her goodbye.

Joey's uncle.

Molly shifted into gear, stepped on the gas and turned the wheel sharply. Instead of backing out, she made a tight U-turn and drove away fast.

"Thank you, Manuel." Molly handed bills to the gangly Mexican-American teenage boy. His face lit up as he quickly examined the amount before stuffing the bills into his jeans pocket. She'd paid him more generously than usual tonight.

"I guess I'll be going." He was already taking loping steps toward the foyer.

Molly followed behind him. At the front door, he paused to let her catch up with him. "You gonna need me to sit with Joey the night of that potluck supper and dance at the community center a couple of weeks from now?" he inquired nonchalantly.

"If you don't have a date. It's on a Saturday night."

The boy blushed and shuffled his feet, which looked huge in his black high-top athletic shoes. "That's okay. It's easy money. Joey's not a brat like most little kids are."

"No, he isn't a brat." Ever the adoring aunt and surrogate mother, Molly was quick to agree. "Plus he admires you too much to act up."

The idea of himself as a role model brought on more blushing and shuffling of feet. "Well, so long."

"Good night, Manuel."

He bolted toward his battered compact car. But before he folded his lanky body behind the wheel, he stopped long enough to say, "Oh, yeah, I almost forgot. The cookies were good."

"I'm glad you enjoyed them."

Molly closed the door and locked it, reliving the scene with Joey in the kitchen when they were making the homemade cookies for a treat for him and Manuel.

The cookies had been the slice-and-bake variety. Molly had sliced and Joey had placed the rounds of dough on the baking pan, patted them flat and created faces or designs with chopped nuts and chocolate chips.

"Cut a fat one," he'd urged. "I want to make a big cookie specially for Manuel."

Molly had done his bidding and watched lovingly as the five-year-old flattened a round of dough twice as large as the others and labored over decorating it with a smiley face. "Very nice," she complimented, leaning over to kiss him on the forehead.

"We need to hurry and get them cooked before Manuel gets here," he said.

"There's plenty enough time for the cookies to bake and for you to take a bath and put on your pj's," Molly assured him.

Still he made quick work of fashioning the remaining cookies, then scrambled down from his tall stool while she was sliding the pan into the oven.

"I'll wear my Batman pajamas! Manuel thinks they're cool!" With those eager words, he made a dash for his bedroom.

Molly set the timer and followed behind him, thinking that she ought to try to find a good man to marry, a guy who likes kids. Her little nephew's hero worship of a teenage male sitter brought home the fact that not only was Joey growing up fatherless, but without any male relatives. Obviously he was hungry for masculine company.

Joey had an uncle and a grandfather, but they didn't

know he existed. She'd sighed. She couldn't risk having them know about him.

Briefly she'd visualized Jonah Rhodes's face, which had been etched in her memory years before. She'd felt the whole range of disturbing emotions associated with him, some of which had nothing to do with Joey. Then, an hour later, she'd looked out and seen Jonah in the flesh. For one shocked moment, nightmare and fantasy and naked reality had clashed and merged.

Now she wondered how he would react to the truth. What if she told him, I am Susan Gulley. No, the truth would be: I was Susan Gulley before I became Molly Jones. My sister, Karen, is dead. I'm raising her precious son. He's your nephew, too, because his father was your brother, Joel.

Would Jonah be ready to forgive and forget the past? Would he have it in his heart to love Joey and become a real uncle to the little boy?

Molly couldn't answer those crucial questions without putting Joey in harm's way, and she wasn't willing to do that. Plus the elder Rhodes parents posed another unknown. How would they treat the news that they had a grandson? Could they love him despite the tragic circumstances? Also, there was the danger that they might wage a legal battle for custody of Joey.

So might Jonah.

She couldn't take the risk.

This wasn't the first time Molly had debated this whole troubling issue of secrecy since Lynette's death. Always she came to the same conclusion. But tonight was different because Jonah Rhodes was *here,* in southwest Texas. She could actually have carried on that imagined conversation with him.

Minutes earlier, when Molly had gotten home, she'd looked in on Joey immediately, needing to make sure he was okay. He'd been sound asleep. Now she made her way again to his bedroom, turning out lights as she passed through the living area of her two-bedroom condo.

Joey slept in the same position, lying on his back, an angelic smile on his face. Love flooded Molly's heart as she bent over and kissed his warm little cheek. It was the same maternal love, tender and yet fierce and protective, that had flooded her when she'd held him as a newborn infant. More than anything else, that love had brought about the change in Molly, transformed her from a timid mouse into a lioness.

Gazing at the sleeping child who couldn't have been more precious to her if she'd given birth to him herself, Molly knew she'd acted in his best interest tonight, deceiving his uncle. It wasn't selfishness on her part. She'd provided Joey with a secure home. In her nurturing care, he'd grown into a happy, well-adjusted five-year-old.

She promised herself she would try harder to find him a daddy.

Undressing in her bedroom, Molly reviewed her prospects. The park ranger Roger Mason was at the top of the short list. With the least encouragement, he would ask her out. Tonight he'd hung around her during the break, but he might as well have been a lifesize cardboard figure for all the impact he made.

Molly doubted there was a man alive who could have captured her attention with Jonah Rhodes in the same room. Even if fear hadn't been a factor.

That was part of the reason she was still unmarried.

The fifty-mile drive back to the Basin campground seemed twice as long, and the location twice as remote to Jonah. His fellow campers had all turned in for the night, probably hours earlier. As he undressed in the darkness of his tent and slid into his sleeping bag, he didn't hear so much as a mumble of a human voice.

Jonah hadn't minded his solitude the past few nights, drifting off to sleep to the yap of coyotes and the quiet rustle of wild predators on the prowl. But tonight he felt lonely. And down in the dumps, out of all proportion.

A woman had turned him down cold and for perfectly understandable reasons. He shouldn't be moping like a damn pimply teenager.

Maybe he should just pack up and move on in the morning, Jonah thought.

But no, he told himself, quashing the idea, he would stick around a couple of weeks, like he originally planned, and hike some more trails and…

And look up Molly Jones in the Mexican Village.

He wanted to see her again. He wanted to talk to her and find out more about her.

As for there not being any future in seeing her, if future translated to marriage, Jonah would have to resign himself to living like a monk and not enjoying the company of women. He didn't intend to speak wedding vows ever again. They obviously had no holding power.

As far as he was concerned, a bride and groom would do just as well to step over a broom, or follow some other quaint ritual, as they would to promise to stay together for the rest of their lives.

Jonah brushed aside the cynical train of thought and made his plans. He would get up early and go for a hike in the morning, then drive to the Mexican Village in the early afternoon.

There were still some unanswered questions niggling at the back of his mind, even though he was ninety-nine percent satisfied that Molly and Lynette Jones weren't Susan and Karen Gulley. What was the family link between Molly and Lynette? Were they sisters? Sisters-in-law?

Cousins? How had they happened to be living together in Amarillo?

If Lynette had also relocated here to Big Bend country, Jonah wouldn't mind getting a look at her, just to erase the one percent of doubt.

Chapter Three

Jonah got out of his pickup in a cloud of red dust he'd created and surveyed the Mexican Village. Built of stucco with red tile roofs, the strip mall formed an L-shape and had been designed to look like side-by-side single-story structures. A long, planked boardwalk fronted the shops and businesses. Blooming flowers spilled out of huge, ornate clay pots that had undoubtedly been imported from nearby Mexico and placed along the boardwalk to serve as planters.

The developers had left the parking area unpaved, as apparently was common down here in this dry, rocky country with its sparse population. Concrete must cost a fortune, Jonah reflected, taking a moment to appreciate the magnificent natural backdrop of rugged foothills and mountains before he made a beeline for Clementine's Closet.

On the boardwalk in front of the shop, he stomped his

hiking boots to shake off the dust while he appraised the window displays on either side of an elaborately carved door. He hadn't expected such fashionable-looking apparel, although Molly Jones's appearance last night should have served as a clue about the merchandise she sold. The keynote was Western, but Western-with-a-feminine-flare.

Entering, Jonah stepped onto a plush oval rug and set off the strains of "My Darling Clementine." While he was taking a quick glance around, his lungs were filling with the flowery scent of potpourri blended with perfume. He had that feeling of being a bull in a china shop that he usually got when he went shopping for a gift for a female.

"Buenos dias, señor." The greeting in Spanish came from a brunette woman who was straightening folded merchandise on shelves in a tall armoire. Its open doors supported hooks for hanging garments.

"Buenos dias," Jonah replied, searching for Molly. Disappointingly she was nowhere in sight, but the armoire and several more like it blocked portions of his view of the shop interior.

"Can I help you?" inquired the saleswoman in accented English as she approached, smiling.

"I was looking for your manager, Molly Jones. Is she here?"

Her smile changed subtly as she gave him a once-over with interested dark brown eyes. Jonah had the half-amused impression that she had gauged his height and weight and probably his belt size. Turning her head aside, she called, "Molly, a handsome gentleman wants to speak to you."

After a second or two of silence, Molly's voice answered, coming from the rear left corner of the room. "One moment, Delores."

Jonah felt his pulse speed up with male anticipation.

* * *

Molly needed the moment to reason away her flare of panic at the sound of Jonah Rhodes's voice, which she'd recognized instantly. He hadn't sounded grim or angry, like a man on a mission. He'd sounded relaxed and pleasant. There was no cause to assume that the status quo had changed since last night, when he'd seemed quite satisfied that she wasn't Susan Gulley.

Once again it was crucial that she not raise his suspicions. You're not Susan. You're Molly. Jonah's a nice-looking man you met last night, who is making a nuisance of himself and interrupting you on the job. With shoulders squared, Molly walked to the front of the shop, the heels of her boots striking firmly against the Mexican-tile floor.

Jonah had advanced several yards inside the door and stood near a rack of scarves and belts. He greeted her before she could greet him. "Hi, Molly. Nice shop."

Relief swept through Molly. Nothing had changed since last night. Unless he'd grown even better looking and more masculine in his jeans and hiking boots and an open-throated cotton shirt. It was almost impossible not to broadcast the message, It's good to see you.

"Thanks, but it isn't mine," she said. "I'm just the manager." A fact she hadn't mentioned last night, when she'd awarded the prize for a fifty-dollar gift certificate for a purchase at Clementine's Closet. Obviously he'd found out somehow on his own.

"I'll bet you do the buying yourself." He inspected her outfit a second time, his gaze blatantly complimentary.

Her fawn skirt fell past mid-calf, swishing over the tops of suede Western-style boots. A matching fawn vest covered most of the bodice of her snug-fitting white knit blouse. The outfit was much more sedate than the one Molly had worn last night. Before now, she hadn't felt provocative.

"Yes, I do the buying, along with keeping the accounts and placing ads. I'm pretty much in complete charge since the owner moved to California. Could I help you with selecting a gift?" she inquired, having established how busy she was.

"Actually I'm not on a shopping trip. I was on my way to the Cactus Café to have that Texas-size mug of coffee and big slice of homemade pie you recommended so highly last night." He reached his right hand behind him, pulled a folded envelope from his jeans pocket and brandished it as a reminder of his bingo prize. "I was hoping you might be ready for a coffee break and would join me."

"I'm in the middle of marking down price tags for a sale that's starting tomorrow. And it's time for Delores to take her break." Molly looked over at her saleswoman, who'd retreated to the counter with the cash register and was fussing with a display of costume jewelry, making a pretense that she wasn't listening to every word.

"You go ahead, Molly," Delores said. "I'll take my break later on. It's no problem."

"I don't want to upset the schedule and put anybody out," Jonah protested. "I can meet you for coffee whenever you say."

Molly was caught in a trap of her own making, since she'd resorted to putting him off with excuses instead of stating point-blank, I don't care to join you for coffee. The problem would have been saying those words with conviction when she truly wished it wasn't necessary to turn him down. If things were different, she would have accepted in a heartbeat.

"Since Delores doesn't mind, I guess I can go with you now," she said.

It was terribly dangerous to spend further time in his company. Molly would just have to be on her guard every second and not do or say anything to give herself away. Plus, she didn't dare encourage him. That wouldn't be easy, since she found him just as attractive and personable now as she had six years ago. Or maybe even more so. No longer a shy virgin, Molly could add virile to the list of adjectives that described him.

"Where are you staying?" she asked as he escorted her along the boardwalk to the Cactus Café.

"I'm camping in the national park. Rudimentary camping," he added. "Sleeping on the ground in a tent. I haven't done it since my college days."

"Is this some sort of reunion vacation with college buddies?" Molly couldn't imagine that he was on vacation alone, and he must not have brought a woman friend.

"No, I'm by myself. And single, in case you're wondering. I've been divorced for a year."

"After how many years of marriage?" He'd been single when she met him.

"Three and a half years. Which was about three years too many. My ex-wife and I were both glad to call it quits. She'd already found herself a guy who was making bigger bucks than I was, a hotshot trial attorney. So the divorce was friendly. She didn't try to take me to the cleaners, and I was spared big alimony payments since she remarried right away."

"You don't seem bitter."

"I'm not bitter, just very cynical about marriage."

"Am I to consider myself forewarned that you're not a husband prospect?"

Jonah grinned and didn't deny her ironic assessment of his purpose in sharing his matrimonial history right away. Molly had to fight the male charm of that grin and remind herself to stay on her guard.

They'd reached the café. Inside, he guided her past two empty tables, apparently headed for the line of booths against the wall. The courteous touch of his hand on her back touched off a sense of déjà vu, and for a moment Molly saw another café interior back in her hometown in Georgia. Six years ago they'd sat across from each other in a booth. Some previous customer, probably a teenager, had scratched "I LUV U" in the thick layer of varnish on the table.

Molly halted in her tracks. "Do you mind if we sit at a table? I've never liked booths."

"No, a table's fine." He pulled out a chair for her and then seated himself, not opposite her but to her immediate left. To Molly's relief, his expression wasn't odd or thoughtful. The details of that past meeting probably weren't so clear in his memory as in hers. The reflection brought a silly stab of hurt.

A waitress was already headed their way. She took their order and left.

"Back to our conversation," Molly said. "You said your ex-wife found herself an attorney who earns bigger bucks than you. What do you do for a living?" She knew the answer, but she wanted to keep him talking about himself. Partly to keep the spotlight off her and partly out of genuine interest in what he had to say.

"I was with a major brokerage firm in Atlanta." He named it.

"Past tense?"

"Past tense. A couple of years ago I started developing a bad case of burnout. I was also up to here with living in a big city and fighting traffic." He drew a forefinger across his throat.

"You're unemployed?"

His smile was amused. "Don't worry. I have those gift coupons. You won't have to pay our tab. Seriously, I'm not a bum. I inherited money from a great-uncle who died recently. Between that and my own investment portfolio,

I'm pretty solvent. I decided to take off six months or a year and do some traveling. I've never seen three-quarters of the U.S. This is my first trip to Texas.''

''And then what, after you've seen the other three-quarters?''

He shrugged. ''I'm keeping my options open. I'll probably go into business for myself.''

''In Georgia?''

''Not necessarily. If I go back to Georgia, it won't be Atlanta or Columbus, my hometown.''

''What's wrong with Columbus?''

''Too many bad memories. And my father still lives there.'' His voice had hardened with contempt. ''He and I don't speak to each other.''

''What about your mother?'' Both his parents had been alive six years ago. Joel Rhodes had talked about them.

''She's dead.''

''I'm sorry.''

Their waitress had returned. The conversation lapsed while she served them. As soon as she'd gone, Jonah declared with a note of apology, ''Hey, I didn't mean to bore you with my whole life story. I'd much rather talk about you. Last night you mentioned that you have a little boy.''

Molly let a nod suffice for her answer and bought a few seconds by sampling her cherry pie, hoping that she wouldn't choke on it. So much hinged on being able to overcome her innate honesty and lie convincingly, since it wasn't possible simply to give misleading information.

''He's five years old and is enrolled in kindergarten,'' she told him, lifting her mug for a swallow of black coffee.

''Is Jones your married name?''

''No, it's my maiden name. There's no daddy in the

picture," she went on. "I'm Joey's only parent. That's why being a parent takes precedent over everything else."

He was eating his lemon meringue pie with evident enjoyment. Molly was almost sure that simple curiosity, not suspicion, lay behind his questions.

"The younger woman who shared the apartment with you in Amarillo. Lynette Jones. Who is she, if I'm not being too inquisitive?" he asked.

This was the hardest lie of all to tell. Molly forked a bite of pie, her gaze directed at her plate. "My cousin." A vision of a roadside cross on a desolate stretch of highway brought a big lump to her throat and the sting of tears to her eyes. Molly blinked hard with the unexpected onslaught of raw grief. Being so tense had left her vulnerable.

"What's the matter?" Jonah asked gently. "You look so sad all of a sudden. Did something…happen to Lynette?"

"She was killed in a horrible highway accident."

"I'm sorry." He reached and gave her shoulder a comforting squeeze. His fingers were strong and warm. "If I'd had any idea, I wouldn't have brought her name up."

"You couldn't have known."

"Say, I could use a refill on the coffee. What about you?" He signaled their waitress, who came right over with the coffeepot. By the time she'd left, Molly had recovered her poise. The small incident had shown her a compassionate side of Jonah Rhodes. Was there a possibility that he could forgive and forget the past?

For Joey's sake, Molly had to try to find out. It meant inching over territory mined with explosives.

"Pardon my curiosity," she said hesitantly. "Last night you mentioned that the two sisters you were trying to locate were connected to a family tragedy. You meant your family?"

Jonah nodded. "The younger sister, Karen Gulley, got my sixteen-year-old brother killed," he stated bitterly. "She was a seasoned juvenile delinquent who'd already been arrested several times when she masterminded a scheme to break into a pharmacy in Columbus.

"Joel had started dating Karen earlier in the year. Before that he'd always been a great kid. Made As and Bs. Lettered in junior varsity sports. Worked at part-time jobs. Thanks to her bad influence, he started experimenting with drugs and acting rebellious. He got into a few scrapes, but nothing serious until the pharmacy break-in." Jonah had laid down his fork, and his big hand was clenched into a white-knuckled fist. "There were six kids involved. The burglar alarm went off. The police came. One of the kids had a gun and fired it. All hell broke loose. Joel ended up dead. The police caught the others except for Karen Gulley, the ringleader. She hightailed it back to her sister's place and the two of them took off together. Karen got away scot-free."

"What a terrible tragedy." Molly's voice came out barely louder than a whisper. Only the thought of Joey kept her from speaking up and telling her own emotional version of the story. He was the sole reason Molly had changed her identity. She'd never meant to go permanently into hiding with her hysterical, grief-stricken sister when the two of them left town that nightmarish night.

Jonah went on, fortunately too wrapped up in his grim narration to notice Molly's upheaval. "The police put out a state-wide bulletin, but there was a big search on at the time for a serial killer. Locating a juvenile delinquent charged with breaking into a place of business and attempting to burglarize it was small potatoes. What Karen Gulley was morally guilty of was manslaughter. And as far as I'm concerned, her older sister was an accessory." Jonah unclenched his hand and picked up his mug and took a big swallow. "Now you can understand why I made the statement last night, 'I'm glad you're not Susan Gulley.'"

"If I were her, you obviously wouldn't have invited me for coffee and pie today."

His answer was quick and definite. "No, that's for sure. But enough about the Gulley sisters. Let's talk about more pleasant subjects."

"I have to get back to the shop."

"But we haven't finished our pie."

"Stay and finish yours. Please. I insist."

But Jonah rose to his feet, too, when Molly pushed back her chair and stood up.

"I'll walk with you," he said.

"That's not necessary."

He ignored her protest and laid the gift coupons and money for a tip on the table before he accompanied her outside.

"Next time, no heavy conversations," he said.

"There isn't going to be a next time," Molly stated. "And I mean that, Jonah."

"How about letting me take you and your little boy out to supper? Then you wouldn't be neglecting him."

"No."

"We could take him hiking this weekend. Or horseback riding. Bring along a picnic lunch. When I was a kid his age, I loved picnics."

"Jonah, don't make this so hard!" Molly hoped he didn't hear her note of desperation. "I thought I made myself very clear last night. I'm not interested in going out on a few dates with you, with or without Joey. So, please, enjoy your vacation and forget about me."

He breathed out an audible sigh. "That's asking a lot."

They'd reached Clementine's Closet.

"Goodbye, Jonah," Molly said and went quickly inside, leaving him there on the boardwalk. She stood just inside the door, waiting for what seemed a century before she heard the thud of his boots.

Molly moved over to the window and watched him walk with long strides across the parking lot to a silver-gray pickup truck. Like last night, he hadn't said goodbye, but this time she really had seen the last of him. The sense of certainty should have flooded her with relief, not tightened a band around her heart.

It was for the best that he came today, Molly reflected dully as she turned away from the window after the pickup had driven away. Now she no longer had to agonize about whether she was doing the right thing, keeping Joey's existence a secret from his father's family. Jonah's bitterness over his younger brother's senseless death was easy to understand, but it could do her beloved little nephew no good to expose him to that bitterness and quite possibly to rejection.

Molly doubted that Jonah could ever get past the fact that her sister was the birth mother of his dead brother's child.

"Enjoy your vacation and forget about me." Jonah played Molly's words over in his head as he drove back to his campground. What she was really saying was, Go away and don't bother me again.

"Okay. If that's what you want," he said aloud, his tone more gloomy and frustrated than determined.

It would have been easier to accept being turned down flat a second time if Jonah's gut instinct didn't tell him that the attraction was mutual. Molly had looked him over today while he was looking her over. Unless he was fooling himself big-time, she liked what she saw, too. Maybe not as much as he liked what he saw.

Because Jonah couldn't find a flaw in her.

Molly Jones wasn't just a pretty face and a shapely body. She had depth and character and dignity. He was impressed by her air of competence, her directness, her honesty.

Dammit, he wanted to spend some more time with her, get to know her better. But he would abide by her wishes and not bother her again.

Back at his campsite Jonah got out his stack of books and pamphlets he'd purchased at the park Visitors' Center and did some reading, sitting in front of his tent in a lightweight folding chair. His mind kept drifting and the splendid nature photographs faded away into close-ups of Molly's face. What was the story behind her being an unwed mother? he found himself wondering. Had the father of her child died before he could marry her? Jonah was inclined to reject that explanation. He hadn't detected sadness or pain when she stated, "There's no father in the picture."

It was hard to imagine that a man could be intimate enough with Molly to get her pregnant and then abandon her and the child. Maybe she was one of those women who wanted to be a mother and not a wife. Somehow that explanation didn't hit him right, either.

Jonah was puzzled about one minor little thing. Why hadn't the old fellow in Molly's apartment building in Amarillo been able to figure out she was the mother? Kids were talking by the age of two and usually said Mommy with some frequency.

The daylight began to fade, and Jonah's stomach growled. He stowed away his reading material, disgusted with himself for his lack of concentration.

The prospect of a supper cooked on his camp stove raised little enthusiasm, but Jonah heated up a can of beef stew and followed the directions on a package of freeze-dried vegetables. By the time he'd eaten and washed up his few dishes, it was dark. He sat out under the stars, listening to the wild night sounds of the park, his thoughts always circling back to Molly Jones.

Strange that I'm not sorry our paths just happened to cross, Jonah reflected. Despite the damage to his male ego from being turned down twice, he wouldn't have missed meeting her. Even talking briefly about Joel's death today had been as therapeutic as it had been painful. Jonah had schooled himself not to think about his dead brother, much less talk about him. Blocking out the bad memories had meant blocking out a lot of good memories, as well. Maybe he was gradually becoming less bitter and would eventually reclaim those good memories.

In this philosophic frame of mind, Jonah turned in for the night and slept soundly until close to morning when he had a disturbing dream in which he was twenty-eight years old again and single. *The phone rang in his Atlanta apartment, and the caller was his mother. Jonah's heart sank at the sound of her tearful voice. More trouble with Joel. Sure enough, the kid had just gotten himself suspended from school for three days for cutting classes. "He won't listen to me or his father, Jonah!" Mary Rhodes had sobbed.*

"I'll come home Saturday, Mom," Jonah promised. "I'll read my little brother the riot act."

"He's having sex with that girlfriend of his. When I was going through his jeans pockets before putting them into the washing machine, I found a condom."

"At least he's showing some sense if he's practicing safe sex."

The scene shifted, and Jonah was walking along a street in his hometown with Susan Gulley, escorting her to a café. The name was lettered on the plate glass windows, but it was the wrong name. "I could have sworn this place was called The Coffee Pot," Jonah remarked, holding open the door for her. "It recently changed to the Cactus Café," she explained.

Inside, he led her toward a booth. They'd almost reached it when Susan stopped short and whirled around. "Do you mind if we sit at a table?" she asked. "I've never liked booths." Her voice was completely different, brisk and self-assured. Her drawl was more Texan than Southern. In fact, she had undergone an astounding change, even though she still had Susan Gulley's facial features. All trace of shyness had disappeared. She wasn't even wearing the same outfit. Something weird was going on here.

"Who the hell are you?" he demanded.

Jonah woke himself up, mumbling the answer aloud. "Molly Jones."

The gray light of dawn was filtering into the tent. Jonah lay there a couple of minutes, snug in his sleeping bag, shaking off the effects of the dream before he rose and got dressed, shivering in the chilly air.

That day Jonah went for an all-day hike and arrived back at his campsite physically tired. After he'd showered in the bathhouse, he got out a can of spaghetti to heat for his supper, then put it back, climbed into his truck and drove to the only restaurant in the park, located conveniently in the Basin area. He was tired of roughing it.

The next morning he broke up camp and drove to Study Butte. After filling his gas tank at Casey's gas station, he bypassed the few motels and headed straight to the Mexican Village to drop in on another acquaintance from the bingo fund-raiser, Flora, the real estate agent.

Jonah figured she was his best source of information about vacation rental property.

"Hi, Delores. Is Molly around?"

Flora Holmburg's throaty voice carried clearly into

Molly's small office, where she was seated at the computer desk, her hands on the keyboard. Molly sagged in her chair, her tense muscles going lax. Every time someone entered the shop, she reacted with this same spurt of panic despite the certainty that she'd seen the last of Jonah Rhodes.

"She's in her office paying bills," Delores was answering.

"I'll just pop in and pay her a quick visit. I have some news."

Molly focused on the screen and sighed with impatience at herself as she deleted several letters her fingers had struck in error to the strains of ''My Darling Clementine.''

"I thought Delores said you were paying bills," Flora spoke from the doorway a short time later.

"I am," Molly replied. "I type in the information and print out the checks."

"Computers!" Flora made a batting motion with her hand, which was laden with silver rings. A shake of her head set her elaborate dangling silver earrings into motion. "Give me a ballpoint pen and a checkbook anyday."

"What's up?" Molly asked, reflecting fondly as she had before that the real estate agent, who was originally from New York, must add an extra pound onto her weight with her jewelry.

"I came to give you the scoop on your new neighbor."

Flora owned a condo in Molly's complex, which she used as vacation rental property. Molly surmised from her statement that it had just been rented to a new tenant.

"Neighbor? Singular?"

"Singular. Male."

Molly raised her eyebrows. "Rich?" Flora's price

wasn't cheap, and she rented the condo by the month, not on a weekly basis.

"Not filthy rich, but the type who doesn't mind paying for what he wants. You've met him. He was at the bingo fund-raiser. Big, tall, handsome guy from Georgia?"

The bottom had dropped out of Molly's stomach. "The man who was sitting at the table with you and Casey Doyle?"

"That's him! He didn't pay a bit of attention to his bingo cards because he kept his eyes on you. I had to tell him he'd spelled out bingo. His name is Jonah, remember? Jonah Rhodes."

Molly's mouth had gone so dry she had to swallow before she could speak. "He came into your office today?"

"This morning. When I went to unlock the door, he was standing there, waiting. He's been camping in a tent in the park and decided he'd had enough discomfort. He was looking for a place he could rent by the week, but I didn't have anything like that available. Rather than send him away, I gave him the big pitch on my condo. He looked at the pictures and was sold." Flora's smile was smugly gleeful.

"You didn't mention that I would be his neighbor."

"No, indeed. Well, I'll let you get back to your checks. I have a client coming who's interested in buying property." The real estate agent waved and left.

It all sounded innocent enough, Molly told herself. With luck Jonah might come and go and never be the wiser.

Still, his presence would destroy her peace of mind. Every night when she tucked Joey in, she would be aware that his uncle was nearby.

And every night when she took off her clothes, slipped on her nightgown and got into bed by herself—

Molly cut off that disturbing train of thought.

Chapter Four

Jonah had spent the afternoon exploring the former mining town of Terlingua and playing tourist. He'd even taken along his camera and snapped a few shots of the adobe ruins. And, yes, he'd browsed in the book section of a so-called trading post and added to his supply of reading material.

Today had been a nice change of pace. As he got into his truck and headed for his new, more luxurious quarters, he had to grin at his relief that he wasn't headed to his campsite. Renting the nicely furnished two-bedroom condo for a month had been extravagant, but, damn, he looked forward to being back in the lap of civilization.

The small condo complex was located on the same huge tract of land as the Mexican Village and had been built by the same developers, information Jonah had learned from Flora, his landlady. She'd shown him the master plan, which included a future hotel and additional condos. Out of curiosity he'd inquired about the purchase price of a condo, and it wasn't astronomical.

The thought had occurred to him that he could buy a unit and make it pay for itself by using it for vacation-rental property, like Flora was doing. He could reserve it for his own use a month or two out of the year. She'd seemed to read his mind and had reeled off some figures to try to sell him on the idea.

Jonah liked this Big Bend country a lot. He liked the rugged scenery and the feeling of being uncrowded. He liked the people he'd met who lived here. They all seemed to be real individuals. This was a place that could draw him back year after year.

And if he were a property owner, maybe he could get better acquainted with a certain beautiful blond resident. Jonah was honest enough with himself to zero in on that incentive.

Today hadn't been as bad as yesterday, but he'd still lapsed into thinking about Molly Jones. As he drove along the road leading to La Hacienda condos, Jonah suffered one of those lapses. He remembered following behind Flora's Cadillac that morning and wondering where Molly and her little boy lived.

Don't ask, because it doesn't matter where they live. You're not bothering her again, remember? he'd reminded himself. To his credit, he hadn't asked or brought up Molly's name.

The next few nights he would face another challenge—not to look her number up and phone her in a weak moment. Jonah planned to meet that challenge tonight by logging on to the Internet and visiting his favorite financial sites to catch up on the happenings on Wall Street. Before now his state-of-the-art laptop he'd brought along had been useless to him without an electrical hookup and a phone jack.

La Hacienda condos came into view. In the late-afternoon light, the single-storied structures made of adobe-colored stucco blended pleasingly into the natural desert setting. The backdrop was magnificent with rocky foothills marching off in the distance to massive mountain ranges.

No grass to cut. That's a nice feature, Jonah reflected as he drove along the only street, noting again with approval the lack of landscaping. It was nice, too, that the dozen buildings, each housing two units, were spaced fairly far apart. This morning the gravel driveways had been vacant. Now automobiles were parked in the majority of them.

Jonah braked suddenly as he came abreast of a driveway with a dark green sports utility vehicle. It was the same color, make and model as Molly's SUV. He'd spotted it in the parking lot at the Mexican Village and looked it over in the daylight.

"Don't tell me," he murmured, half dismayed and half excited.

It would have been great news to him to discover she and her son were his neighbors, if only she would react the same way. But she wouldn't, Jonah was fairly certain.

He had to find out, one way or another. He couldn't sleep tonight not knowing for sure whether she was within easy walking distance.

Jonah pulled over to the side of the street and killed his engine, acting on the old maxim that no time was better than the present.

Two large terra cotta pots, similar to those at the Mexican Village, flanked the front door. Intent on his mission, Jonah didn't pay much attention to the glossy-leafed shrubs growing in the pot except to note absently that they looked oddly familiar and out of place.

The doorbell worked fine. He heard faint chimes, then

rapid footsteps and the shout of a boyish voice, "I'll see who's at the door!"

Molly's son? What was his name? Joey. Easy to remember because you substitute an *l* for the *y* and you spelled his brother's name, Joel.

The door swung open to reveal a small brown-haired boy dressed in jeans, striped polo shirt and high-top sneakers. He regarded Jonah with curious blue eyes that held no distrust of a stranger.

"Hi," Jonah greeted him. "Is your mother home?"

"She doesn't live here. She's in Heaven." The little boy imparted the information cheerfully.

Jonah could feel his own face fall as he deduced that he was talking to a stranger's cute offspring. "Then you're not Joey Jones."

"Do you know me?" The inquiry was interested.

"Joey, who's at the door?" Molly's voice preceded her. She soon appeared in the foyer, dressed more casually than he'd seen her before, in jeans and a pale pink knit blouse that hugged her breasts. "Jonah!" she exclaimed.

"It's not what you think," he hastened to assure her. "I was just driving by and thought I recognized your car. By pure coincidence, we're going to be neighbors for a short while."

She'd come up beside Joey and drawn his small, sturdy body against her hip. Her posture was maternal and protective as though Jonah represented some threat. "Flora told me you'd rented her condo," she said.

That explained why she didn't act more stunned.

"Honest to God, I had no idea where you lived."

Several phones had begun to ring in the condo. "Joey, would you run and answer the phone, please?" Molly gently turned the little boy's body when he didn't respond with alacrity.

"Promise you won't go away before I come back?" he

called to Jonah over his shoulder as he tore away, his sneakers pounding the Mexican tile floor.

"Cute kid," Jonah commented. "Is he adopted?"

Molly looked startled. Or was that a flash of alarm in her face? "What makes you ask?"

"When he opened the door, I asked to speak to his mother. He said she was in Heaven."

She nodded and seemed to hesitate slightly. "Joey is Lynette's son. My cousin who died. She was still in her teens when she got pregnant with him. I've taken care of him since he was a newborn infant."

Jonah's mind was running on two tracks, listening to her and trying like hell not to let his gaze stray over her figure. Roger's words came back to him: "She's so fine." Obviously the park ranger had seen her in jeans and a blouse that clung to her curves. The thought aroused a pang of jealousy.

"Some lady wants to talk to you!" Joey yelled at the top of his lungs as he raced to join the adults again. Rounding a corner into the foyer, he skidded and had to do a pinwheel with both arms to keep his balance.

Jonah grinned in amusement.

"Excuse me," Molly said to him.

"Do you want to come in?" Joey invited, positioning himself in the open doorway before Molly could close the door and send Jonah on his way. "While Molly's on the phone, you and me could play a Nintendo game."

"Only if it's okay with Molly for me to come in," Jonah said after leaving a pause long enough for her to speak up and cancel the invitation. It both surprised and pleased him no end that she hadn't.

"Is it okay, Molly?" The little boy beseeched her with his hopeful expression as well as his tone.

"I guess so, but let Mr. Rhodes decide for himself whether he has time." She ruffled his hair and bent down to kiss him on the cheek before she departed, giving Jonah a rear view of her jeans.

"Do you have time?" Joey inquired.

"Lots of time," Jonah replied indulgently.

He closed the door behind himself and followed the small boy, who was grinning from ear to ear with his delight over having a grown-up playmate.

The floor plan of the condo was identical to Flora's. The living room, dining room and kitchen all flowed together without walled partitions. Jonah had always liked this modern "great room" concept, but he especially liked it now as he sat down on a thick area rug with Joey in front of the TV in the living room. Molly was carrying on her phone conversation in the kitchen, perched on a tall stool. Jonah could turn his head forty-five degrees and see her.

He didn't deliberately eavesdrop on her conversation, but he couldn't help overhearing enough to surmise that she was probably discussing a potluck supper/dance coming up at the community center. Flora had mentioned it to him and stressed that he would be welcome to attend. Maybe he would, if this impromptu visit with Molly and Joey broke the ice and caused her to be more friendly toward him.

He would bet money that ole Roger the park ranger would be on hand, sporting a fancy Western shirt and lining up to dance with Molly. The picture that rose in Jonah's mind caused that same stab of jealousy he'd felt earlier.

"Here's your control, Mr. Rhodes." Joey had been busily occupied with getting the Nintendo game started. Now he gave Jonah a black plastic hand control unit attached to a long cord. "You want to go first?" The offer was obviously halfhearted, prompted by courtesy.

"Why don't you?"

"Okay."

Jonah smothered a grin at the little boy's eager agreement and watched with amusement as small nimble fingers worked the control unit that looked much larger in the boy's hands. It wouldn't have been necessary to follow the action on the TV screen or listen to the noises. Joey's animated face and his vocal reactions told the tale of his successes and failures in racking up points. "Oh, man!" he muttered one second and then exclaimed, "All *right!*" a few seconds later.

"Hey, you're pretty good at this," Jonah declared when the final score flashed up. And it wasn't a bad score for a five-year-old. "I've got my work cut out for me." He was rewarded by that ear-to-ear grin of boyish delight.

"Your turn."

Jonah hadn't played this particular game, but he'd played similar ones. He could easily have maxed out the points on the beginning level, but he was careful to rack up a score slightly lower than Joey's.

"Whew, you almost caught up with me," the little boy said. "You're pretty good, too, huh?"

Molly had finished her phone conversation. She came over to perch on the edge of the sofa. Joey glanced at her. "I beat Mr. Rhodes," he boasted happily.

"I saw," she said, her gaze meeting Jonah's.

"Want to play the next level, Mr. Rhodes?" Childlike, Joey had basked in his triumph long enough.

"Sure. If I'm not holding up your supper."

"Our supper isn't ready, is it, Molly?"

"No, I was just about to go into the kitchen and fix it."

"Fix something that takes a long time," Joey urged.

Do you want me to go? Jonah asked Molly silently.

She looked at the child she plainly doted on and shook her head no.

Jonah was ready to believe she'd been telling the truth when she told him three nights ago at the fund-raiser, "I'm afraid I don't have time for a social life, not while my son is small." She took her role of single parent as seriously as she would have if she'd been Joey's birth mother instead of his adoptive mother.

Joey was a hell of a lucky little kid.

Molly sat there a few minutes longer and watched the Nintendo competition between the small boy she adored and his uncle before she rose and went into the kitchen. Then she kept glancing into the living room, her eyes drawn like a magnet. The picture man and boy made sitting side by side in front of the TV tugged at her heartstrings and raised troubling doubts about whether she really was doing the right thing, keeping Jonah in the dark.

It would be easier to sort through her emotions if Jonah weren't so handsome and virile. And if Molly didn't feel this strong attraction to him.

He seemed to be enjoying himself, playing an electronic game with a little boy who'd literally pulled him in off the street. If this was an act and Jonah was just trying to make points with her, he was an awfully good actor.

Just how much difference would the truth make? Would he want to make points with her if he knew who she was? Would he be this wonderful with Joey if he realized the little boy was his dead brother's child and Joey's birth mother, Lynette, was the same teenage girl he blamed for that brother's death?

There was simply no way to know the answers to her questions. And so much was at stake.

Molly set two places at the breakfast bar when she'd finished her simple supper preparations. Jonah was in the midst of taking his turn at Level Five by now. She waited until his score flashed up on the screen to call the Nintendo session to a halt.

"Supper's ready, Joey. Say goodbye to Mr. Rhodes and run to the bathroom and wash your hands."

"Can't we play one more?" he pleaded.

"You heard her, champ." Jonah ruffled Joey's hair and got to his feet, rising to his full height of six foot one or two.

The little boy scrambled up, too. He sniffed. "Hmm. Are we having some of those tamales you buy from Manuel's mom?"

"You told me that's what you wanted for supper tonight, remember?" Molly replied.

"I forgot, after Mr. Rhodes rang the doorbell," he confessed, walking with Jonah toward the breakfast bar, where she stood. "They taste real good. Manuel's mom makes them herself." This explanation was directed to Jonah. "Do you like tamales, Mr. Rhodes?"

Molly had seen that question coming.

"I've only eaten the frozen ones you buy in the supermarket, and they haven't been all that tasty," Jonah said. "If Manuel's mother sells her tamales to the general public, maybe I'll buy some and give them a try."

"Or you could eat supper with us and try them," Joey suggested, looking at Molly.

"No, I'd better go and not wear out my welcome." Jonah's glance took in the two place settings at the breakfast bar as he refused tactfully, saving Molly from having to be ungracious.

She had extra tamales in the refrigerator that she could have quickly heated in the microwave and she had additional salad makings. It wouldn't have been a problem to include him for supper. Part of Molly wanted very much to include him, but the cautious, fearful part of her advised against taking that step.

She would be opening a door that would be very hard to close.

Molly's main concern was protecting Joey from being hurt, but she was extremely vulnerable herself where Jonah Rhodes was concerned.

"'Bye, Mr. Rhodes." The little boy called out his farewell over his shoulder as he dashed away to wash his hands, as he'd been instructed.

"'Bye, Joey." Jonah smiled and shook his head. "Such energy. Does he ever wind down?"

"Only when he sleeps." Her tone was loving and maternal. "Have you been around children a lot?" she asked.

"Not a lot. I was thirteen when my brother Joel was born, so there was no sibling rivalry. I played with him, and he tagged around behind me. Also, I've had friends and acquaintances who were parents."

"You're so good with Joey."

"He's a cute, bright kid. And well behaved. It's nice to see a kid who doesn't throw a tantrum to get his way."

"He throws a tantrum now and then. But he is a sweet-natured little boy."

"I'm sure personality figures in, but you should take some credit as a parent for bringing him up right."

"Thank you."

"Well, I'd better go." Jonah reluctantly turned to leave. The tamales smelled delicious, but even if a cabbage aroma had permeated the room—cooked cabbage being his least favorite dish—he would have jumped at the opportunity to stay and share their supper in order to prolong the visit and have the pleasure of their company.

Molly was accompanying him to the door, ushering him out. "I'm sure you'll be very comfortable in Flora's condo," she said. "It's so nicely furnished and decorated."

"Yours is a lot more homey."

"With a small boy, you get that lived-in look."

They reached the door, and she opened it, commenting, "I gather you're extending your original two weeks."

"It kind of looks that way. When I went to see Flora, I didn't have in mind renting a place to live for a whole month," Jonah admitted honestly. "But I don't think I'll have any trouble finding things to do to occupy myself. This Big Bend country grows on you."

"Molly, I'm ready to eat!"

Joey's shouted announcement cut the conversation short, much to Jonah's regret. He said good-night and drove to his rented condo, wondering whether he'd made any headway with her.

Whether he had or not, Jonah's resolve not to bother Molly anymore was down the drain. Seeing her again had reignited the urge to spend time with her and get to know her. To hell with male pride. He would keep trying.

"Where does Mr. Rhodes live?" Joey asked, climbing into bed.

Molly pulled his covers up. "His home is in Georgia. That's another state, like Texas is a state, but not as big. I can show you on your puzzle map of the United States tomorrow." If he remembered to ask. She wouldn't bring up the subject of Georgia or their male visitor, who'd made a big impression on him. Several times her little nephew had popped up with questions about Jonah.

"Read me my new storybook about the astronaut," he said drowsily. His five-year-old mind had skipped on to their nightly ritual of his choosing a storybook for her to read to him.

He'd fallen sound asleep before she turned to the final page. Molly closed the book and leaned over to kiss him on the cheek. "Sweet dreams, precious boy," she whispered and sighed a troubled sigh, gazing at the childish face.

He wasn't the spitting image of his father or his mother, but had inherited physical traits from each of them. He had Joel's long curly eyelashes and dark brown hair and Karen's eyes, which were a lighter blue than Molly's. Karen's hair color had been a medium brown. As Joey grew older, he might show a more marked resemblance to one parent or the other, but now his impish grin and features were his own.

Fortunately Jonah hadn't looked at him and seen a miniature Joel Rhodes or a miniature Karen Gulley. Molly bent and kissed her nephew's other cheek before turning out the lights except for his night-light.

Outside in the hallway she had taken several steps toward the living room when she stopped suddenly, struck by an alarming thought. Changing direction, Molly pivoted and walked to her bedroom, which was located across from Joey's. The door stood wide open, as it had earlier when Jonah was here in her condo. If he'd stood in the doorway, he could have glanced inside and seen the framed photographs sitting on her chest of drawers.

There would have been nothing preventing him from taking a closer look at one photograph that stood out among the various shots of Joey.

Jonah hadn't left the living room, Molly reminded herself as she moved over to the chest of drawers to gaze at her sister's laughing face. It had seemed safe enough to display a single picture of Lynette in Molly's bedroom, where she never entertained company.

It was safe if she didn't allow Jonah inside her condo again.

Molly sighed and stroked a gentle finger on the glass of the frame.

*   *   *

Jonah didn't fall asleep until well after midnight. It wasn't exactly relaxing to lie in the comfortable queen-size bed in the larger of the two bedrooms and think about Molly in her bed just down the street. And try as he might not to think about her, his mind kept circling back and imagining her in a silky nightgown.

Finally he dropped off and slept soundly. Then right before waking up, he dreamed that crazy disturbing dream in which he was escorting Susan Gulley into a café in Georgia and she turned into Molly. Evidently his subconscious wasn't convinced they weren't the same woman, Jonah reflected as he stepped under the spray of the shower. His conscious mind must be fully satisfied because he hadn't given Susan Gulley a thought yesterday during that all-too-brief time in Molly's company.

He hadn't even glanced around in search of a photograph of Lynette Jones, Joey's mother. There hadn't been one, he was quite sure. His memory served him well enough that he could visualize the portion of the condo interior which he'd seen, and the only photographs had been several large studio portraits of Joey. Plus some snapshots of him on the refrigerator along with scribbled notes and lists and kindergarten artwork.

If there had been a picture of Lynette, Jonah was satisfied that he wouldn't recognize her, even though she seemed cut of the same cloth as Karen Gulley. Lynette obviously hadn't been much of a mother to Joey, turning him over to Molly's care. Jonah would have expected the same kind of behavior of Karen if she'd gotten pregnant and carried a baby to term.

He could imagine Susan Gulley taking responsibility for a newborn nephew and assuming the role of parent, as Molly had done. But there the parallel ended. Susan would be working at a lesser job and earning a smaller income and struggling to make ends meet if she were a single parent somewhere. She wouldn't be providing the kind of upbringing Molly was providing for Joey.

It wasn't worth thinking about, especially in light of that phone conversation with Jonah's mother his subconscious had dug up and replayed in a dream several nights ago. For all his poor judgment in other respects, sixteen-year-old Joel had practiced safe sex when he dated Karen Gulley. Thank God, Jonah didn't have to worry too much about the possible existence of a nephew—or niece, for that matter—who would be roughly Joey's age.

Brushing aside the whole train of thought, Jonah concentrated on his plans for the day. He'd decided to drive the El Camino del Rio, or River Road, a stretch of Highway 170 leading to the small border town of Presidio, formerly a Spanish mission village. His guidebook touted El Camino del Rio as one of the most spectacular—and hazardous—scenic routes in the state of Texas.

Molly's driveway was vacant when Jonah passed it on his way out at nine o'clock. Not surprisingly, she'd already gone to work and Joey was undoubtedly in his kindergarten class at school. Jonah's gaze fell on the familiar-looking shrubs growing in the terra cotta pots. What were they called? Azaleas? No, wrong name. Camellias? Wrong again. An image of his mother's yard flashed up on a mental screen, and Jonah zeroed in on the same shrubs, but they were studded with white flowers that perfumed the air with a heavy, sweet gardenia scent. Bees hovered around the shrubs. It was summertime.

"Cape jasmine," he said aloud, snapping his fingers.

Cape jasmine bushes could be seen in most yards in his hometown. Evidently they were available at plant nurseries in Texas.

Out on the highway Jonah turned west toward the small town of Lajitas. He pronounced it silently, la-HEE-tahs, reviewing what he'd read about it. Originally it had been established as an army post in 1915 to protect settlers from Pancho Villa, the infamous Mexican bandito. Looking out at the rugged landscape, Jonah had no trouble conjuring up a scene out of an old Western movie, with cavalry men on horseback chasing a band of outlaws.

Once he'd passed through Lajitas, the roller-coaster ride began as the narrow highway began to climb steeply and descend just as precipitously, with the Rio Grande river flowing along on his left-hand side. After he'd passed several colorful teepees that served as picnic shelters on a scenic spot overlooking the river, the highway slanted upward at a fifteen-degree grade for the next five miles. No wonder the guidebook used descriptions like "major engineering feat," reflected Jonah.

Not surprisingly, there had been automobile fatalities. Small wooden crosses decorated with artificial flowers served as sobering reminders. At the summit of the long uphill ascent, Jonah pulled into an overlook and got out to gaze at the spectacular view. "Damn!" he murmured appreciatively. Volcanic rock formed sheer walls of the canyon on one side, and on the other side he could gaze off for miles to the horizon. It had been worth the trip to Big Bend country just to drive El Camino del Rio, Jonah decided as he climbed back into his truck twenty minutes later.

A short distance farther on he encountered his third automobile since leaving Lajitas, a mud-spattered small compact car that careened around a curve, straddling the center line. Jonah reacted fast, jerking the steering wheel and pulling over as far as he dared toward the shoulder on his side. The driver of the compact car veered and avoided collision at the last moment.

Jonah had gotten a glimpse of a teenage girl with another girl as her passenger. Relief that they hadn't been maimed or killed wiped out most of his anger over the carelessness that could have been tragic. His adrenaline was still coursing through his veins when he passed another roadside cross no more than a quarter of a mile from the near accident.

It stood out because it wasn't a wooden cross, like the others. It was black wrought iron with a graceful scrolled design. The silk flowers attached to the base of the vertical bar were starting to fade, but their colors were still vivid. Bright yellow and red.

A bouquet wouldn't stay bright long in this southwest Texas sunshine, Jonah reflected, glancing in his side mirror for a final glimpse of the roadside memorial.

Fortunately, the rest of the trip to Presidio was uneventful. After exploring the small downtown district on foot, browsing in the few stores and eating lunch in a restaurant where the only language he heard spoken among the other patrons was Spanish, he decided to make an excursion across the border into the sister village of Ojinaga.

It was nearly five o'clock when Jonah set out on the return trip. The scenery was just as magnificent heading east, though more harsh and somber and seeming even less accessible to humans with the darkening shadows heralding eventual nightfall.

Once again he passed the black wrought-iron cross and soon entered the same blind curve, but this time there was no heart-stopping incident, thank goodness.

Jonah relaxed his vigilance when he came to Lajitas and had reached the end of El Camino del Rio. Five minutes later his stomach let out a rumble, making him realize he was hungry. The Cactus Café would be open. He decided to go there and eat his supper.

Twenty minutes later he was pulling into the parking lot of the Mexican Village. He saw a cluster of eight or ten automobiles parked over in front of the Cactus Café. Among them was Molly's SUV.

Jonah didn't waste any time getting out of his truck and hot-footing it to the boardwalk. He peered through the windows of the café as he strode along in front of it toward the door. His heart speeded up with pure gladness as he located Molly and Joey seated at a table. Good. They hadn't been served.

Joey was facing the door. A big smile of recognition broke out on his face when Jonah entered. ''Mr. Rhodes!'' he called out in greeting, waving his arm wildly.

Molly turned around, and her expression mirrored more surprise than welcome, but Jonah headed over, anyway.

''Hi, Joey,'' he said. ''Hi, Molly. Mind if I join you?'' He was already pulling out a chair.

''No, we don't mind,'' Joey answered for the two of them.

''Have you already ordered?'' Jonah asked after he'd sat down. He directed his words to her.

''No, we just got here.''

''What lucky timing for me. I had resigned myself to eating alone.''

A waitress arrived with menus and three glasses of water.

''I'll have a soda to drink,'' Joey announced, looking at Molly for her reaction.

''Make that milk,'' she said pleasantly to the waitress. ''Bring me an iced tea with extra wedges of lemon.''

Joey poked his bottom lip out.

''A big glass of milk sounds good to me,'' Jonah said. A bottle of cold beer would have definitely hit the spot, but it wasn't a big sacrifice, especially when Joey's sulkiness instantly disappeared.

''I want a big glass, too,'' the little boy stated.

The waitress left to fill the drink orders, and Molly and

Jonah opened their menus. He glanced at his and saw that there were popular Mexican-American selections like burritos and tacos, more standard fare like hamburgers and also plate dinners like meat loaf and mashed potatoes that he might have seen on a café menu in any Southern town. "What do you two recommend?" he inquired.

Joey promptly listed his favorites, "Burritos and fried chicken and tacos."

"Everything's good, depending on your taste," Molly said. "Gloria Zachary, the owner, supervises the kitchen herself and trains her cooks."

"I play with Brad sometimes," Joey piped up.

"Brad's her six-year-old," Molly explained.

The waitress returned with the drinks, and the three of them ordered, with Joey speaking up first, asking for a beef burrito. He wriggled with delight when Jonah asked for the more ample adult version of the burrito plate, opting for it rather than a steak and baked potato.

"Mr. Rhodes and me are having the same thing," the little boy stated proudly to Molly, as though she might not have been listening.

Jonah half expected a grammatical correction, but instead Molly smiled at her adopted son and said fondly, "I heard him take your recommendation."

The café was fast filling up. A number of people who came in spoke or waved to Molly and Joey. Several came over to hold brief discussions of the upcoming potluck supper and dance at the community center. It was apparent to Jonah that Molly was a key person in the planning and success of these local functions that brought the spread-out population together and fostered a spirit of neighborliness while providing old-fashioned fun and entertainment. Just like pioneer days, he reflected.

Their food came, and it was hearty and delicious. The ceasing of any further interruptions allowed Jonah to carry on a conversation between bites. He inquired about Joey's day at kindergarten and Molly's day at the shop.

"It was an interesting day," she said, dry amusement in her voice. "One customer tried on clothes in the fitting room and left her panty hose behind. Another lady walked out and left her purse on the counter and didn't come back to claim it for several hours. But the funniest story of all— an older gentleman who was waiting around for his wife had a coughing attack and spit out his dentures."

"I hope he didn't break a tooth," Jonah said, grinning.

"No, fortunately he didn't." Molly smiled back at him, shaking her head in recollection. "What did you do today?" she asked with what sounded like genuine interest.

"I drove to Presidio and went across the border into Mexico. On the way I almost had a head-on collision along that scenic route the guidebooks call El Camino del Rio."

Her smile faded. "That's such a horribly dangerous stretch of highway. I would have cautioned you if I'd known you would be driving it."

"Those crosses along the roadside serve as their own warning."

She seemed to go pale and looked almost frightened— or haunted—for just a second. "Thank heaven you made it back safe and sound."

Jonah changed the subject, resisting the urge to quiz her gently about whether she'd had a harrowing experience herself on El Camino del Rio. Obviously something had instilled this horror in her.

Chapter Five

When Molly had said to Jonah, "Thank heaven you made it back safe and sound," her fervor had been genuine.

The roadside cross he'd mentioned earlier had been erected in memory of her sister, whose life had been snuffed out on El Camino del Rio. The fact that he hadn't identified that one particular cross as relevant to him in any way brought a different kind of intense relief to Molly but also intense regret and guilt. She wished with all her heart that secrecy and deception weren't necessary.

And maybe secrecy and deception would prove not to be necessary. A little time around Jonah would tell. It would be so good to share the whole story with him. Molly hadn't fully realized before now just how isolating it had been not to take anyone into her confidence.

"Have you used a computer at kindergarten?" Jonah was asking Joey.

Molly put aside her thoughts and focused on the present.

The little boy nodded his head to Jonah's question. "It has a little TV screen and a mouse! A mouse!" he repeated, giggling.

"I'm impressed with your local school," Jonah said to her. "That's great that Joey's learning computer skills before he even enters first grade."

"We parents are buying extra computers. That's one of our projects that we're financing with our fund-raisers."

"Molly says Santa Claus might bring me my own computer for Christmas." Joey wanted his attention back.

"That'll be fun. There're all kinds of neat computer games that are educational, a lot of them free on the Internet at university web sites." Jonah snapped his fingers. "Hey, I can download some for you on my laptop computer and save them on a floppy disk."

"Where is your laptop computer?" the little boy wanted to know.

"Back at my condo."

"Can I see it?"

"Sure. I'll show you how to operate it."

"After we leave here?"

"Mr. Rhodes didn't necessarily mean tonight," Molly put in. "He meant sometime."

Jonah grinned, looking over at her. "No time like the present for a five-year-old."

"Exactly." She smiled back at him, pleasure flooding her like a warm tide.

"When?" Joey persisted.

"How about tomorrow afternoon after school?" Jonah offered the suggestion to Molly. "That'll give me time to download some games tonight."

"Please, Molly," her little nephew urged.

"Are you sure?" she pressed Jonah. "This is your vacation. Don't let yourself be railroaded."

"I'll look forward to it."

Joey clapped his hands. "Me, too!"

Me, too, Molly echoed, hoping that she wasn't being railroaded herself for the wrong reasons. Doing what was best for Joey was her top priority.

"I don't guess there's a computer store anywhere close," Jonah said, frowning at a thought.

"The closest place to buy any kind of computer-related items would probably be Alpine, and it's a hundred miles away."

He shrugged broad shoulders. "That's not so far. I'll drive there tomorrow."

By this time they'd finished eating. "Could I bring you some coffee or dessert?" the waitress inquired as she cleared away dishes.

"Nothing for Joey and me," Molly said.

"Same here. I'll just take the check," Jonah said, pulling out his wallet and extracting a credit card.

Molly objected to his paying for their meals, but he insisted. She gave in, rather than haggle, and thanked him.

The café owner, Gloria Zachary, had been manning the cash register. A short, plump redhead, she came over personally to return Jonah's credit card and get his signature on the charge slip. Molly introduced Jonah as Flora's tenant.

"Did Flora invite you to our potluck dinner next Saturday night?" Gloria said to him.

"She did, and I'm planning to be there," he answered. "How does it work, anyway? Do the single guys bring a dish of food, too? Or could I donate money toward buying things like paper plates and napkins or beverages?"

Gloria waggled her free hand. "Either way is fine. Interesting you should bring up paper plates and napkins and beverages, though. We're low on all those things and need somebody to make a supply run to Alpine." She raised her eyebrows, looking at Molly questioningly as though to say, Any ideas?

"I can take off from work in the early afternoon one weekday and go myself," Molly said. "I need to do some shopping, anyway. Maybe you could pick up Joey from kindergarten and let him play with Brad."

"No problem. Just let me know the day," Gloria declared. "Joey can spend the night, if he wants. Brad has a tent pitched in the living room. His grandparents sent it to him for his birthday. He's been after me to invite a schoolmate over to sleep in it with him."

"Can I play with Brad tomorrow after kindergarten and spend the night and sleep in his tent?" Joey begged, bouncing up and down in his chair. He'd been following the conversation. "Can I, Molly? Can I?"

"What about learning to operate Mr. Rhodes's laptop tomorrow afternoon?" she reminded him.

"We can postpone that until the following afternoon," Jonah spoke up. "Why don't you and I ride together to Alpine since I was going anyway? I'll drive you. We can load a lot of stuff into the back of my pickup."

"Sounds like a workable plan to me, but I'll leave the details up to you two," Gloria said, looking over her shoulder at the cash register. She started backing away. "So I'm picking Joey up tomorrow afternoon?"

Molly answered in the affirmative. Joey would have a good time, and tomorrow afternoon was as convenient as a different afternoon.

"What time?" Jonah asked as though she'd agreed they would ride together.

There was no reason to balk at the arrangement, and she really didn't want to balk. The prospect of an excursion to Alpine with him aroused a keen anticipation that overrode caution and apprehension. What harm would it do to spend time alone with him and treat herself to the pleasure of his masculine company as long as she stayed on her guard? None. And possibly a lot of good if she could get more insight into how he was likely to react to learning that Joey was his nephew.

"One-thirty?" she said.

"One-thirty suits me." His tone and whole manner said any time she set was agreeable.

The three of them walked together outside and said good-night. Jonah's truck followed behind them as Molly drove to her condo. When she pulled into her driveway, he tooted his horn and continued past.

Joey was keyed up with excitement over his plans for the next day. He didn't fall asleep until Molly had read him several storybooks. "Who's going to read *me* to sleep?" she reflected as she left his bedroom after quietly tidying up. The evening had been stimulating for her, too.

In the living room Molly sank down on the sofa and picked up the TV remote, but she held it in her hand without clicking a button to bring the blank screen to life. Her mind was too full of its own vivid images. She relived that moment tonight when she'd turned and seen Jonah entering the café, tall and ruggedly good-looking, gladness written on his face. Her heart had given a leap of feminine delight even as panic clutched her in the instinctive reaction she still experienced each time she saw him.

He'll recognize you, warned that frightened voice of a fugitive inside her. Grab Joey and run and hide!

Yet he continued not to recognize her as Susan Gulley, a fact that shouldn't amaze her since she didn't look in the mirror anymore and recognize herself as that shy, unsure young woman she'd once been. She'd changed during the process of starting over in a strange place with a whole new identity.

"Let's go somewhere far away where nobody knows us," her sister had begged that night of the pharmacy break-in. "People won't look down at us. We won't be those two Gulley sisters who grew up in foster homes. We'll change our names, be whoever we want to be. I'll be different, I promise. I'll never get in trouble again."

The plea had struck a chord of longing in Susan that weakened all the arguments against fleeing from their hometown. She'd still made the arguments, but been swayed into going along temporarily when Karen threatened to harm herself. Then Karen had turned up pregnant with Joel's baby, and there had been no going back because of the threat of having the baby taken away from them as soon as it was born. Maybe even having it born in a juvenile institution.

"I'm not sorry," Molly said aloud. Or least not sorry that she'd made a complete break with her past. Not sorry that she'd gotten Joey in the bargain. He'd been a complete joy to her. As for the sacrifices she'd had to make, she'd made them willingly.

The necessity for secrecy hindered making really close women friends, the kind who knew your background and shared deepest confidences. It hindered the kind of intimacy with a man that led to love and marriage. Reaching a certain point, she either had to break off the relationship or else confide, "Oh, by the way, Molly Jones is an alias."

Last year she'd stopped dating altogether. She didn't like leaving Joey with a sitter frequently, nor did she think it was good for him to have a series of men in his life. He became attached quickly when a man showed him attention.

Like Jonah was doing.

Molly sighed, tossing down the TV remote and getting up to walk over to the sliding glass doors leading out onto her patio. A full moon flooded the patio with silvery light.

A perfect setting for romance, she thought wistfully, and slid open the door to step outside into the cool air. Overhead the sky formed a vast inky backdrop for the luminous moon and myriad stars. Molly shivered and hugged herself.

What was Jonah doing? Watching TV? Surfing the Internet on his laptop? It was easy to visualize him doing either of those things in Flora's condo. The images touched off a longing inside her and raised more intimate questions, questions she'd entertained in other weak moments like this one. How would it feel to be in Jonah's arms? To have him kiss her?

Don't fantasize about him....

The admonition went unheeded because the path to this particular fantasy had been traveled before. Molly closed her eyes and gave her imagination full rein. She moaned softly and brought her eyes open.

"You might be disappointed with the reality," she said aloud to counteract the ache of dissatisfaction.

On the other hand, the reality might be even better.

"That's what worries me," Molly said aloud.

It would be so easy to experience the real thing. All she needed to do was give Jonah the opportunity, and he would take it.

But only because she'd deceived him.

The truth would probably kill any desire he had to kiss her.

Jonah woke up aroused and faintly ashamed of himself. He'd gone to bed last night thinking about Molly and had dreamed about her. X-rated dreams. At least he hadn't dreamed that goofy dream in which Susan Gulley turned into Molly, he reflected as he stepped into a cool shower.

After he'd dressed, he made coffee and took his first cup out on the patio. The air was cool and bracing. Bathed with hazy morning light, the mountains off in the distance looked ethereal and delicate instead of massive and heavy. He didn't think he could ever get tired of this view, he thought, taking a swallow of coffee and savoring it.

He was glad he'd rented the condo. Spending a month here in Big Bend country seemed an altogether pleasant prospect, with Molly and Joey as his neighbors. He was in no hurry to move along to his next destination.

Molly hadn't exactly encouraged him last night, but she hadn't given him the cold shoulder, either. She'd agreed fairly readily to make a joint trip to Alpine. Damn, he was looking forward to the hours alone with her. In fact, Jonah couldn't remember the last time he'd been this eager to be alone with a woman. Certainly not since his divorce.

Maybe never.

That bit of honest insight caused Jonah to choke on his swallow of coffee. You're just hungry for female company with this traveling alone, he chided himself. Plus you're horny.

Jonah went back inside and fixed himself some breakfast and ate with the TV playing on a cable channel with financial news. But he barely paid attention. What was happening on Wall Street and in boardrooms seemed unimportant. After he'd washed his few dishes, he selected a couple of books from his pile of reading material about Big Bend country and took them out on the patio. Sunshine had dispelled the morning coolness and cleared away the haze on the mountains.

Seated comfortably in a chair, Jonah opened one of the books, but ten minutes later he closed it in defeat. Was Joey having this much trouble paying attention in kindergarten class? he wondered wryly, recalling the little boy's excitement last night over playing with Gloria's son after kindergarten today and sleeping in a tent in her living room.

If things got friendlier between Jonah and Molly, he would like to take her and Joey on a weekend camping trip. They could cook on Jonah's camp stove and sleep in his tent in the outdoors. Go hiking on some easy trails and take a picnic lunch. Joey would have the time of his life.

He was a cute kid. For some reason, he reminded Jonah of his brother Joel at that age. Probably the big ear-to-ear grin. Memory flashed up a photo that stabbed Jonah with a bitter sadness. Why the hell had Joel gotten himself messed up with the likes of Karen Gulley? He'd had so much going for him. He would have turned into a fine man.

If only Jonah could have done something to save him....

"You tried and failed," he reminded himself, his voice bleak and hard.

Jonah tried to rewind his thoughts like a videotape and conjure up more details of a camping trip with Joey and Molly to erase the sense of defeat, but eventually he gave up and went inside to log on to the Internet and write e-mail messages to friends and former co-workers in lieu of the postcards he hadn't sent.

"Hi. You're right on time."

"I've worn out my watch, looking at it," Jonah replied with a self-deprecating grin. "Say, I like that outfit." His eyes had already made the same complimentary statement as he took in her white knit blouse and blue denim skirt that ended above the knees. She was wearing her red

Western boots and a red bandanna knotted around her throat.

"I decided to go comfortable."

"Every woman should look that good in 'comfortable,'" he said. His tone turned good into sexy.

"I could pay you the same kind of compliment," Molly countered, pulling the front door closed behind her. She treated herself with giving him a thorough once-over. He wore his usual jeans and hiking boots. A jade green cotton shirt open at the neck revealed the strong column of his throat and hugged broad shoulders and a muscular chest.

He made a rueful face, looking down at himself. "I hate shopping for clothes."

His hint of embarrassment was totally charming to Molly. One thing that had appealed to her six years ago and appealed to her now was his seeming lack of egotism, for being such a handsome man.

"Shall we go?" she suggested.

"Sure thing."

Molly's glance fell on the terra cotta planters. "Oh, dear! I forgot to water these shrubs again!" she exclaimed.

"We've got plenty of time. Water them now."

"I will, if you don't mind. They're starting to wilt." She went over to an outdoor tap on the side of the condo and filled a plastic watering can.

"Here. Let me do that for you." Jonah took the watering can from her and emptied it on one shrub, saturating the dry soil. Then he returned to the tap, refilled the watering can and emptied the contents on the other shrub. "There. They already look happier, don't they?"

"Yes, they do. Thanks."

"We have these cape jasmine shrubs in my hometown in Georgia."

"Oh?" The phony response stuck in Molly's throat.

"I always liked them. My mother had several in her yard. They would get covered with white blossoms in the summertime and smell so sweet."

I always loved them, too. They were my favorite flower when I was growing up in your hometown, which was my hometown, too. Molly wished she could speak the words aloud that she was thinking. But, of course, she couldn't.

"They're a variety of gardenia," she said. "I ordered them from a nursery catalog."

"I wondered whether they were grown locally."

There didn't seem to be any note of suspicion in his voice, and he didn't pursue the subject. Apparently he placed no special significance on her choice of a common Southern shrub. A part of Molly regretted that he'd overlooked a clue to her background.

"Was your mother a gardener?" she asked when they were riding along in his truck. Joey's grandmother.

"Not a vegetable gardener. She liked flowers and blooming shrubs and took pride in her yard. Until my younger brother was killed. He was only sixteen. After that she was so overcome with grief that she lost interest in everything. The yard. The house. Friends. Church."

"How sad," Molly said. "I've heard people say that the death of a child is the most devastating loss to recover from. How long did her depression last?"

"She never pulled out of it. She lost weight and became frail and sickly, and she had always been a healthy woman before. A year and a half after we buried Joel, Mom developed a bad case of pneumonia and died."

"I'm so sorry." Molly touched his arm to convey her deep sympathy. "And your poor father became a widower."

"Don't waste your sympathy on him." Jonah's voice had hardened with contempt. "He didn't stay a widower long. He'd already started a courtship on the sly. The dirt hadn't settled on my mother's grave before he was taking a new set of marriage vows, promising to love and cherish a different woman in sickness and in health.''

Molly stated the obvious, her voice troubled. ''You have hard feelings toward him.''

''I haven't spoken to him since he phoned me in Atlanta three months after my mother's funeral to invite me to his wedding.''

''He still lives in your hometown?''

Jonah nodded. ''He moved into Edna's house. She was a widow. Her husband died of cancer. My father had the gall to assure me he hadn't been unfaithful to my mother while she was alive. He'd turned to Edna for comfort, according to him.''

''Maybe it's true,'' Molly suggested gently. ''Your father must have grieved over his son, too, and from what you've described of your mother's mental state, it might have seemed as though he'd lost his wife at the same time.''

''She'd been a good wife to him for thirty years. He could have toughed out a few bad years and not gone sneaking off to Edna's house.'' Jonah uttered a sound of disgust. ''How did we get off on this subject, anyway?'' he asked, suddenly apologetic. ''I didn't mean to bore you with my family history.''

''I'm not bored.'' Just saddened by what she'd learned about Joey's grandparents. And disturbed over the estrangement between Jonah and his father, which didn't cast a favorable light on either of them. It made the elder Rhodes appear a man of weak character and Jonah appear judgmental.

Wasn't Joey better off without a grandfather and uncle who hadn't spoken to each other for over four years?

''I guess it's just as well under the circumstances that

you didn't give your father a grandchild," she commented. "At least you haven't mentioned being a father."

"I'm not. My ex-wife and I put off having a family."

"You must have been glad you did."

"Actually I'm as sorry as I am glad because I wanted to be a father eventually. I don't foresee getting married again. So that pretty much rules out children."

"Your marriage left you that disillusioned?"

"In combination with what I saw happen with my parents' marriage. I don't buy the whole notion of enduring love between a man and woman. Romantic love between a bride and groom is largely sexual attraction. When that dies, if a couple is lucky, they discover they like each other and develop affection. That was the situation with my parents, until my brother hit sixteen and started dating the wrong kind of girl."

"Karen Gulley." My sister. Your brother's teenage lover. Joey's birth mother.

"Yes. Karen Gulley. Call me vindictive, but I hope she's serving a prison term somewhere. You can bet that older sister of hers, Susan Gulley, is making regular visitations and telling anyone who'll listen that Karen is a good girl."

"You sound as though you hate them both and blame them entirely."

"I don't blame them entirely. I blame myself, too. I was wrapped up in my career off in Atlanta, working eighty-hour weeks. I should have done more than I did to save Joel, when talking to him and trying to enlist Susan's help didn't work. I met with her and asked her to do what she could to stop Karen from dating Joel," he explained. "She made excuses for her sister, bringing up their background. They were raised in foster homes."

"There might not have been much she could have done."

"I doubt she made any attempt to break them up."

I had hoped Joel would be a good influence on Karen, not vice versa.

"So tell me your life story," Jonah said. "I hope it's more upbeat than mine."

"No such luck. It's every bit as dreary," she replied. "My father deserted my mother when I was in grade school." Karen was a toddler at the time. "She dealt with her situation by becoming an alcoholic. They're both dead now." The sketchy facts were all true. Was he familiar enough with the Gulley sisters' family history to detect a similarity?

"You weren't kidding. That is dreary," he commiserated, giving her a compassionate glance. "No sisters and brothers?"

She shook her head, amending the answer. Not living.

"Are you a Texas native?"

"No, I was born in Birmingham, Alabama, but lived there only a short time." Her parents were both from rural Alabama. When Molly was a baby, they'd moved to Columbus, Georgia, for her father to take a job that hadn't lasted.

"I definitely don't detect an Alabama accent," he said. Nothing she'd told him seemed to have sounded an alarm. Evidently he hadn't done much research on the Gulley sisters. "Where did you go to college?"

"Here, there and yonder. I didn't get a degree." I had to work at jobs to support myself and my sister.

"You've done well for yourself without a degree."

"I have done well," she agreed with a note of pride. "One of these days, though, I plan to finish up my college education, just for the satisfaction. First I have to raise Joey and send him to college."

"As bright as he is, he may get a scholarship if he applies himself in school."

"Did you get a scholarship?"

"Yes, as a matter of fact, I did, which left the college fund my parents had set aside for me largely intact for financing Joel's education." His tone was bleak.

"Then Joel died and didn't use the fund, either."

"Right."

Molly's heart went out to him. She knew what it was like to survive a younger much-loved sibling. Karen had lived only a few years longer than Joel. But those two, for all their irresponsible behavior, and despite the grief they'd caused, had left a wonderful gift to the world. Joey.

If only Jonah didn't hate Karen so much, Joey could be a joy and consolation to him, too. And perhaps to the elder Rhodes, as well.

Molly would gladly share Joey, if introducing him to his close paternal kin would enrich his young life. But she wasn't willing to expose the little boy to bitterness and enmity between father and son, not to mention the threat of a custody battle.

There was simply no way of knowing—at least at this point—how Jonah would react when he learned the truth.

"Enough conversation about heavy topics," he declared, breaking into Molly's somber reflections. "Let's talk about books. Or movies. Or hobbies. Multiple choice," he said, smiling his wry, charming smile.

Molly smiled back, her heart doing a little flip-flop of pleasure. "I'll start with hobbies, selection C."

They passed through Study Butte and picked up Highway 118, heading north. From time to time she interrupted to point out a landmark or the gate to a ranch that encompassed thousands of acres.

Molly reminded herself every now and then to stay on her guard, but it was difficult because she was enjoying his company so much.

Too much.

If only...

She didn't let herself finish the wistful thought.

Chapter Six

"Where are the ranch houses?" Jonah asked about the seemingly endless expanse of open range. He could see no sign of human habitation other than miles of barbwire fencing and the occasional unimpressive gate with a rutted road leading off into nothingness. It was a scenic drive in its own way, but his eyes were always drawn back to Molly like a magnet. And not only was she lovely to look at, she was intelligent and had a sense of humor. He wouldn't have minded if the distance to Alpine were three hundred miles.

"They're out there somewhere out of sight," she replied. "I've only seen one, and it was quite luxurious with a swimming pool and a runway for the owner's small airplane."

"This owner. Was he a bachelor?" Jonah looked inquiringly at her. When she nodded, he felt a stab of jealousy.

"He's divorced," she said. "I dated him awhile."

"Filthy rich?"

"Yes, but hardworking. He's a born-and-bred rancher."

"You said you dated him 'awhile.' How long?"

Molly lifted a shoulder in a shrug, and the stretchy white fabric of her blouse pulled across her breasts. Jonah's groin tightened in response.

"Five or six months, I guess."

"You must have liked him to date him for that period of time."

"I did like him, but he started getting serious."

"That was bad?"

She gazed out her side window so that Jonah couldn't see her expression. "I wasn't in love with him. Also, there were...other obstacles to marriage."

Jonah waited, but she didn't elaborate. "Did he and Joey get along?"

"They got along fine. The fact that Joey became attached to Chad made it twice as hard to break off with him."

So what were these *other obstacles?* Jonah wondered. "From a purely selfish standpoint, I'm glad the match didn't work out," he said. "Your last name wouldn't be Jones. I wouldn't have gone to the fund-raiser on the off chance that you were Susan Gulley. We wouldn't be on our way to Alpine today."

She was slow to answer, a fact that disappointed him. He would have liked her to share his sentiments.

"You didn't just happen to go to the fund-raiser?"

"No, I was in the main Visitors' Center in the park at Panther Junction and overheard Heidi and her co-worker Roger talking. Your name came up during their conversation about the fund-raiser. I was doubtful that you were the same Molly Jones who'd lived in Amarillo, but my conscience insisted I make certain. The rest is history, as they say.''

She was gazing out her window again. Jonah took advantage of the freedom to feast his eyes on her. His fingers were itching to comb through her sun-streaked blond hair, stroke her smooth, lightly tanned skin. He didn't dare let his male imagination roam any further, not with her denim skirt riding up on shapely thighs.

''You said you weren't in love with the rancher. Has there been a special guy in your life you wanted to marry?'' he asked. ''I'm assuming you haven't ever been married.'' It occurred to Jonah that he hadn't been this deeply inquisitive about his ex-wife's past love life when they'd covered the same territory during their courtship. Although in truth he really hadn't courted Darleen. She'd pursued him.

''You assume right. I haven't ever married,'' she said, looking over at him and subjecting him to a thoughtful inspection that sent the blood humming through his body. ''As for a special guy, I knew a man very briefly who kind of overshadowed all the other men I met after him. It wasn't mutual.''

''Was he blind?'' Jonah demanded, that stab of jealousy getting him in the gut again. What was going on with him? he wondered. He'd never been the jealous type, and at this point in his relationship with Molly, he shouldn't mind this much that she'd been crazy about some other guy.

''Obviously you've had at least one special woman in your life,'' she remarked.

''You mean my ex-wife, Darleen.'' Jonah shrugged. ''I sold myself on the idea that she was the woman for me. Mainly I'd reached that stage a lot of men reach when I was tired of the single life and thought it was time to settle down. By then Joel and my mother were both gone and there were no family connections.''

''How did you meet Darleen?''

''She introduced herself to me. We were both sitting in a restaurant at adjacent tables. I was meeting a client for a business lunch, and he was a few minutes late. Darleen was with her boss, who'd gone to the ladies' room.'' Jonah added, smiling, ''The boss was a woman, naturally.''

''So you followed up and asked Darleen out on a date?''

''Actually she called me and saved me the trouble. We started dating and got married six months later. We'd been living together for three months. I knew I wasn't in love with her,'' he admitted, ''but we were sexually compatible, and I thought we had a future together. I expected a deeper affection to develop with time. As things turned out, it didn't develop.''

Jonah decided to make a clean breast of it. ''Darleen didn't love me either, I found out. She told me in one of our more candid discussions during the divorce proceedings that she'd set her cap for me because she liked my looks and considered me a good catch. She realized she'd made a mistake when I started getting burned out with city life and talked about a career change and a simpler life-style. At that point she cut her losses and found herself a better catch.''

Molly reached over and laid her hand on his arm. ''I doubt that,'' she said.

He covered her hand with his and squeezed it, seizing the opportunity to touch her and connect with her physically. ''Thanks for saying so, anyway.''

Their eyes met and Jonah was sure she caught her breath, too, with the intimacy and the flare-up of the man-woman chemistry between them.

''Where were we on that multiple-choice list of conversation topics when we got off on my failure at matrimony?'' he asked when she pulled her hand away with a seeming reluctance that pleased him deeply.

''We'd worked our way through hobbies and movies. That leaves books,'' she answered.

''So what are you reading now?''

She mentioned the title of a nonfiction book that was about single parenting and, in response to his questions, told him about the author's approach to the subject of single parenting.

''I feel at a real disadvantage, being from a dysfunctional family background,'' she explained. ''So I read all the experts.''

''You're doing a great job bringing up Joey.''

''He's a total joy to me.''

''That's part of the reason he's such a lucky little boy.''

Jonah's matter-of-factly earnest words seemed to ignite a glow in her that made her even lovelier. He hadn't spoken them to get into her good graces, but some tension eased between them allowing them both to relax and be themselves. For the first time he heard her laugh in response to a joking comment he made. The sound gave him such pleasure that he put himself out to amuse her and hear it again.

The whole excursion took on a carefree element as the wheels of his pickup ate up the miles to their destination. It occurred to Jonah that he hadn't felt this happy and centered in the moment for a long, long time. Probably years.

The realization was a little scary.

When they neared Alpine, Molly described the county seat of Brewster County as a combination cow town and college town that had kept its west Texas character while keeping up-to-date on offering modern amenities. Jonah noted the saddle shops and feed stores and numerous pickup trucks, some of which were attached to horse trailers. But he also noted bookstores with cafés and ever-popular coffee shops, chic jewelry stores, clothing boutiques, art galleries and pottery showrooms.

Finding a store that sold computers and computer accessories turned out not to be a problem. Molly went inside with him. "You're buying a mouse?" she commented with slight surprise.

"My laptop has a trackball," he explained. "But Joey is already familiar with using a mouse, which is better for a child's hand-eye coordination. I'll plug it into an external port on the back."

"How thoughtful. But why don't you let me buy it?" She held out her hand for the small box.

Instead of giving the box to her, Jonah placed his palm on hers and intertwined their fingers. "Don't be silly," he chided. When he tugged her in the direction of the checkout counter, she went willingly, holding hands with him.

At the cash register he needed both hands to uphold his end of the transaction, but on the way toward the store entrance, he pushed his luck and loosely circled her waist with his free arm. She let him get away with it for a second before she nudged his arm away.

"Jonah, don't," she said.

"Why not?" he answered.

"Let's just be friends. Please."

He held the door open for her, feeling wounded. "If that's what you want," he said when they were out on the street.

"It's what's best."

Jonah took consolation in the fact that she didn't seem especially happy, either, about holding the line to friendship. He frankly doubted they could be around each other and not give in eventually to the chemistry sizzling between them, but maybe he was mistaken.

"Where to next?" he inquired.

"I'd like to go to a store a couple of blocks down that sells candles and silk flowers." She gestured. "We could split up and meet back here at the truck in about a half hour."

"I'll just go with you, unless you're trying to get rid of me."

"No, that wasn't my intention."

Jonah took her at her word. They walked together in the direction she'd indicated.

"This is the store," Molly announced when they'd gone a couple of blocks. Inside she picked up a shopping basket and headed for a section with candles. Jonah would just as soon have tagged along, to be near her, but instead he browsed on his own, giving her some space. She sought him out after about ten minutes, saying, "I'm ready to check out."

At the cash register he noted her purchases with interest. Evidently she liked candles. She'd selected half a dozen. She'd also chosen silk flowers for some kind of arrangement, he assumed. The colors—coral and yellow and bright blue—were especially vivid in contrast to the more subtle hues of the candles. Some vague memory nudged at Jonah's mind, but then vanished as Molly turned to him, shopping bag in hand.

"This is not a very exciting way for a person on vacation to spend a day," Molly said.

"I'm not complaining," Jonah replied good-naturedly.

They'd driven in his truck to a discount store and were both pushing shopping carts along the aisles, loading them up with paper plates, napkins, paper towels and other items on Molly's list to buy for the community center.

Jonah had made himself handy, lifting packages and cartons off shelves.

"I appreciate your help."

He grinned his wry, attractive grin. "Good. I'm knocking myself out to be indispensable."

Molly smiled back at him and felt her pulse quicken as they gazed at each other, the attraction between them like a magnet pulling her toward him. "What am I looking for?" she said, consulting her list. "Toothpicks."

"Right up there ahead of you."

She took several steps, searching. "Where? I don't see them." It was hard to concentrate and focus on anything but him.

He left his cart and came to stand beside her, close enough that she imagined she could feel the heat of his body.

"Oh, I must be blind," she said as he reached for a small carton.

"How many?"

"A couple, I guess."

He tossed them into her shopping cart.

"Thanks," Molly said distractedly. When he didn't move away, she glanced up at his face, tried to look away and couldn't.

"This is a first for me, wanting to kiss a woman in a grocery aisle," he said, his gaze falling to her mouth. His low voice with its forced humor was a seduction in itself.

A dozen protests half formed in Molly's brain, but they weren't strong enough to muster the necessary willpower to turn her head aside as Jonah's head lowered and he brought his mouth to hers. The contact was warm and seeking. Molly's lips clung, and she swayed, feeling a rush of weakness and exhilaration all the way to her fingers and toes.

Jonah's hands grasped her waist to steady her. All too

soon he raised his head and drew in a breath. "Was that as good for you as it was for me?" he asked, the unsteadiness in his voice undermining his attempt at lightness.

"Jonah—"

"You aren't going to get upset over a kiss that innocent," he chided, gently stroking her bottom lip with his thumb.

Molly breathed out a sigh. "I'm not blaming you any more than myself."

"How does blame enter in? We're a couple of single adults with the hots for each other. Maybe a kiss or two will cool us off a little. The hands-off approach isn't doing the trick, is it? So what's next on your list?"

A better question was Where was the list? It had fluttered to the floor from her nerveless fingers, forgotten. Jonah retrieved it and they proceeded with their shopping mission.

Maybe he was right, Molly reflected. By trying to hold him at arm's length, perhaps she was making matters worse. A more casual attitude might defuse the sexual attraction. For him, anyway. She doubted anything could make her less responsive to him.

"Has there been a special guy in your life?" he'd asked her on the drive to Alpine, never dreaming that he'd swept her off her feet six years ago when she was a shy twenty-one-year-old full of romantic yearnings. He might have been her own modern—but oblivious—Prince Charming. After that one meeting, she'd imagined conversations with him, fantasized about him, dreamed about him. It had only been a foolish crush, but he'd still overshadowed all other men.

Until he'd shown up here in Big Bend country, Molly had convinced herself that she'd built Jonah Rhodes up larger than life. But she hadn't. He was as tall and good-looking as she remembered, as intelligent, as personable, as virile. His voice was as deep and sexy. Also, he seemed every bit as much a decent guy with admirable qualities as she'd made him out to be, on such short acquaintance.

And this time around he looked at her and smiled at her the way he had in her dreams. Of course, his smile would die if she told him the truth.

Whether or not she did was a decision that had little to do with his good or bad opinion of her and everything to do with what was best for Joey.

Her nephew. His nephew, unbeknownst to him.

Their nephew.

To Jonah's immense satisfaction, Molly didn't try to get rid of him with a suggestion that they go about their grocery shopping separately and meet at the front of the store later. He wouldn't have gone for such a plan, anyway. Supermarkets held very little fascination for Jonah— in and out as quickly as possible had always been his motto—but he could happily spend an hour or two pushing his cart up and down aisles with Molly, a measure of how bowled over he was by her.

"Did you go grocery shopping with Darleen?" she asked as they moved on beyond the canned soups. He'd tossed several cans into his cart to her dozen cans.

"Rarely, unless we were together and stopped to pick up a few things, like milk and bread. Neither of us was really into cooking. We mostly ate take-out if we ate at our apartment."

"She had a career?"

"Bridal consultant."

They'd arrived at condiments. "I guess I need ketchup," Jonah said.

Ketchup was on Molly's list, too. They got sidetracked from the subject of his marriage, which suited him fine.

It wasn't painful for him, satisfying her curiosity, but the here-and-now was far more interesting to Jonah.

In fact, when had the here-and-now ever been this vitally interesting?

"Do you like steak?"

"I live in southwest Texas," she reminded him. "Of course I like steak."

"Then let's have a steak dinner tonight. At my place." He made the offhanded invitation more a statement than a question.

"Jonah, I don't think—"

He didn't let her finish what was shaping up like a reluctant refusal. "Okay, your place."

She sighed. "The place doesn't matter."

"I agree. And we can have something besides steak, if you'd rather. Pork chops? Ribs? Chicken? I'm easy."

"No, you're not 'easy.' Not if *easy* means being a pushover."

"Look, I'll buy the steaks, and you make up your mind later. If you've had enough of my company by the time we get back and prefer a quiet evening by yourself over having dinner with me, I'll take a simple no for an answer." He put the package in his cart.

"If I say no, it won't be a simple no," she said.

When she didn't elaborate, Jonah didn't press her to explain. There was more than a fifty-fifty chance, he thought, that the part of her that wanted to say yes would win out.

If it didn't, Jonah was going to be disappointed. In fact, he would probably go back on his word and resort to persuasion.

They'd just emerged from the supermarket after passing through a checkout line. Her cart was overflowing, while his was only partially full.

"I can handle this," Jonah said when they'd reached

his truck and he'd unlocked the rear panel of the camper top that converted his pickup into a carryall. "Why don't you sit in the cab?"

"I'll hand you the bags," Molly insisted. "That's only fair since the majority of them are mine."

A minute later she wished she'd taken his suggestion when she glanced and saw a ruddy-faced young man in a border patrol officer's uniform gazing at her. God, no, she thought, her heart sinking.

"Hi, there," he called and headed toward Jonah's truck. "I thought I recognized you." He covered the distance and came to a stop. "Remember me? Andy Post?"

"Of course I remember you. How are you, Andy?" Molly forced a smile and shook hands with him.

"Can't complain. Nobody would listen anyway, right?"

"This is a neighbor of mine, Jonah Rhodes."

"Nice to meet you," Andy said, leaning forward to shake hands.

"Same here," Jonah replied.

"Guess you heard about that bad motorcycle accident last month on the River Road," the younger man said to Molly, his tone grave. "It was almost in the same exact spot on the big hill—that's what we call Santana Mesa."

Molly knew the color had drained out of her face. She sensed Jonah's concerned glance at her. "I did hear about the accident," she said.

"Same kind of motorcycle, a Harley. A guy and a girl." He shook his head, his expression sober. "They were both killed, too."

"It's such a dangerous highway."

"It sure is when you treat it like a roller-coaster ride. Say, how's your sister's little boy? He must be about, what, five years old now?"

"My cousin's little boy," Molly corrected him.

Andy looked slightly puzzled. "I thought she was your sister," he said slowly. "That's why I got a little confused—"

"To answer your question, Joey is five years old," Molly cut in before he could finish his sentence. She knew what had confused him. The words "Beloved Sister" in the scrolled design of the wrought-iron cross she'd erected on Santana Mesa. "He's in kindergarten and is loving it."

"That's great. Well, it was good seeing you."

"Take care, Andy."

The border patrol officer waved and walked off toward the supermarket entrance.

Molly handed Jonah a bag without meeting his eyes. "Lynette and her boyfriend were killed in a motorcycle accident on Santana Mesa. The motorcycle was a Harley. That's on the same highway you traveled yesterday to Presidio," she explained, reaching for another bag. "El Camino del Rio is Spanish for the River Road."

"No wonder you reacted the way you did last night at the Cactus Café when I mentioned I'd almost had a head-on collision on El Camino del Rio," he said gently. "I figured that highway had some really bad association for you."

"The worst possible association. Maybe I will sit in the cab." Molly turned away from him, the combination of sadness and guilt more than she could handle. If there weren't Joey to consider, she would blurt out the whole truth to Jonah. She was so sick of secrecy.

"You'll need the keys," he said gruffly. But instead of handing them to her, he pushed aside the shopping cart separating them and gathered her into his strong arms. Molly couldn't help herself. She knew it was wrong for her to bury her head against his shoulder and lean into him, letting him comfort her. She was accepting his sympathy under false pretenses. Sympathy that would vanish if she were honest with him.

His admiration and interest in her as a woman would vanish, too, as would his good opinion of her. The knowledge sent a wave of anguish through Molly.

She couldn't bear to tell Jonah the truth, for selfish reasons, not just because she had Joey's welfare to consider. The insight into her own mixed motives made Molly pull away from the haven of Jonah's arms.

"I'm okay now," she said. "Thanks for the hug."

He hugged her tighter before he released her. "Anytime."

His words and the caring expression on his face sent the wave of despair through Molly again. She took the keys from him and walked blindly around to the cab of the truck, facing up to another not-so-startling revelation. It was going to break her heart when he left in a month, either knowing or not knowing that Joey was his nephew.

When Jonah slid behind the wheel, Molly was combing her hair. She dropped the comb in her purse and flipped up the visor, asking, "Would you like me to drive?"

"No, I don't mind driving." He was glad to see her normal color was back in her cheeks, and she seemed herself again.

"Gas is cheaper here in Alpine," she commented as Jonah pulled out onto the street.

"I noticed. But what the heck. I'd rather pay a little more at Casey's gas station and give him my business."

"That's what I do. I never fill up here in Alpine, either."

Their shared support of the local economy of Study Butte and that pocket of Brewster County struck a note of rapport between them.

Five minutes later they were headed south on Highway 118, the open highway in front of them. A border patrol vehicle heading north whizzed past in the other lane. Jonah didn't need the reminder of the recent incident in the supermarket parking lot. It was fresh in his thoughts. Apparently fresh in Molly's thoughts, too, he surmised when she spoke up.

"Andy and his partner were driving from Presidio toward Study Butte that day Lynette was killed. They came along immediately after the accident had happened. Andy couldn't have been kinder when I came from Amarillo and made funeral arrangements."

Her reflective tone of voice freed Jonah to follow up with questions.

"So you were still living in Amarillo at the time?"

"Yes. I moved down here soon afterward and took the job I have now. Joey was two."

"You've never mentioned Lynette's parents."

"For all practical purposes, she had no parents. I like to think if she had grown up in a close family with a real home, she would have turned out differently. Oh, she had her sweet moods and bursts of generosity and could be lots of fun, but she was completely self-centered and manipulative. Still, I loved her dearly and I miss her."

Jonah offered the only good thing he could think of to say about her teenage cousin, given how little he knew about her. "At least she didn't take the easy solution to a teenage pregnancy and have an abortion."

"No, but she threatened to. Having her baby was a bargaining point she used with me at the time to get her way."

Jonah had run out of platitudes. He resorted to sympathetic silence.

Lynette Jones sounded like an evil soul twin to Karen Gulley. He could easily imagine Karen being just as manipulative and amoral, threatening to abort an unborn child to bully her older sister into submission when other methods failed.

But never in a hundred years would Susan Gulley ever describe her bad-egg sibling's flaws the way Molly had analyzed her teenage cousin's character, sadly, but with the objectivity of a sociologist. Molly wasn't Susan in disguise. No way.

It was weird as hell, though, the parallels.

Chapter Seven

It was almost seven-thirty when Jonah backed into Molly's driveway and edged past her parked automobile to get as close as possible to the front door. His stomach had been rumbling for at least thirty minutes.

"I'm almost hungry enough to eat my steak raw," he said. "What about you?"

"I'm hungry, too. Lunch seems like a long time ago."

So far, so good, Jonah thought. Now to go for broke.

"I'll help you bring in your groceries. Then I'll go and start fixing dinner. You can come along to my condo as soon as you put your perishables away."

"Okay. I can help when I get there."

Her reply following the briefest pause made jubilation rise up inside him. Yes! When had he ever reacted like this to a woman's agreeing to let him cook dinner for her?

Never.

Jonah shoved aside the slight uneasiness. It was probably the element of challenge, he rationalized. Molly hadn't been deliberately playing hard to get, but the effect on him had evidently been the same.

"Do you want to transfer the supplies for the community center into my car, so that I can drop them off?" Molly asked while they were making trips back and forth from his truck to her kitchen.

"No, I can drop them off myself tomorrow."

"Are you sure you don't mind?"

"Positive."

"That'll be a big help. I'll give you a key to the building."

"You trust me with a key?" he joked, but underneath he was pleased. Of course, he would have been even more pleased if she'd elected to go with him some time tomorrow and unlock the building herself.

You've got a bad case, Rhodes.

But a bad case of what?

"That's the final haul," he said as he put down several bags on the island. Molly had remained in the kitchen on this final trip and was busily stowing food items in the side-by-side refrigerator/freezer.

"Thanks a million," she said, casting him a grateful smile.

"Don't mention it. Well, I'm off. See you in a few minutes."

"I won't be long. I promise."

"I'll leave the front door unlocked. Just come on in."

"Okay."

Jonah stood there a second longer and finally managed to tear himself away. Damn, he'd been with Molly for six straight hours. Anyone would think he'd be ready for a short breather. Instead he was regretting being separated from her for fifteen or twenty minutes.

At Flora's condo, Jonah made short work of carrying

in his groceries and putting away purchases that didn't figure into the dinner menu. Next he found a corkscrew in a drawer and opened a bottle of red wine. What next? he asked himself after he'd set out two stemmed glasses in readiness. Scrub the potatoes? Start on the salad? While Jonah was deliberating briefly, mentally scratching his head over priorities, the phone on the kitchen wall pealed to life. He stared at it like he might have eyed his worst enemy and muttered a curse.

If that was Molly calling to cancel out on him—

Flora's voice came over the line. "Hi, Jonah, just checking to make sure my tenant is happy."

Jonah sagged with his relief. "You've never had a happier tenant," he assured her. Nor would she ever have had an unhappier one if he'd had to reconcile himself to an evening alone. This from a man who'd set off on a lengthy vacation by himself with nary a qualm about solitude.

After he'd hung up, Jonah took the potatoes over to the sink and subjected them to a thorough cleaning. Maybe he should back off after tonight. Molly had made her wishes plain. She didn't want to get involved with him. And Jonah didn't want to get involved in anything serious either. He'd had it with marriage.

Yes, better to back off. At least slow down.

He set the potatoes aside and started washing the lettuce.

"It's me, not a burglar," Molly called out from his foyer in her sexy Texas accent. The front door closed with a click.

Jonah dropped the lettuce and snatched a paper towel to dry his hands. His heart was racing with a surge of sheer gladness that she'd arrived. The light tapping of her boots on the Mexican tile might have been music to his ears.

"You said to walk on in," she reminded him, appearing in the doorway.

"Great, you're here," he said. "Now I can pour us a glass of wine to enjoy while I'm fixing dinner." She couldn't have looked any lovelier to him if he'd already drunk the whole bottle. He was taking in the sight of her, streaked-blond hair, pretty face, blue eyes, knockout figure.

"By all means," she said, moving over toward him. "Now, what would you like me to do?"

Kiss me. Touch me. Make love with me....

"Er, how about making the salad?" Jonah glanced around at the sink, realizing that, in his excitement, he'd left the faucet running.

"I can handle that."

But could he handle working in close quarters with her and managing to keep from touching her and kissing her? Not easily, was the answer.

Jonah did succeed in restraining himself. Hunger helped. Also, savoring the companionable atmosphere helped.

The stove in Flora's condo was equipped with a grill. He cooked the steaks inside and microwaved the potatoes while Molly created a delectable-looking salad and set two places for them at the dining room table.

When the food was all prepared and their meals served on plates, Jonah played maître d' and pulled out Molly's chair. Then on impulse he returned to the kitchen, doused the bright lights and lit the tall tapers that formed part of Flora's elegant table centerpiece.

"Candlelight?" Molly said, but she sounded more charmed than resistant to the idea.

Jonah took his chair and raised his glass of wine. Molly clinked her glass with his, and they both took a sip, gazing at each other in the soft, flickering light.

Had she made a private toast? he wondered, but he didn't ask because she might ask him the same question. And he had made a private toast he was reluctant to share with her. A sentiment that had sprung from within him. To us. And to many more evenings like this.

"I'm glad you recommended this wine from one of your Texas vineyards," he said. "It's really good."

"I like it a lot," she said. "Of course, I'm not a wine connoisseur by any stretch of the imagination."

They both took another sip, and Jonah's taste buds came even more alive to the subtle range of flavors on his tongue. On her tongue…

"Shall we dig in?" he suggested, setting down his glass abruptly and picking up his knife and fork.

She followed suit and sampled her steak. "Hmm. Delicious." The genuine pleasure in her voice uncoiled a spool of satisfaction in him.

"Cooked to your liking?"

"Perfect."

Jonah's chest swelled with the pride of a gourmet chef. His steak was succulent and grilled exactly the way he liked. In fact, it was probably the best damn steak he'd ever eaten, and he'd dined in some fine restaurants in Atlanta.

"Hope the potatoes don't have marble hearts," he said, forking up a mouthful of baked potato.

"Mine doesn't. You thought of everything—even sour cream. I'm impressed."

She smiled at him, and Jonah caught his breath. The candlelight had probably been a mistake. God, she was lovely.

"So the way to earn your favor is feed you?" He smiled at her, and, damn, he could see her catching her breath.

"You catch on quick," she said several seconds too

late. "I have to wonder about your ex-wife's judgment. She didn't know when she had a good thing."

"That's the kind of comment a divorced man likes to hear."

Jonah was on the same wavelength with her and trying to cooperate in her attempt to dispel the intimacy by bringing up Darleen. But it didn't work. Whatever subject they talked about, however mundane, that other more-compelling conversation was going on.

I like you a lot and find you incredibly attractive, she told him.

I feel the same way, he answered.

This is wonderful, just the two of us here together.

Yes, wonderful... But it's scary, too.

Very scary.

The combination of utter contentment and suspense underlaid with vague apprehension that had Jonah in its grip was an entirely new experience for him. He had ventured into unexplored emotional territory. *Whoa!* a voice inside him cautioned.

"Sorry, no dessert," he said when they'd laid down their knives and forks, hunger satisfied. Hunger for food, anyway. Jonah had no sense of being sated with the delights of her presence.

"I don't need any dessert. But I could offer you pie from the Cactus Café—" She broke off. "Or maybe I can't. On second thought, we might have eaten it."

Attuned to every nuance of her voice and the play of expressions on her face in the flickering candlelight, Jonah knew the pie probably hadn't been eaten. She'd decided in mid-thought against offering him dessert, for whatever reasons.

"I don't need dessert, either," he said, pushing back his chair.

They both got up from the table. When she started clearing dishes, he tried to stop her.

"Let's just leave the dishes."

"I'll help you load them in the dishwasher. Then I'll say good-night."

The little voice inside Jonah was advising, "Call it a night," but the urge to detain her another few minutes overrode it.

"First we can finish our wine." He picked up both glasses, which were three-quarters full and led the way toward the living room. After a moment of obvious reluctance, she followed.

Jonah paused at the sofa, briefly imagining himself sitting next to her. Too much temptation. "How about some fresh air?" he suggested, continuing toward the sliding glass doors onto the patio.

"It might be cool out…" Her voice drifted off. He was already clicking the latch.

"You're right. It is cool out. Feels nice." Jonah advanced several steps out onto the tile patio. Molly came to stand near him. She accepted her glass, but didn't take a sip of wine. Instead she tipped her head back, gazing upward. Jonah admired the graceful line of her throat and followed it down to the swell of her breasts before he jerked his head back to gaze up at the sky, too.

"Damn, look at the size of that moon," he marveled. No wonder he could see her so clearly. The patio was flooded with silvery moonlight.

"Isn't it beautiful? So luminous." Her voice held a wistfulness that made him want to lay some fabulous gift at her feet.

"How many stars do you suppose there are up there?"

"Millions."

So much for avoiding temptation in the living room. Jonah took Molly's arm and drew her over to a bench near a big terra cotta planter with a blooming shrub that trailed long tendrils. The sweet scent of its blossoms, whatever kind of shrub it was, added another touch of enchantment.

"When I suggested getting some fresh air, I honestly wasn't setting the scene for seducing you," Jonah said as they sat down on the bench. His tone was ironical. "I stepped out here last night and should have remembered the moon was full, but I didn't."

"I was out on my patio last night, too. And I did remember."

Still she'd come out here with him. The indirect confession, spoken with the wistful note, sent a reckless warmth coursing through Jonah. He sipped his wine, and she sipped hers. They looked at each other in the moonlight, and Jonah knew that her pulse was hammering in rhythm with his.

When he took her glass from her hand, she didn't resist. Nor did she utter a word of protest as he set both glasses down out of the way, though his intentions were surely as plain to her as had been his intention to kiss her today in the discount store.

"I've wanted to do this all day," Jonah said in a voice husky with his desire. He combed his fingers through her hair. "And this." He caressed her face.

She closed her eyes, shivering.

"Cold?" he asked with concern.

"Warm," she murmured.

Jonah brought his mouth to hers and nuzzled the luscious fullness of her bottom lip. She brought her hands up and clasped his head, but not to stop him.

"Kiss me," he whispered.

And she did. Jonah learned the wisdom of the maxim, Be careful what you ask for. The blood in his veins seemed to become effervescent, like champagne filled with bubbles.

Her lips were warm and eager, pressing against his mouth. She was pleasuring herself, a fact that compounded his pleasure a thousandfold. Jonah took over and kissed her the same way. Then she kissed him again. Back and forth, they traded kisses, with the moonlight bright against his eyelids.

Jonah's breathing had quickened, and so had hers, even before their tongues touched for the first time and a more intimate exploration began. He tasted the heady flavor of her wine and experienced a period of drugged happiness during which a burgeoning need came to life, demanding more pleasure than kissing.

Up to now Jonah hadn't even been conscious of his hands, which grasped her at the waist. Suddenly he could feel the warmth of her body through her clothes. His fingers loosened on their own, and he slid his palms up and down her back. The friction burned his skin, and the heat traveled through him like a hot transfusion. Molly moaned softly in her throat, and the sound unleashed more urgency in Jonah.

He tugged her blouse from the waist of her skirt and thrust his hands under the stretchy knit barrier to caress the satiny warmth of her bare skin. Her arms were around his neck now and she was kissing him back with a hunger that matched his hunger, her tongue mating with his. Jonah's heart was pounding. He was rock hard, fully aroused. Dimly he heard the yap of coyotes off in the distance.

I thought you decided to back off, the little voice of his rational self reminded, but seconds too late. Jonah's hands had made their way around to Molly's midriff and were moving up to take possession of her breasts.

Her back arched and she turned her head aside to rest

her cheek against his, her arms tightening around his neck. She murmured his name, her voice soft with ecstasy, "Jonah…"

"God, have I wanted to touch you here," he murmured, discovering for himself that the silk bra she wore was totally unnecessary. It was thin enough that he could feel the hard peaks of her nipples. Rubbing them with his thumbs brought a transitory pleasure. Touching wasn't enough. Jonah wanted to kiss them and worry them with his tongue.

Nothing was ultimately going to be enough except making love to her.

"Jonah, please. We have to stop." Her plea was all the more desperate and earnest with the mixture of ecstatic pleasure and regret.

"Why?" Jonah withdrew his hands and put his arms around her, drawing her close in a tight embrace. "I want you more than I've ever wanted another woman." That confession had slipped out. He immediately wished he could take it back.

"But you don't really know me. There are things I've done in my life that might lower your opinion of me—things I'm not at liberty to tell you."

"I can't imagine that you've done anything that bad. You're not wanted by the law for a heinous crime, are you?"

"No." She sighed a troubled sigh. "Forgive me for letting this happen tonight."

"There's no harm done, other than some frustration. Blame it on the moonlight," Jonah suggested lightly, rubbing his cheek against her silky hair.

"I'd better go."

The coyotes yapped again. Either they were closer than before or else Jonah was able to hear them better now that his heartbeat had calmed down and his pulse wasn't creating a roar in his ears. The voice of caution spoke more clearly, too.

This is all for the better.

Jonah loosened his embrace reluctantly. "This checkered past of yours. The man you mentioned today—the one who spoiled you for marrying any other guy—does he figure into the story somehow?"

"Yes."

"I see." Jonah dropped his arms away and stood up, jealousy a sour taste in his mouth.

Molly paused to pick up the two wineglasses before she followed him inside. "I'll help you clean up," she said, sounding apologetic.

"Thanks, but I can handle it." The apology he couldn't handle.

She didn't insist, but said good-night and left. Jonah waited until he'd heard the click of the front door closing before he moved over to the dining room table. The candles had burned out. The remnants of the dinner looked anything but appetizing.

Now for a few chords of "The Party's Over," he thought.

The sarcasm didn't help a bit to ease his frustration, which went much deeper than physical dissatisfaction.

She had told him about that rancher for a reason. He should take it as a warning and not fall for her and try to compete with Super Guy, whoever the hell he was.

Jonah intended to follow his own advice.

Especially in view of the fact that he wasn't in the market for a serious relationship with a woman, anyway. And this thing with Molly felt awfully intense. He'd only been divorced a year and was in between careers.

Yes, common sense said to cool it with Molly.

That didn't mean Jonah couldn't see her with Joey present as a buffer. After all, he'd promised the little boy a session with the laptop computer tomorrow afternoon, and he wasn't one to break his promises.

His mood considerably more cheerful, Jonah scraped the dirty dishes and loaded the dishwasher.

Molly's footsteps seemed to echo in her condo. With Joey absent, it was unnaturally quiet and empty. She paused in the doorway to his room, taking comfort in the sight of his furniture and toys and books.

Having Joey in her life was enough to make her happy. Or it had been enough, before Jonah showed up and awakened in her a woman's unfulfilled needs that being a mother couldn't satisfy.

What was she going to do?

The answer came at once. She had to do whatever was best for Joey. His welfare came first. But what was best for him?

Jonah was his uncle and had so much to offer the little boy as an uncle. But once Molly told Jonah the truth, how would he react? She couldn't predict—or at least not at this point—that he would want to forge a permanent bond with his little nephew. Everything depended on whether blood kinship could win out over bitterness and hatred of Joey's birth mother.

Once Molly enlightened Jonah, confessing her real identity—or more accurately, former identity, she might be exposing herself to a custody battle. That possibility was so frightening. A judge could rule against her and she could lose Joey. Her fugitive status might very well reflect badly on her character. The news media were full of nightmarish stories in which good birth mothers had their children literally torn from their arms. Molly was only an aunt, even if she did love Joey as much as she would love her own child.

True, Jonah had made comments, praising her for her

maternal skills. He'd even said that Joey was a lucky little boy. But could Molly depend on his fair-mindedness? His praise had been for Molly Jones, not Susan Gulley.

It has too big a gamble to say anything until she was sure she would be accomplishing good rather than causing harm to Joey.

The decision made, Molly turned to go across the hall into her bedroom, her heart dragging as heavily as her feet. Whether she told Jonah the truth tonight or delayed in telling him, the consequences would be the same for her personally, she feared. His interest in her as a woman would instantly die. He might even be repulsed that he'd kissed Karen Gulley's older sister and desired her. Almost surely, he would be angry that he'd been taken in.

God knows Molly had tried to discourage him. After failing, she'd tried to keep him at arm's length, but she was human.

Karen's face smiled at her from the chest of drawers. Molly walked over and picked up the small framed photograph, remembering that moment tonight when she'd issued her dessert invitation and then quickly taken it back. She'd suddenly visualized her sister's picture. Under the spell of the candlelight dinner, Molly had recognized the very real danger that she might end up in her bedroom making love with Jonah.

She must never let what happened tonight happen again, she resolved. It wasn't right to melt in Jonah's arms when she was deceiving him. From now on, she would make sure they weren't alone together.

The fact remained that Molly no longer felt safe with the picture out on display, not as long as Jonah was around and didn't know that Lynette and Karen were one and the same. She had to put it away, as much as she hated to.

Molly opened a drawer and gently buried the photograph.

The next morning Jonah rolled out of bed with a groan. He hadn't slept worth a damn and had dreamed more crazy, disturbing dreams. In one of them he'd made passionate love with Molly in the middle of the desert under a full moon, surrounded by a whole pack of snarling coyotes.

After a shower and shave, he felt more ready to face the day. One thing he needed to accomplish was delivering the supplies to the community house, he reflected as he walked into the kitchen with coffee on his mind.

"The key," Jonah said aloud, snapping his fingers. Molly hadn't remembered to give it to him. He glanced at his watch and then at a clock on the wall as though double-checking the time. Only seven-thirty. She wouldn't have gone to work yet. He probably should get the key from her now. She might not think to take it with her to Clementine's Closet.

What the heck, he thought. He would pick up the key from Molly and go have breakfast at the Cactus Café.

Maybe she would join him, Jonah thought as he acted immediately upon his impromptu plan. He was standing outside Molly's front door, pressing the doorbell button when it occurred to him that he could have phoned first.

To his relief—okay, his disappointment, too—she wasn't wearing a flimsy see-through robe when she opened the door. She was dressed and had on makeup.

"Jonah," she said in surprise.

"We forgot the key to the community center last night."

"I know." She moved back, pulling the door open wider. Jonah responded to the unspoken invitation to enter, stepping into the foyer.

He inhaled. "Is that coffee I smell?"

"Yes. Would you like a cup?" On second thought, I take the offer back, her expression stated clearly.

"I only make passes at beautiful women in the moonlight," Jonah said wryly. He shrugged. "And occasionally in discount stores. Never before breakfast."

She smiled, relaxing. "In that case."

He followed behind her as she led the way to her kitchen.

"Actually it's good to see another human face," she said. "I was feeling lost this morning without Joey. He very seldom spends the night away from home."

Jonah pulled out one of the high stools at the island and sat on it. "Thanks," he said when Molly served him a mug of steaming hot coffee.

"I was about to make some toast. Have you eaten?"

"No, but I was all geared up to be adventurous and order *huevos rancheros* for breakfast. I noticed that the Cactus Café has it on the menu."

"I doubt you'll get better *huevos rancheros* anywhere else in the state of Texas. Gloria uses corn tortillas made locally and the salsa is her own recipe."

"*Huevos* are eggs, right?"

"Yes. So you've never had it before. Then you definitely should."

"Forget the toast and join me."

"Since you've twisted my arm, I will."

They smiled at each other, and Jonah suddenly felt on top of the world. He also felt the powerful pull of that magnetic field between them. God, but he wanted to touch her, kiss her.

"Ready?" he said, and took a hasty gulp of his coffee before setting it down and standing up.

"I'll drive my car and meet you there."

"Great. Thanks again for the coffee." Jonah didn't hang around.

Chapter Eight

"Sorry, all the tables were taken," Jonah said with a note of apology. "I remembered that you don't like booths, but I thought I'd better grab this one while it was still available."

He'd stood and waved his arm when Molly entered the Cactus Café, arriving minutes after he had.

"I'm not that opposed to sitting in a booth. This is fine." She slid in opposite him. There was little sense of déjà vu to make her uncomfortable. His attentive manner toward her said this breakfast was purely for enjoyment, whereas he'd been carrying out a grim mission on that past occasion when they'd shared a booth.

She fished into her purse. "Before I forget, here's the key."

"Oh. Right. I'll just put it on my key ring. Then I won't be likely to lose it."

Molly watched, taking pleasure in the sight of his well-shaped hands accomplishing the minor task with dexterity. Last night they'd felt so wonderful on her body, stroking her bare skin, cupping her breasts....

"What a unique key chain ornament," she said, sucking in a breath. Intimate recollection had speeded up her pulse and sent a surge of delicious warmth through her.

He held the round-shaped copper ornament so that she could inspect it better. It looked like a boy's crafts project. Indentations that had probably been created with a nail and a hammer formed a buffalo design. More than likely, the buffalo on a nickel had served as the model.

"My brother, Joel, made this in Cub Scouts," Jonah said. "He gave it to me for Christmas one year." His thumb caressed the copper disk, and from his faraway expression, she was almost certain he was reliving a holiday scene. "We were opening presents, and he couldn't wait for me to open his. He dug it out of the pile under the tree and presented it to me so proudly. Naturally, I made a big deal about how much I liked it. He grinned from ear to ear."

Molly had a sudden vision of Joey grinning. "You've had it on your key chain ever since, I'll bet," she said gently.

"No, I took it off after he was killed. For a few years, I couldn't stand reminders of what had happened."

"I'm so sorry. Such a sad thing, losing your only brother." Her heart aching for him, Molly covered his hand with both of hers.

"Such a senseless thing." He shook his head slowly. "That's what was so hard to come to grips with. If Joel had come down with a terminal disease, I would have grieved just as much, but there wouldn't have been the same guilt that I hadn't intervened somehow. Or the same anger."

"At Karen Gulley?"

"At her. And her sister."

Molly drew her hands back. Conveying sympathy and understanding seemed horribly hypocritical.

"Good. Here comes a waitress," Jonah said, stuffing his keys into his jeans pocket. "Smart lady. She's bringing a coffeepot with her."

By now Molly wasn't very hungry anymore, but she let him persuade her to order *huevos rancheros,* too. Despite the fact that resuming the conversation wouldn't do anything to restore her appetite, she needed to resume it.

"That anger you talked about. I can tell that it hasn't gone away entirely."

"No, it hasn't." He took a sip of his coffee. "I get all stirred up inside any time I think about the fact that Karen Gulley probably went on to corrupt God knows how many other Joels. So I don't think about her."

"What would you have done if you'd found her living in Amarillo, this many years later?"

"Performed a citizen's arrest and hauled her back to Georgia. I wouldn't have harmed her physically," Jonah assured her. "I'm not into vigilante justice. To be honest, I went to Amarillo hoping that Lynette Jones wasn't Karen Gulley. I want to close that whole chapter of my life permanently and put it behind me."

"How is that possible without coming to terms with your guilt and anger?"

"Maybe I'm depending on the old maxim that time heals all. I go for six or eight months at a time now without any thought of the Gulley sisters crossing my mind. Maybe eventually I'll be able to blot them out altogether. A shrink probably wouldn't recommend that tactic of dealing with traumatic memory, but it works for me." He made a rueful face.

"My resemblance to Susan Gulley doesn't disturb you?"

"No. After that night of the fund-raiser, I stopped being conscious of it."

Otherwise he wouldn't enjoy being around her. Molly could draw the troubling inference for herself and expand on it. Jonah wouldn't choose to be around her period if he knew who she was.

He hadn't wanted her to be Susan Gulley any more than he'd wanted Lynette to be Karen. That explained a lot about why he was so quick to accept Molly's denial of having any ties to Georgia. It explained his lack of suspicion when clues to her identity had cropped up, like her having a younger female relative who was a rebellious type. When the border patrol officer yesterday had referred to Lynette as her sister, even that incident hadn't tripped an alarm for him.

What a seemingly hopeless situation insofar as uniting Joey happily with his uncle. Molly doubted that Jonah could stand being around the little boy if he knew who Joey's mother was.

As for any chance of a future between Molly and Jonah, there was none. It was cruel that fate had brought them together.

"Hey, cheer up," Jonah chided. He reached across the table and chucked her gently under the chin. "Don't get all down in the dumps on my account. Life has never looked better to me. My main regret is not buying myself a pair of cowboy boots in Alpine yesterday." His grin was sheepish and utterly disarming. "I may have to make a trip back there."

Molly found herself smiling back at him, her depression lifting. "There's a men's store here in the Mexican Village that sells cowboy boots."

"That's good to know. I'll check out their selection."

"They also sell fancy Western shirts and belts with silver buckles and cowboy hats," she said teasingly.

"I doubt I have the nerve to go the whole nine yards," he replied, charming her again with his sheepish grin that confessed he might spring for those items, too, if he worked up the courage.

Their food was served. Molly was able to eat most of hers, while Jonah cleaned his up, obviously savoring every bite. He didn't put up a big fuss when she reached for the check and stated that she would buy his breakfast.

Molly had halfway hoped he would. Why does he have to measure up to all my standards? she asked herself. One of her pet peeves was men who always insisted on paying.

Outside the restaurant, Jonah got his keys from his pocket. Molly caught a glimpse of the copper ornament, and her earlier depression came creeping back.

"I'll return the community center key this afternoon after you and Joey get home," he said, walking along with her toward Clementine's Closet. "Remember, I promised to show him how to operate my laptop computer."

"I doubt he has forgotten. Otherwise I would let you off the hook."

"I don't want to be let off the hook," he declared, sounding completely sincere. "I'm looking forward to it myself. I downloaded some games from the Internet, like I mentioned doing. It'll be fun."

"Did you plan to come to our condo? Or would you rather we come to yours?"

"Whatever suits you best."

It didn't require a great deal of deliberation to choose. Her condo hadn't been the scene of a candlelight dinner or a romantic interlude in the moonlight.

"Our place then."

They settled on an approximate time. By that point they'd reached the door of the shop. Jonah bade her a casual, but warm goodbye and strode off across the parking lot toward his truck.

How I wish…

Molly didn't finish the thought. She entered the shop and began her workday.

Moping and wallowing in regret wouldn't change a thing in the whole chain of events that had brought her to Texas. Feeling sorry for herself was equally as futile. So what if she'd had a rough time of it growing up and never really knowing what it was to feel carefree and secure. There were far worse horror stories than hers. She'd done well for herself and had darned few hangups, considering her background, if she did say so herself.

One of those hangups was Jonah. He'd stolen her heart when she was particularly vulnerable, and she'd indulged in fantasy about him. Other men just hadn't measured up. And now that Jonah had appeared in person and she'd actually gotten to know him and had experienced heaven in his arms, it was doubtful any other man would ever come close to measuring up to him.

I really do feel I'm falling in love with him now. Molly made the admission to herself between customers.

She also recognized that there was no happy ending in store for her. Just an ending not even preceded by a brief, glorious love affair. After this afternoon she would ask Jonah to stay away from her and Joey.

It would be best for Jonah never to know he had a nephew. Why give him knowledge that would only place him in a dilemma and torment him?

Jonah backed his truck up as close as he could get to the door of the community center building. He figured he might as well save himself some steps when he unloaded the supplies he and Molly had purchased yesterday in Alpine.

As he singled out the new key to unlock the door, Jonah paused to finger the copper ornament, recalling the conversation with Molly at breakfast. Odd how painless it had been to tell her the background story, he reflected. He'd felt more sweet nostalgia than sadness as he'd remembered that long-ago Christmas.

What had he given Joel that year? Jonah propped open the door, letting his mind travel back. The model plane operated by remote control. That had been Jonah's present. God, had the kid been thrilled. They'd spent the whole afternoon playing with the damn thing, Joel and Jonah—and their father.

They deserted their poor mom, he remembered, but she just teased, "Next year I'll know what to get Jonah and your dad, Joel."

Jonah could visualize her, smiling and happy.

Those had been happy days for the Rhodes family. They'd had lots of great Christmases. Until Joel hit his sixteenth year.

But Jonah didn't want to think about that year. Today stretched before him, full of options for how to spend his time enjoyably. When late afternoon rolled around, he would get to see Molly and Joey. With luck he might manage to include himself in their supper plans.

Life seemed very good.

A carryall vehicle pulled up just as Jonah was making his final trip inside the building. A man he recognized from the fund-raiser got out. His first name rang a bell when he introduced himself as Charlie Pendergast. He was a retiree and had come to do some volunteer handyman work.

"Could you use another pair of hands?" Jonah asked.

"You bet," Charlie answered.

By noon they'd finished a series of small jobs. Charlie insisted on buying Jonah lunch at a burger restaurant across from Casey's gas station. Casey came in and joined them, after first greeting Jonah like an old friend.

Jonah found himself thinking how much he liked this small-town socializing. He glanced out a window at the two-lane highway that the station owner had walked across without any hazard to his life. Traffic was intermittent.

If he lived here, what would he do as a means of livelihood?

The tidbits of news the other two men threw out during conversation presented a couple of possibilities that might have been worth checking into if Jonah were seriously interested in putting down roots in rocky Big Bend soil. The elderly owners of an RV park had just put up a For Sale sign. The Mexican Village management wanted to bring in someone with advanced computer know-how. Jonah qualified.

As far as that went, he could pursue his old career in financial investment from a home office anywhere in the country. All he needed was state-of-the-art computer equipment and a telephone. But the idea didn't have as much appeal as doing something new and different once he did settle down somewhere.

After he'd parted company with his lunch companions, Jonah drove by the RV park slowly, purely out of curiosity. It looked fully occupied with mostly new-looking expensive motor homes and travel trailers.

He was curious about the price, but not being a serious prospective buyer, Jonah decided he wouldn't feel right inquiring and taking up the owners' time with pertinent questions.

Maybe he would do a little research into the RV park business, find out the pros and cons. Again out of curiosity.

During the afternoon, Jonah visited Lajitas on the Rio Grande, a private retirement/resort community which boasted a small golf course and a landing strip in addition to amenities like tennis courts and swimming pool. He strolled along the boardwalk in front of the Badlands Hotel, which was flanked by shops designed, like the hotel, to be replicas of buildings in the Old West. Before heading home, he stopped in at the original Lajitas Trading Post which supposedly Pancho Villa and his men once patronized.

A boy-size cowboy hat caught Jonah's eye. On impulse he bought it for Joey.

Molly had said to come about five-fifteen. Jonah was back at his condo by four-thirty. He watched national news on satellite cable TV until time to drive the short distance to her place.

Joey was playing outside in the front yard. His face lit up when he spotted Jonah's truck and he came running toward the driveway, blue eyes shining with excitement.

"Hi, Mr. Rhodes!" he yelled out.

What a nice reception this is, Jonah thought, feeling a wave of gladness. "Hi, there, Joey."

He climbed out and Joey came up to him. Jonah reached out and ruffled his hair affectionately. "How was kindergarten?"

"Fun. I brought home some papers. You want to see them?"

"Sure, I do. Shall we go inside?" Jonah slung the strap of his black leather carrying case over his shoulder. Inside it were laptop and disks and assorted computer paraphernalia. He remembered the cowboy hat and retrieved it. "Here. I bought you something."

"Wow! A cowboy hat!" Joey wasted no time trying on his gift. He tightened the string under his neck and took off for the front door, motioning Jonah to follow. "Let's go show Molly!"

Jonah's pulse picked up with a less-juvenile enthusiasm

as he walked with long strides in Joey's wake, pausing in the foyer to close the front door behind them.

"Molly! Molly! Look what Mr. Rhodes gave me!"

She came out of the utility room adjacent to the kitchen.

Jonah noted that she'd changed into black jeans and a red knit blouse after arriving home from work. Her shoes were black canvas with straw soles. Mentally he whistled his male appreciation and tried not to remember slipping his hands up under her blouse out on his patio last night.

"Look what Mr. Rhodes gave me!" Joey was repeating. "A cowboy hat!"

"How nice of him," she said, but she seemed very taken aback.

"I was in Lajitas today and saw the hat at the old trading post and thought Joey might like it," Jonah explained awkwardly. He hadn't meant to overstep his bounds, but apparently he had.

"I do like it," Joey declared.

"Did you thank Mr. Rhodes?" she asked her nephew.

The little boy turned to Jonah, an endearing trace of shyness in his blue eyes. "Thank you."

"You're welcome." He squeezed Joey's shoulder and then felt even more awkward under Molly's unsmiling scrutiny. What the heck was the matter? "Where did you want us to set up our computer station?" he asked her.

"Anywhere that's comfortable for you."

Jonah had been half expecting her to show him the door. "The dining room table okay?"

"The dining room table is fine."

"Oh, boy! This is going to be fun!" Joey clapped his hands and received a loving glance from her.

I'd like for her to look at me with that open-ended approval, Jonah thought to himself.

"Shall I get a booster chair to raise him higher when he sits in a dining room chair?" she asked.

"Actually it will be better for him to sit on my lap so that we can both look directly at the screen." When she nodded comprehendingly, he didn't consider it necessary to explain that frontal viewing was a privacy feature of many laptops since businessmen used them on airplanes and in other public places.

Five minutes later he and Joey occupied a chair in her dining area with the laptop open on the table and booting up.

"May I watch?" she asked.

"Sure," Jonah said, inserting a diskette. He was pleasantly aware of her standing about a foot behind them as he patiently led Joey through the steps of moving the cursor, a small white arrow, around on the screen and clicking the control gadget called a mouse. Soon the little boy was engrossed in a cyberspace visit to a zoo, complete with sound track. He laughed delightedly at the noises the animal made.

"What a neat program," Molly marveled, moving up closer and bending lower to gaze over Jonah's shoulder. He was inhaling the scent of her perfume mixed with the pleasantly earthy scent of active small boy. It was a thoroughly nice combination. Jonah eased back enough to make firmer contact with her arms, which she'd folded along the back of the chair.

Feeling the warmth of her body through his shirt, he was perfectly content to be right here, doing what he was doing.

Molly eventually disappeared into the utility room, leaving him and Joey to continue the session without her supervision. The little boy didn't even seem to notice she'd gone.

Ten or fifteen minutes later she reappeared with a laundry basket of folded clothes and headed toward the hallway to the bedrooms. Jonah smiled at her, and she smiled back, but her lovely blue eyes were shadowed with worry as her gaze touched on Joey. Something definitely was bothering her.

After she'd returned, the phone rang and she carried on a conversation, perched on a kitchen stool. Jonah tuned out her end of it, but he glanced over often, enjoying looking at her and hearing her voice.

She hung up just as Joey came to the end of his computer tour of the imaginary zoo. A voice on the soundtrack said, "Please come and visit again soon."

"That was fun! Can I start over?" the little boy asked, his tone eager.

Molly spoke before Jonah could reply. "I'm sure Mr. Rhodes is getting tired."

"I could stretch my legs for a bit," Jonah admitted. "How about getting that booster seat you mentioned earlier?"

"Please, Molly."

She retrieved the seat. Jonah got the little boy settled in front of the computer again. Undaunted, Joey began to point and click, manipulating the mouse with his small hand.

The two adults stood behind him, watching.

"He already has the hang of it," Jonah said to her in an undertone. "What a bright little character he is."

"You're a wonderful teacher. So patient."

Why that troubled note beneath her praise? Jonah wondered.

"I can stand here and keep an eye on him and help him if he needs instruction," she suggested, speaking at a normal level.

Joey obviously overheard her. "I want Mr. Rhodes to help me," he announced.

"You don't look like you need much help from either of us, cowboy," Jonah remarked indulgently.

The cowboy hat sat to one side on the table, Joey having reluctantly taken it off earlier. Jonah picked the hat up and plopped it on the little boy's head. Joey giggled, pausing long enough to tighten the string under his neck before he resumed pointing and clicking.

"Would you like a beer?" Molly asked Jonah.

"That sounds good. But I don't like to drink alone."

They moved over into the kitchen. She got out two amber-colored bottles of a popular Mexican beer and cut up a fresh lime. When he'd refused her offer of a glass, she sat beside him on a stool at the breakfast bar, apparently not wanting a glass, either.

Jonah squeezed a small piece of the lime into his beer while she was doing the same. He picked up his bottle and was about to salute her when he remembered that silent toast last night at dinner. Instead he took a big swallow of the cold, tangy beer.

"This hits the spot," he said, watching her as she tilted back her head and drank from her bottle. His pulse had picked up speed. Damn, just having a beer with her was arousing.

"The phone call I got a few minutes ago was from Charlie Pendergast's wife," she said.

"Nice guy. I ran into him this morning at the community center."

"So she told me. That was certainly generous of you to donate several hours of labor."

"Actually it felt good to be useful," Jonah admitted. "And I enjoyed Charlie's stories about his work in the offshore oil drilling industry."

"He and his wife both are good people."

"It seems that all the locals I've met fit in that category." He smiled at her. "Including you."

She looked pleased but also uncomfortable with his sincere commendation of her character. "Well, thank you."

Last night she'd said to him, "But you don't really know me. There are things I've done in my life that might lower your opinion of me—things I'm not at liberty to tell you."

Jonah couldn't believe she'd done anything immoral or illegal. She struck him as being a highly conscientious person. He couldn't remember ever having a higher regard for a woman he was attracted to. Maybe the combination of admiration and chemistry accounted for this sense of treading on unfamiliar ground, which Jonah didn't expect to be experiencing in his thirties.

He tabled that thought in favor of resuming the conversation.

"I also saw Casey today. He had lunch with Charlie and me at that burger place across from his station."

"You must have learned all the news, between the two of them. Casey is always a font of information. He's such a gregarious type and chats with his customers."

"He did pass along some news. The owners of the RV park just down the highway from Casey's place of business have put up a For Sale sign."

Molly nodded. "Fred and Sherrie Hapstead. She came into the shop today and was telling me they plan to move to Oregon to be nearer to their grandchildren."

"Did she mention the selling price?"

"Yes. Delores tends to be inquisitive, and she asked Sherrie."

"How much?"

She told him.

"No kidding. That's quite a bit lower than I would have guessed. Maybe I'll go and talk to them."

"You mean with the idea of buying their business and reselling it at a profit?"

"Not necessarily. I really like it so far down here in

Big Bend country. Running an RV park might be a nice change of pace from sitting behind a desk.''

Molly stared at him.

''Hey, I'm not that bad a neighbor, am I?'' Jonah's attempt at a light touch failed miserably. Her reaction disappointed him terribly. But didn't surprise him, he realized.

''You're not serious,'' she said.

''Halfway serious.'' Jonah took a swallow of his beer, and it tasted flat and bitter.

''Could you come and help me, Mr. Rhodes?'' Joey requested. ''I forgot how to feed the monkeys.''

''Sure thing, Joey.''

Molly slid off her stool, too, and began supper preparations. Jonah noticed when he glanced over that she'd also left her half-full bottle sitting on the counter.

He felt disappointment—and, yes, hurt—that she hadn't expressed even a mild enthusiasm over having him around permanently. Not that Jonah could accuse her of being wishy-washy. She hadn't given him any encouragement from the get-go, not any deliberate encouragement.

Jonah didn't understand himself. Why was he being so persistent, when she was obviously fighting the strong attraction between them for her own reasons?

''Can I visit the farm now?'' Joey asked, having completed his second zoo tour.

Molly spoke up from the kitchen. ''No, supper will soon be ready. Go and wash your hands.''

''Can Mr. Rhodes eat supper with us so I can visit the farm after supper?'' the little boy pleaded.

''Mr. Rhodes is welcome to eat supper with us, if he likes, but afterward you'll need to get ready for bed.'' Molly's voice was sympathetic, but firm.

Joey poked his bottom lip out and contorted his features

in a pantomime of unhappy small boy, but he climbed down from his chair and trudged off down the hallway.

"Most kids his age would pitch a fit," Jonah remarked, touching a button to turn off the laptop.

"I set a place for you, in case you wanted to take potluck," she said. "We're having macaroni and cheese and steamed broccoli."

"Did you make enough?"

"I made plenty."

"In that case, I accept. Can I do something to help?"

"No. Everything's ready."

"Guess I'd better wash my hands, too."

"Feel free. The layout is the same as yours."

Jonah could feel her gaze on him as he left the laptop sitting on the dining room table and started down the hallway.

By this time Joey was returning.

"How about showing me where your bathroom is," Jonah said.

"It's right down here, next to my bedroom." With all the self-importance of a guide at the nation's Capitol, the little boy changed directions and changed body language, his sulkiness vanishing. "That's Molly's bedroom across from mine."

Jonah couldn't resist glancing through the open doorway.

When he joined Molly and Joey in the kitchen, Joey had already climbed up on the center stool. Jonah sat on his right, grateful that the architect had designed a slight curve in the breakfast bar so they weren't lined up in a row. Molly served their plates, giving him ample helpings, before taking the remaining place.

"You must have gone to Lajitas today," she said. "You mentioned buying the hat for Joey at the old trading post there."

Jonah replied and the two of them talked about the Lajitas on the Rio Grande development, with Joey piping up occasionally between mouthfuls of his food. The meal couldn't have been more different from last night's candlelight dinner, but it was enjoyable in its own way.

"We have ice cream and leftover pie for dessert," Molly announced after they'd finished. She added for Jonah's benefit, "Joey and I hadn't eaten the rest of that pie, after all."

They polished off dessert. Afterward Jonah volunteered his and Joey's help in loading the dishwasher.

"Shall I make some coffee?" Molly asked.

"Coffee sounds great." He'd been resigned to saying good-night and leaving.

Chapter Nine

"Don't worry about me. I can entertain myself," Jonah assured Molly.

"Help yourself to coffee," she said as she departed with Joey to do her duty as a mom and help the little boy get ready for bed.

"Thanks. I will." He settled back on her sofa and flipped on the TV.

About twenty minutes later he was watching a program about an archeological dig when Joey came in, fresh out of the tub and wearing his pajamas and his cowboy hat. Molly followed behind him. The little boy stopped a few yards away, suddenly attacked by shyness.

"He insisted on showing you his pajamas that go with his hat," she explained.

Jonah surmised that she probably hadn't been in favor of the idea. "Hey, I like them," he declared, beckoning Joey closer. "Are those horses wild mustangs?"

Without Jonah realizing quite how it happened, the next thing he knew Joey had scampered up onto his lap. The five-year-old looked cute and adorable and smelled like soap and toothpaste. Jonah acted without thinking and gave him an affectionate hug.

"Time for bed," Molly said. Her voice sounded odd. She looked odd, Jonah saw when he glanced over at her.

"Your foreman just gave you some orders, partner." He set Joey on his feet and gave him a gentle swat on the bottom. "Off to bed with you."

"Will I see you tomorrow?"

"You just might." He didn't dare be more definite, though he would have liked to be.

"Tell Mr. Rhodes good-night," Molly instructed, and the little boy complied.

Jonah got up after they'd left the room again and poured himself more coffee. He resumed watching the TV show, but he couldn't concentrate on it during the short interval before Molly came back. She got herself a cup of coffee before joining him. Jonah patted the sofa cushion next to him, and she sat down.

"Did he fall asleep?" he asked.

"Surprisingly he went out like a light. I expected him to be too excited to go to sleep right away." Her voice was distracted and faintly troubled.

A silence fell, and Jonah could feel himself tensing. It dawned on him that she'd wanted him to stick around tonight in order to tell him something. Something that he probably didn't want to hear.

"What's on your mind, Molly? Something has been bothering you ever since I got here this afternoon. Is it my giving Joey the cowboy hat without first getting your permission?"

She leaned forward to put her still-full cup on the low table next to his empty cup. "I think buying him the hat was an extremely nice thing to do, but I would rather you hadn't. He's more apt to blow your kindness out of proportion than other little boys his age who have dads.''

''Maybe he needs a dad as well as a mother,'' Jonah stated.

''Of course he does.''

''How is he going to get a dad if you treat every man who wants to date you like you've treated me?''

She eyed him with mixed astonishment and irritation. ''I seem to recall you making it quite clear at our second meeting that you weren't planning to remarry any time soon. Wasn't I supposed to take you at your word?''

Jonah squirmed. ''You have me there, I guess. On the other hand, you told me on our first meeting that you didn't have time for a social life while you were raising Joey. Remember?''

''Yes, I did say that.'' She sighed. ''You're pushing my guilt button. I'm well aware that I'm letting him down by not finding him a good dad. Every now and then I evaluate my prospects. But it's not as simple as picking out a nice man and marrying him.''

Had she evaluated him as a potential dad? Jonah wondered, but he lacked the nerve to speak the question out loud. The answer might be too crushing.

''Anyone I know among the group?'' he asked. ''Like Roger the park ranger?''

Her expression confirmed that he'd made an accurate guess. Jealousy zigzagged through Jonah.

''You've gotten me off track,'' she said. ''This isn't the conversation I needed us to have. I've decided, Jonah, that it would be best for Joey—and me—if we didn't fall into a habit of seeing you regularly.''

''Because I'm a transient, just passing through.''

''Mainly, yes.''

So there were other reasons, too. Damn, it hurt that she

was making still another concerted attempt to get rid of him.

"Joey is already making you out to be a hero. You're about twelve feet tall in his eyes." She touched his arm as though wanting to soften the blow of rejection.

Jonah put his hand over hers, capturing it. "Every person in his world can't be permanent, Molly. You can't protect him from life. And I'm seriously kicking around the pros and cons of living here." She had it in her power to tilt the balance toward the pro side. Surely she was able to figure that out for herself.

"Please don't make this more difficult than it already is."

"So what you're asking—at least for the third time—is for me to get lost?"

"It's better this way, Jonah. For you, too."

"Thanks for looking out for my best interest." His tone was heavily ironic.

Releasing her hand, he stood up.

"I'm truly sorry," she said, rising to her feet, too.

Jonah led the way to the door. He was reaching to open it when Molly spoke behind him, sounding as miserable as he felt.

"Your laptop. You're forgetting it."

"Keep it awhile and let Joey use it. You have enough computer know-how to walk him through the instructions."

"That's awfully generous. But you must have brought the laptop on your trip to use it yourself. Plus I can tell by looking at it that it was expensive."

Jonah shrugged off her reservations, figuring they weren't the main one. "If you're worried about returning it to me, just leave it with Flora at the real estate office."

"Okay, I'll keep it a few days. Joey was enthralled with the zoo program."

With the issue settled, they looked at each other.

"So this is goodbye?" he said brusquely.

Instead of answering, she stepped forward and raised up to kiss him on the cheek. "Take care of yourself."

Jonah's combined hurt and disappointment couldn't keep him from putting his arms around her and drawing her close. She resisted for barely a second before surrendering to his tight embrace. He could feel the lush warmth of her breasts against his chest, her thighs against his thighs. The scent of her perfume filled his lungs.

"I have to kiss you at least one more time," he murmured.

"Please don't..." Her protest sounded dazed and desperate.

Jonah thrust his fingers into the silky strands of her blond hair and tilted her head. He brought his mouth down on hers, the blood surging through his veins. Their kiss was hard and passionate and hungry. Molly's arms circled Jonah's neck as she returned the bruising pressure of his lips. When he demanded entrance into her mouth, she opened and coupled her tongue wetly with his ardent tongue.

Groaning with urgent arousal, Jonah picked her up and held her hips tight against his groin. They both turned their heads aside at the same instant, pressing cheek to cheek and breathing raggedly. Jonah could feel her heart pounding in wild rhythm with his thunderous heartbeat.

"God, I want you," he whispered, the pain of desire in his voice. "More than I've ever wanted a woman before. How can you just break it off between us?"

"I have to," Molly replied with heartbreaking certainty.

Jonah's arms loosened, and he put her down. She clasped his forearms a moment, steadying herself. Then she backed away, giving him room enough to jerk open the door and walk out, closing it behind him.

As he strode toward his pickup, Jonah swore that this was the last straw. He would not set himself up to get knocked down again.

The beams from his headlights spotlighted the cape jasmine bushes when he was backing out of her driveway, for the last damn time. The sight of them increased his anger and agitation.

The fact that she'd planted his favorite shrub could have been—but wasn't—one more indication that fate had brought them together because they were meant for each other.

Molly listened to the sound of Jonah's pickup roaring off and fought the wave of despair that made her want to sink down on the floor and cry her heart out. Her only consolation was knowing she'd done what was ultimately best for Joey, for Jonah and for herself. This parting tonight was painful and hard, but if she'd let things go on, the three of them would have been subjected to a more devastating parting.

She'd protected Joey from getting attached to Jonah, and she'd spared Jonah's peace of mind. Still, it was impossible not to be flooded with a multitude of regrets for what might have been.

This afternoon and evening had filled a mental picture album with beautiful snapshots. Molly tortured herself by reviewing them as she picked up the coffee cups in the living room and carried them to the kitchen. Jonah with Joey on his lap at her dining room table, patiently tutoring the little boy in navigating the computer program. Joey seated between the two adults at supper. Strangers seeing that snapshot might mistake them for a family. Then later the touching good-night scene in the living room, Jonah giving his small nephew a hug.

A band had tightened around Molly's heart as she'd watched. Memory tightened it again.

How I wish...

What did she wish for? The answer was easy. For Jonah to fall so deeply in love with her that it wouldn't matter who she was. For him to adore Joey as much as she did and want to raise him. For her and Jonah to marry and be parents to their little nephew. For them to have a child together.

None of that was possible because the tragic past cast a big shadow over the present. Sadly, the truth about Molly's and Joey's identities would only deepen the gloom rather than dispel the shadow and let healing sunshine brighten all their lives.

"I'm going outside to play," Joey announced, sliding down from his perch behind Jonah's laptop at the dining room table. He was wearing his cowboy hat. Each morning he donned it first thing.

"Okay." Molly smiled at him. "I'll call you in for supper in about thirty minutes."

The kitchen window faced out onto the front yard. She glanced out frequently to check on him. He galloped back and forth, riding an imaginary horse. Every couple of minutes he stopped and looked toward the street.

The poor little guy was keeping a watch out for Jonah, as he'd done the two previous afternoons. Molly offered up her same prayer: Please don't let Jonah drive by.

Today the prayer wasn't granted. She had just gone to the front door to summon Joey inside when the little boy shouted, "There's Mr. Rhodes!"

Sure enough, the big silver extended-cab pickup with a stylish camper top had come into view.

"Time for supper," Molly said firmly, but Joey paid no heed. He was hopping up and down, waving one arm excitedly.

The pickup didn't slow down as it passed in front of her condo, but Jonah tooted the horn as he came abreast of Joey.

"Mr. Rhodes didn't stop," the little boy complained, looking crestfallen.

"He probably realized we're about to have our supper," Molly said gently. "Come in and wash your hands."

He trudged toward her. "Doesn't he still like us?"

"I'm sure he must, but he's down here on vacation. He may have been sight-seeing all day and gotten tired."

Her soothing words didn't cheer him up. He was subdued during supper. Molly battled her own depression and tried not to keep reliving the earlier episode. Jonah's gaze had been so somber when he looked at her standing in the open doorway and then looked at Joey. Evidently he intended to abide by her request for him to keep his distance.

This is best for him, too, she thought.

The reminder didn't ease the ache in Molly's heart.

"Was everything okay?" the waitress inquired.

"Fine," Jonah answered.

He barely remembered what he'd eaten. He'd meant to have supper at his condo after hiking all day. Then he'd driven past Molly's condo and seen her and Joey. The incident had been so upsetting that Jonah had turned around and headed back to the highway again. He'd ended up at this motel restaurant in Study Butte. He'd wanted some place that was impersonal, without any associations with Molly.

Jonah was haunted by the memory of Joey waving at

him, eager expectation written on the little fellow's face. Driving on past without stopping had been one of the hardest damn things Jonah had ever had to do. He'd made the mistake of glancing in the side mirror and had cursed with his dismay. Joey had been gazing after the pickup, looking like a kid who hadn't found a single present under the tree at Christmas.

In the background Molly hadn't looked much happier. Although she had looked relieved.

I should pack up and leave.

As Jonah drove back toward the condo complex, he tried to imagine himself leaving Big Bend country for good, leaving Molly and Joey and never seeing them again. The thought was intolerable.

Despite everything, he didn't want to go.

Earlier he'd bypassed the turnoff to the Mexican Village. Reaching it on this return trip, he took the road and was soon pulling into the familiar parking lot. The lighted windows of the Cactus Café seemed to have a homey air that beckoned Jonah.

Gloria was at the cash register. She smiled and waved when he entered.

Casey and Flora were sitting at a table with Charlie Pendergast and a woman Jonah assumed was his wife. They'd just been served coffee and dessert. Jonah responded to their chorus of friendly greetings.

"Come join the crowd," Casey called, getting up to grab a chair from an adjacent table. Flora was scooting her chair over to make room.

After Jonah had sat down, Charlie introduced his wife. In the meanwhile Casey had already summoned the waitress over. Jonah ordered coffee and the dessert special of the evening, blueberry cobbler.

No one treated him like a guest. He might have been one of them, a local person who was a regular customer at the café. Jonah's morale had lifted considerably by the time the subject of the potluck supper-dance came up. Gloria had come over to chat with them and announce that a local rancher had donated steaks for the supper.

"We'll need at least a couple of guys to be in charge of cooking the steaks on the big grill at the community center," she said.

"Count me out," Charlie said. "I'm the world's worst when it comes to cooking meat on a grill. Right, Betty?"

His wife patted his arm, agreeing with him.

Gloria looked inquiringly at Casey and Jonah.

"Sure," Casey said. "I cook a mean steak, if I do say so myself. Jonah, you want to be my cochef?"

Jonah was thinking about the steaks he'd grilled for Molly and himself the evening after they'd gone to Alpine. "If I come, you can count on me."

"What's this 'if I come' business?" the gas station owner demanded. "Of course, you're gonna come."

The other four of them all chimed in, insisting that he had to attend.

"Put me down as Casey's cochef," Jonah said to Gloria.

Committing himself meant he would have to stay at least until after the potluck supper, which was scheduled for next weekend.

Molly hadn't specifically asked him not to attend, and with a crowd of people present, she shouldn't having any trouble avoiding him, Jonah reflected. Undoubtedly she would hear, through the grapevine, that she could expect to encounter him, but he would give her advance warning anyway.

I'll call her, he decided as he left the café.

Approaching her condo a few minutes later, Jonah slowed to a crawl while he debated with himself. Joey would be in bed by now. What would be the difference between phoning Molly and just stopping by long enough to alert her to the fact that he would be at the upcoming community social event?

A big difference. A phone conversation that led to another dead end wouldn't be nearly as hard as walking out without touching her.

Jonah accelerated.

At Flora's condo, he called immediately, telling himself he might as well get this over with.

Yeah, sure, the cynical little voice inside him taunted. Any excuse to talk to her.

On the second ring she answered.

"Hello."

"It's me. Jonah."

"Jonah." Her voice held surprise and, God help him, a note of gladness. "I thought I heard your truck go by."

"I started to stop by a minute."

"If you had, you could have gotten your laptop. I packed it up in the carrier earlier."

"Shall I come and get it now?"

His heart thundered during the suspenseful pause. He could hear her sharp intake of breath, sense her forming her answer.

"Not unless you really want to use it tonight. I could hand it out the door. I'm in my robe," she explained.

God, don't tell me that, Jonah thought. He let his own silence fall as he rejected inappropriate questions that came to mind. What color is it? Could you describe it for me? Are you wearing anything underneath it?

All questions a lover would ask, and he wasn't her lover and wouldn't be.

"You did call about the laptop," she said with a questioning inflection.

"Actually, no. I called about something else. Before tonight I had pretty much ruled out going to the potluck supper at the community center. But it turns out I will be going.''

"Oh."

Jonah waited for more reaction. When there was none, he continued, "I ran into Flora and Casey and the Pendergasts at Gloria's café and ended up being assigned a job at the supper. Casey and I are cooking steaks that some local rancher is providing.''

"I heard about the free steaks.''

Suddenly a question occurred to him. "This rancher isn't the guy you dated, is it?''

"Yes, he is. Chad Worthing.''

"Is he among those husband candidates you review every now and then?''

"He's still single, and occasionally I hear from him.''

The evasive reply amounted to another yes.

"I guess he'll be there, lining up to dance with you right behind ole Roger.'' The speculation was grim.

"The men dance with all the women.''

"So I get to dance with you at least once?''

"If you're not too popular. You'll be in great demand.''

All the contestants for the Miss Universe competition could show up in their sexiest swimsuits and Jonah wouldn't have eyes for anyone but Molly. But he kept that thought to himself, figuring the sentiment behind it was pretty damn apparent.

"Did Joey enjoy the other computer activities?" he asked.

"Very much. Thank you again for going to the trouble of getting them off the Internet.''

"I felt really rotten, passing the little fellow up this afternoon.''

"I can imagine that you did. I felt terrible about it, too,'' she said. "On his behalf. And yours.''

"What did he say?''

"Naturally he was disappointed, but he'll get over it, Jonah."

"Tell me," he insisted.

Her sigh of capitulation came over the line. "I can't remember his exact words, but he concluded that you had stopped liking us."

Jonah cursed savagely under his breath. "And what was your response?"

"I assured him that wasn't the case and made up plausible excuses."

"You're so worried about protecting him, Molly. But how can this be good for a kid? Teaching him that a grown man can be friendly and interested in him one day and not have five minutes to spare to pay him a little attention from then on?"

"A lot of men behave that way with children, Jonah."

"Well, I don't."

"I believe you. I'm sorry to have put you in this position." Her voice was troubled, but resigned. Obviously she meant to keep him in that untenable position.

"Well, I'll say good-night," he said brusquely.

"Good night."

Jonah cut the connection.

He hadn't felt this low and dejected during his separation and divorce. The only halfway cheerful thought he could dredge up was that she evidently still intended to go to the potluck supper herself. He would get to see her, take his place in line behind Roger and Worthing and claim a dance.

A slow dance.

Normally when Molly looked in on Joey each night before going to bed, he was sleeping peacefully. Tonight his covers told the tale that he had been thrashing about. His small brow was furrowed with a frown, and he mumbled something unintelligible, speaking to someone in his dream.

Molly moved quickly over to his bed, her own unhappiness taking a back seat to maternal instinct. She straightened the covers and spoke to him in a soft, loving voice. "It's just a bad dream, Joey. Molly's right here with you." Seated on the edge of the bed, she stroked his face and smoothed his dark brown hair.

The frown disappeared, and he relaxed into a deep sleep without ever waking up, reassured by her voice and her touch. Molly stayed there awhile longer, guarding him from the demons that can invade even a five-year-old's slumber.

In her bedroom she took off her robe, remembering the phone conversation with Jonah. "I'm in my robe," she'd said with no provocative motive whatever. His charged silence had quickened her pulse and made her aware of the silky fabric of her nightgown against her skin.

It had been so good to hear his voice, which affected her like no other man's voice ever had. Ever would. She'd been able to visualize his expressions as they'd talked.

Talking to him on the phone hadn't proved any less risky than talking to him in person, because they were so attuned to each other that every pause, every inflection conveyed messages. Some of those messages like God, I miss you and want to be with you would be incredibly thrilling if only Molly weren't deceiving him. And didn't have to go on deceiving him as long as he was here in Big Bend country.

Other than unburdening herself, nothing good would be accomplished by unveiling her identity and Joey's parentage. Jonah couldn't forgive and forget the past and become a part of their lives.

Secrecy is best for all of us, Molly reflected dully, getting into bed.

She closed her eyes and thought about the potluck supper-dance. Jonah would be there, and surely he would dance with her, at least once. It was something wonderful to look forward to. They'd never danced together.

If the song was slow, he would put his arm around her waist and draw her close. What sheer heaven to move in time to the music with him, the two of them temporarily in complete harmony....

Molly drifted off to sleep with a rapturous smile on her lips.

The next morning Jonah gave himself a stern lecture: there was nothing to be gained from moping and feeling down in the dumps. He had plenty of interesting things to do to kill the days between now and the potluck supper.

He drank his first cup of coffee sitting out on Flora's patio, thumbing through a guidebook and looking up often to appreciate the magnificent view of mountains and desert scenery. After he'd had breakfast, he drove to an outfitter and booked a two-day rafting trip on the Rio Grande.

The owner of the business, who was also a guide, was there at the office. He turned out to be a very likable guy about Jonah's age by the name of Tim Perry. The two of them hit it off right away.

"Man, I'd like to pick your brain about some good stocks to buy," Tim said when he learned that Jonah had a stockbroker's license and had worked in the investment business.

"And I'd like to know where you bought those Western boots you're wearing," Jonah countered.

They ended up spending the next hour and a half talking. Then they went to lunch at the same burger place where Charlie had taken Jonah. This time Casey didn't show up, but Tim introduced Jonah to several local people who were his friends.

The list of Jonah's acquaintances just kept growing by leaps and bounds.

He picked Tim's brain on a few other subjects besides his footwear. One subject was the RV park that was up for sale. Tim had nothing negative to say as he ticked off points on his fingers. "It's pretty much fully occupied year-round. I can't see where there would be much maintenance expense. And Fred and Sherrie Hapstead weren't tied down, running the place. They would go off on trips in their motor home for months at a time."

"They hired a manager?"

"No, they left a camp host in charge." He went on to explain that many retired couples who were avid RVers took camp host positions in parks. They acted as managers in return for free rent and other benefits such as free use of laundry facilities.

"I like that system," Jonah remarked. "It's a win-win for everybody involved."

"If you want to meet Fred and Sherrie and find out more about the business angle, I'll be happy to take you over and introduce you. They're nice folks."

"Maybe another day, if I decide I'm seriously interested. Right now I qualify as a tire kicker."

Jonah couldn't really account for his less-than-serious interest, considering the fact that Molly was giving him no encouragement whatever to stick around.

Nevertheless, he slowed down and looked the RV park over thoroughly from the highway as he passed by it a short time later after dropping Tim off.

Jonah was on his way to Presidio for a return visit to do some shopping. Tim had given him directions to the store where he'd bought his boots and his leather belt, which Jonah had also admired as well as his footwear.

The belt had a filigreed silver buckle, inlaid with turquoise.

It might be impractical to spring for Western boots and a fancy belt, but what the hell, Jonah thought. He planned to show up at the do at the community center next weekend all duded up like a west Texas man.

Once he'd driven through Lajitas, the El Camino del Rio began its steep twisting climb, and Jonah soon sighted the first simple cross along the side of the highway. He stayed alert, while still taking in the magnificent vistas of canyons plunging down to the Rio Grande on his left and rocky foothills and mountain ranges off to his right.

During this section of the drive, five or ten minutes would go by without his encountering another vehicle. Once a pickup truck roared past him around a curve. Jonah cursed and put on his brakes, giving the idiot driver plenty of room to pull back into the right-hand lane.

Eventually Jonah started up the fifteen-grade climb that went on and on for miles before taking him to the summit. On his last trip he'd pulled in at the overlook, but he kept going today, figuring he could stop on his way back if the urge struck him. Soon he came to the blind curve where he'd had his near accident with the red compact car. No vehicle careened into view.

As he executed the curve without incident, Jonah reflected somberly that this must be the approximate location of the recent fatal motorcycle accident the border control officer had referred to. Also the same location where Lynette Jones and her boyfriend had been killed.

The highway straightened out and he saw the small black wrought-iron cross up ahead on the left. There was enough rocky shoulder to pull over safely, which probably explained the placement of the cross. Jonah figured that it had been erected in memory of someone who'd perished in the hazardous curve. Had Molly erected the cross as a memorial to her cousin? he wondered.

The silk flowers formed vivid blots of color, reminding him of those bright silk flowers she'd purchased in Alpine.

Without quite understanding his motive, Jonah parked on the highway shoulder and got out of his truck. When he walked up close to the cross, he could decipher words in the lacy pattern on the horizontal bar and the vertical bar. "Beloved Sister."

Obviously Molly hadn't bought those flowers to replace these. Unless…

Jonah reluctantly finished the thought. Unless she'd lied to him and Lynette was her sister, not her cousin. But why would she do that? Unless… He plowed on past another mental roadblock. Unless Molly Jones and Lynette Jones were assumed names, and the two women were really Susan and Karen Gulley.

No way. A woman couldn't change as much as Susan would have had to change in six years' time. The only similarity between her and Molly was the physical resemblance. Jonah strode back to his truck, shaking his head emphatically.

Even if she'd put the cross there—and she probably hadn't—it didn't mean she'd lied. She might have been expressing the sentiment that she'd loved Lynette like a sister.

Besides, if Molly was Susan, why hide her identity from him if Karen was dead? Molly hadn't committed any serious crimes herself. Jonah doubted the police back in Georgia would even be interested in her at this point in time. They had bigger fish to fry.

Of course, Jonah would definitely have some questions about who Joey's father was, since the little boy was about the right age to be Joel's kid.

But he wasn't Joel's kid. Except for the grin and typical boyhood behavior, he didn't remind Jonah of his brother at that age any more than any brown-haired, blue-eyed, five-year-old boy might.

Chapter Ten

Jonah had worn his new boots and his new belt home from Presidio. He wanted to break in the boots and get used to wearing the belt before this Saturday night.

When he drove past Molly's condo, she was outside filling the water can at the spigot, dressed in jeans and a white T-shirt, her back to the street. She glanced over her shoulder, and Jonah tooted his horn. All it would have taken was a tepidly friendly smile to give him the courage to stop, but she didn't smile.

Jonah watched her in his side mirror and saw her gazing after him, looking unhappy. Where was Joey? he wondered. Had she kept him indoors?

The incident put a real damper on Jonah's good mood.

Inside Flora's condo, he uncapped a beer and flipped on the TV to watch the news. Five minutes later the doorbell rang. Somebody must be lost, he thought, hauling himself up. Or maybe Flora had dropped by.

To his utter surprise, Molly stood outside the door, hugging his laptop carrying case in her arms. "I wanted to return this," she said. Her eyes were taking in his belt and his Western boots.

"Well, what do you think?" Jonah asked, gesturing at himself. He felt ridiculously self-conscious. "Do I make the grade as a cowboy?"

"That's a beautiful belt," she said. "And those boots are really handsome. Where did you buy them?"

He named the store in Presidio, and she nodded.

"I got a shirt, too, but I doubt I'll wear it. It reminds me too much of the fancy shirts you see on men in square dancing groups." She looked intrigued as if she were trying to imagine him in such a shirt. "Want to come in and see what you think?" he asked. "I wouldn't mind an expert fashion opinion."

"You've aroused my curiosity," she admitted.

Still hugging the laptop, she stepped over the threshold and preceded him into the main room.

"Here. Let me take that," Jonah said.

Her expression went blank for just a second, and he realized she'd actually forgotten her errand. He relieved her of her burden and set the laptop out of the way. "I was having a beer. Would you like one?" he offered.

"Thanks, but I'd better refuse."

"I guess Joey's home by himself."

"No, he was invited to play after school at a classmate's house. I'll go pick him up in a little while."

So she hadn't kept Joey inside to prevent him from seeing Jonah. That information made Jonah perk up even more.

"You were going to show me your new shirt," she reminded.

"Oh. Right. If you're not in a big hurry, have a seat." He indicated the sofa.

"I can't stay long." She sat down while he was moving over to the kitchen to retrieve the store bag, which he'd tossed onto a stool earlier en route to the refrigerator.

He brought the bag and handed it to her. "Now don't make fun."

"You're embarrassed." Her face had that same intrigued expression.

"Real men get embarrassed," he joked, sitting down next to her.

She reached inside the bag and drew the shirt out. Watching her as she held it up by the shoulders, Jonah might have been a defendant who'd been instructed by a judge to stand and face the jury. The shirt was a dark-green-and-navy plaid with mother-of-pearl buttons.

"Pretty bad, huh?" he said. "I'd have to learn to do-si-do."

"Don't be silly. You'll look very rugged and masculine in this shirt. I like it."

"Well, maybe I will wear it. If it fits."

"You didn't try it on?" She checked the neck label and then eyed his upper torso as though holding a tape measure to his shoulders and then looping it around his chest. Jonah found her inspection instantly arousing.

"No, the woman waiting on me seemed certain I would take an extralarge."

God, he wanted to touch her hair, kiss her, hug her. But one wrong move, and she'd be up like a flash and gone.

Jonah picked up his beer and took a swallow. He watched her refold the shirt with deft movements. Instead of slipping it back inside the bag, she placed it on top of the bag on the coffee table.

"How was business at Clementine's Closet today?" he asked.

"Slow this morning, but hectic this afternoon. At least

a dozen local women came in shopping for an outfit for Saturday night.''

"You already have the perfect outfit."

"I do?"

Jonah grinned, amused at her startled tone. "I haven't been peeking in your closet. I meant that little red number you wore to the bingo fund-raiser. With your red boots."

"You liked that dress?"

"I liked you in that dress. But I haven't seen you in any clothes that don't look good on you." He allowed himself only the briefest glance at her white T-shirt. Even that played havoc with his pulse.

"I could say the same about you," she remarked.

"Except you've only seen me in jeans."

She didn't answer, and Jonah could sense that he'd jarred the harmony somehow. Change the subject. Quick. Or she'll leave. "Say, I met a nice fellow today. Tim Perry. Do you know him?" he asked.

"Not well. Are you taking a rafting trip on the river?" She'd quickly put two and two together.

"Tomorrow. It's a two-day trip. Our party will be camping overnight. We'll go through Santa Elena Canyon. I hear it's really something to see. Sheer walls and rocks and eddies."

"What a thrilling adventure!" she exclaimed. She'd seemed to relax again while he talked. "I bet this is going to be a highlight of your visit here in Big Bend country."

Jonah could have told her that he would cancel his rafting trip in a second to spend time in her company doing nothing more exciting than what they were doing now. But he kept the thought to himself.

"You haven't rafted the river?" he asked.

"No, Joey isn't old enough. But someday I want to."

I'd love to take you. I'd love for us to do all kinds of thrilling and not-so-thrilling things together.

Jonah didn't dare speak the words aloud. It would upset her to hear them. Actually he found his own word choice, love instead of like, unsettling. Like had slipped out of his vocabulary where Molly was concerned.

"Speaking of Joey, it's time for me to go and pick him up," she said, rising. "Thanks again for lending us the laptop."

He'd gotten to his feet, too, and accompanied her to the door, inquiring whether she'd kept the diskettes with the children's programs. She replied that she'd made copies of them on the store computer and given him back the originals so that he could re-use the diskettes.

"I suppose I'll see you Saturday night," she said as she departed.

What the hell, Jonah thought. Might as well try.

"Are you going with a date?" he asked.

She stopped and turned around. "No."

"Then how about giving me a ride? That way I won't have to worry about my alcohol level." Beer and liquor wouldn't be sold at the supper-dance. However, both would be available on a bring-your-own basis, he'd learned. Jonah didn't plan to overindulge, but making her a designated driver was the best ploy he could come up with to get her to agree to their riding together.

She was slow answering, obviously having been taken aback by his spur-of-the-moment request. "I'll be coming home by midnight, at the latest, to pay my sitter," she said. "The party may still be in full swing, and you might not be ready to leave."

"In that case, I can bother somebody else to bring me home. But by midnight my feet will probably have had enough dancing in these boots."

"Okay," she agreed reluctantly. But not that reluctantly. "I'll pick you up."

"Great."

Jonah would have preferred coming to her condo and seeing Joey for a few minutes before they left, but it was best not to push his luck.

After she'd driven off, he returned to his living room, where the neatly folded shirt brought back the recent scene with the two of them sitting on the sofa. It was worth the price of the darned thing just to lure Molly inside to look at it, Jonah reflected as he discarded the partially drunk beer, which had grown lukewarm, and got himself another one.

She'd meant to ring his doorbell, hand him the computer and leave. If he hadn't appeared in the doorway in his new boots and belt and thrown her off her guard, she'd have done just that.

Yes, the trip to Presidio had been completely worthwhile in earning him that brief visit. Now he was really looking forward to Saturday night. He intended to dance more than one slow dance with her.

"I'll answer it!" Joey was already dashing toward the kitchen telephone.

He and Molly had just walked in. She'd gone directly from Jonah's condo and picked up Joey at the home of his little classmate.

"Hello." When his face didn't brighten, she knew the caller wasn't Jonah. "Just a minute. She's right here." He held the cordless phone out to her. "A man wants to talk to you."

Roger Mason's pleasant voice came over the line, sounding shy as he identified himself and then engaged her in the kind of chitchat they might have exchanged if they'd accidentally run into each other.

Molly sensed that he was leading up to asking her out on a date and was framing a gentle refusal when he got to the point of his call.

"I wondered if you would go with me to the community center Saturday night."

"I'm sorry, Roger. I've already agreed to give a neighbor of mine a ride. But I'll see you there."

"Sure thing."

His disappointment came through in their parting conversation.

She could have said yes to Roger and backed out of going with Jonah, Molly thought after she'd cut the connection. It would have been a method of keeping Jonah at a distance.

A method that wasn't Molly's style because she would be using Roger, who was a very nice man and deserved more honest treatment. She was honest by nature, not manipulative or deceptive. Lying didn't come easily for her.

But she doubted Jonah would ever take that view of her character if the truth came out.

A report on the late news about a terrible highway accident in El Paso, Texas, triggered Jonah's memory of stopping on the way to Presidio for a closer look at the wrought-iron cross. Even if he'd thought about the incident while Molly was at his condo this afternoon, he wouldn't have questioned her about such a morbid subject, he reflected.

It just didn't seem all that important to determine whether she'd placed a cross along El Camino del Rio for her deceased cousin that read "Beloved Sister." Probably she hadn't.

Even if she had, Jonah was certain the explanation wouldn't make him any less eager about Saturday night.

His subconscious mind, however, wasn't so sanguine. That night Jonah dreamed that he was driving to Presidio and saw Molly replacing the vivid flowers on the cross. Her automobile wasn't anywhere in sight. Puzzled as to how she'd gotten there, and also anxious for her safety, he pulled over and parked on the highway shoulder. When he walked toward her, she ran away from him. He pursued her and caught her, only then realizing his mistake. She wasn't Molly. She was Susan Gulley.

Suddenly the setting changed, and he was alone in the cemetery in his hometown where his brother and his mother were buried. The marble vases on the family headstone were filled with the bright-colored silk flowers Molly had bought in Alpine.

Jonah woke himself up, demanding, "What the hell is going on anyway?"

He lay there a few minutes, letting his emotions ebb before going back to sleep. His main emotion in the dream had been bafflement. He hadn't been angry at all.

The two-day rafting trip combined tranquility with the heart-stopping challenge of negotiating the Rock Slide, the Class IV rapid inside Santa Elena Canyon. Just passing through the narrow canyon hemmed in by towering walls was like a religious experience for Jonah.

It was good to eat meals outdoors on the bank of the river, good to feel in tune with nature, good to fall asleep in a tent again after sitting out under the immense night sky studded with stars. He enjoyed the camaraderie that quickly developed among the small party of strangers, all fairly rugged types.

But, most important, Jonah got his head on straight again. He'd barely begun his travels. Sure, Big Bend country was awesome, and he'd seemed to fit right in from the start and feel at home here. He liked all the local people he'd met. But there were other awesome places in the U.S. to visit, to experience. Who was to say he wouldn't like another location better and decide to settle down there?

If he didn't, he could come back here.

Putting some distance between him and Molly was definitely a good idea, Jonah decided. He hadn't thought he was in danger of falling hard for a woman on the rebound, as so many recently divorced guys did. But that must be what had happened to him. Maybe he'd just been lucky up to now, but being rebuffed by a woman he wanted to date was a first for Jonah. The challenge probably accounted for his feeling of walking through a minefield of unfamiliar emotions. Her very elusiveness made him want her more.

Yes, the thing to do was get out of Dodge City before he started imagining being married to her and taking on the role of dad to little Joey. A role she obviously didn't cast him in. Jonah made his plans. He would go to the supper-dance Saturday night and stick around on Sunday. Monday he would head out bright and early.

Before he left, dammit, he was going to say goodbye to Joey.

In his condo, Jonah stared at the screen of his laptop, rereading the e-mail, his hands clenched into fists.

Dear son,
I got your e-mail address from George Plessy, your colleague at Dunton & Meyers. Or former colleague. I learned from him that you've resigned with the idea of changing careers and are taking time off to do some traveling.

I heard in a roundabout way about eight months ago that you'd gotten divorced. At the time I wanted to call you up and say how sorry I was your marriage had failed, but I guess I was afraid you would hang up on me. I hope you read this e-mail all the way through. I went out and bought a computer just so I could write to you. Edna was all in favor of the idea.

I hope you're having a great trip. It would be good to hear from you.

Love, Dad

"Nice lady, Edna. A real peacemaker," Jonah said with heavy irony. His forefinger hovered over the Delete key, but didn't strike it. Instead he went through the series of commands to turn off the laptop.

At some later time he would reply to his father's e-mail once he decided what he would say. The tentative communication was the first offering of an olive branch after more than four years of tense silence between father and son.

Jonah grabbed his key ring with no real notion of where he was going. He'd reached the front door and was jerking it open when the doorbell suddenly chimed.

His visitor was a guilty-looking Joey, wearing the cowboy hat.

"Hi, Mr. Rhodes."

"Well, hi there, Joey. This is a surprise." Jonah couldn't believe how glad he was to see the little boy. "You by yourself?"

Joey nodded and pointed toward the street. "I rode my bicycle. It has training wheels, and one of them rolls crooked. Do you think you could fix it?"

"I'll take a look at it. Where's Molly?"

"She got a phone call just as we were going outside. I was supposed to wait for her," he confessed. "She doesn't want me riding on the street by myself. Not until I can ride better."

"That sounds like the safest plan to me. Come on. Let's check that wheel. I've got a toolbox in the back of my truck."

Joey trotted alongside of him. "I wear my cowboy hat every day," he said.

"I'm glad you're getting some use out of it, partner." Jonah slapped him gently on his small back, and the little boy grinned happily.

The repair turned out to be fairly simple. Jonah was just finishing up when Molly arrived on foot, the picture of an indignant mother. A sexy, indignant mother in jeans and a pullover blouse. "Joey Jones," she scolded, hands on hips. "You know better than to vanish like that!"

"Mr. Rhodes fixed my bike," Joey said meekly. "He wasn't too busy. Were you, Mr. Rhodes?"

"I sure wasn't," Jonah answered. His eyes met hers accusingly.

She made the silent admission, Yes, I told him you were too busy to fix his bike.

"Watch me ride, Mr. Rhodes."

The little boy pedaled off in the opposite direction from Molly's condo.

"Thank you," she said to Jonah. She started walking behind Joey.

Jonah hesitated for a split second and then caught up in a few long strides and walked along with her.

"This takes me back a few years," he remarked.

"To your first bicycle?"

"Not quite that far back. My brother Joel was Joey's age when he got his first bike. I remember doing the same repair on his training wheels when they got wobbly."

"What a lucky little boy to have you for a big brother."

"He was such a cute kid. All bright-eyed and happy like Joey. If he'd lived, he would be twenty-two years old now. My mother wouldn't have grieved herself to death. She and my father would still be married. Instead—" Jonah broke off and apologized tersely. "Sorry, I read an e-mail from my father just before Joey rang my doorbell. Hearing from him got me all stirred up.''

"How did he get your e-mail address?''

Jonah explained and found himself giving her the gist of the message.

"That must have taken a lot of courage on his part to offer an olive branch,'' she ventured.

"I suppose. Yes,'' he amended, "it did. I didn't get my pride and stubbornness from a stranger.''

"Is your dad's remarrying so soon the only thing you hold against him? Was he a good father to you and Joel?''

"A great father.''

"I remember you said he denied that there had been any wrong-doing on his part. Is it possible he simply turned to the woman who became your stepmother for friendship because he was lonely and needed comfort?'' she asked.

"Yes. It's possible.'' Jonah had to pull the grudging answer out. "Mom wasn't any company for him after she went into such a deep depression. I came home from Atlanta most weekends the first year after Joel died and helped Dad out with all his extra chores, but then less frequently. I had my own life and my career.''

They walked along in silence. Jonah figured she was thinking that he'd been very judgmental. He was facing up to that fact himself.

"Does Edna have grandchildren from another marriage?'' she asked.

The question came unexpectedly. Jonah switched mental gears. "No. She and her first husband didn't have any children. He died a couple of years before she and Dad got together.''

The reply seemed to trouble her. "That's kind of a shame, isn't it? Your dad sounds like the type who would enjoy being a grandfather.''

"Oh, he definitely would."

Joey had turned around and was pedaling back toward them. "See how good I ride, Mr. Rhodes!" he yelled, waving one hand in the air.

"Hang on to those handlebars," Jonah called, but the caution came too late. The bicycle toppled over, spilling the little boy on the hard-packed dirt of the street.

Molly and Jonah both headed for him, but Jonah got there first and picked Joey up and stood him on his feet. "You okay, partner?" he inquired gruffly, squatting in front of the small boy and dusting him off with gentle swipes.

Joey's lip was trembling, but he nodded, bravely keeping back the tears.

"Ready to get back on that bucking bronco?" Jonah helped him climb back on. "Attaboy."

Soon the little boy had regained his confidence and was pedaling vigorously. "Are you watching me?" he shouted.

Jonah and Molly called in unison, "We're watching you."

He glanced over and saw the distress mirrored on her face. Jonah knew what he could say to take a load off her mind. "Don't look so worried. Joey isn't going to get attached to me. I'm leaving on Monday."

"Day after tomorrow?"

"Yep. Time to move on."

It was some small consolation that she didn't brighten up at what was undoubtedly welcome news to her. After all, she'd been trying her best to get rid of him from the night they'd met at the bingo fund-raiser.

Leaving on Monday. Leaving on Monday. Leaving on Monday...

The refrain played in Molly's head the rest of the day,

bringing waves of despair. Jonah's absence was going to
create a huge void in her life. She couldn't bear to think
about weeks and months and years without seeing him
ever again, without talking to him, without being around
him.

It was so cruel that he'd come here to Big Bend country, and yet she treasured every tense minute she'd spent
with him. Now her regrets for what wasn't to be were
greater than ever after getting to know him and appreci-
ating all his fine qualities, especially after observing him
with Joey. If only the tragedy of the past hadn't left such
deep scars on Jonah's soul, he could have made his little
nephew such a wonderful uncle. He could have made
Molly the lover and male companion of her dreams, even
if he never wanted to become her husband.

For his sake she had to keep him in the dark. The
knowledge that Joey had resulted from the romance between young Joel Rhodes and the teenage girl Jonah held
responsible for his brother's death would only be a source
of torment and bitterness. Not joy. Not solace.

And the custody issue remained a real concern. An aunt
probably had no stronger legal claim to a child than an
uncle or a grandfather, even an aunt who'd been a surrogate mother since that child's birth. Once the truth was
out, Molly couldn't predict what she would be dealing
with. The fact that Jonah and his father had been estranged for years told her they were both capable of letting
hard feelings rule them. One or both of them might decide
that Karen Gulley's sister wasn't a fit parent. It frightened
Molly to realize that impersonal judges could take a dim
view of a woman with an alias.

There was too much to lose and nothing to gain—other
than a clear conscience—from telling Jonah the truth before he left.

Molly kept coming to that same conclusion.

Chapter Eleven

Jonah had worn the new shirt, Molly noted, sitting behind the wheel of her automobile as she watched him emerge from Flora's condo hours later. He looked even more handsome and virile than she'd imagined him looking in his Western attire.

Leaving on Monday. The heartbreaking refrain made her attempt to arrange her lips into a smile twice as difficult.

He opened the passenger door and whistled his male admiration of her appearance, all the while giving her a once-over that made her breasts suddenly fuller and her figure in general more shapely. "You look as beautiful in that red dress as I remembered," he said, climbing in and bringing the tangy masculine scent of his aftershave.

"It suited my mood tonight." The mood to dress to please him.

Molly's smile felt natural now with her pulse humming

with pleasure at his nearness. She shifted into reverse and backed out of the driveway, aware of her skirt riding up on her thighs.

"How was your rafting trip?" she asked.

"Fantastic."

"Tell me about it."

He complied and she listened with interest, a part of her thrilling to the sound of his deep, resonant voice. Which she might not hear again after tonight. Ever.

She wouldn't think about that, Molly decided. She would make the most of this limited, precious time with him. Tomorrow she would deal with the multiple regrets, the sense of loss, the terrible emptiness of his permanent absence.

At the community center the parking lot was already filling up with automobiles. People were carrying in food containers and coolers.

"I brought some beer and wine over earlier," Jonah said as he and Molly got out. She retrieved a large platter from the back of her SUV, and he took it from her.

Charlie Pendergast hailed them like long-lost friends and they walked toward the building with him and his wife, exchanging other greetings along the way. The atmosphere inside was just as jovial, not to mention festive. Long tables were draped with red-and-white-checkered tablecloths and decorated with novelty centerpieces featuring papier-mâché cacti and candles.

Toe-tapping country-western music was blaring from large speakers on the platform.

Gloria from the Cactus Café bustled up and dispatched Jonah to go and assist Casey, who, according to her, already had the large grill fired up outside to cook the free steaks. Molly observed Jonah threading his way through the crowd, seeming perfectly at home. He paused to say a few words to Flora, paused again to talk to Tim Perry and several other people whom he'd evidently become acquainted with. In just a couple of weeks he'd met an amazing number of local people, she reflected. He was so personable that everyone liked him, including her.

But she also loved him.

"Molly, you can set your platter of tamales over on the buffet table," Gloria was saying.

Molly came out of her trance and obeyed the instructions. Someone handed her a glass of wine, and she sipped it while she socialized. Flora came up to her, silver earrings dangling to her shoulders.

"Well, you're losing your neighbor," the older woman said.

"Yes. So Jonah tells me."

"I did my best to talk him into staying."

"He wants to travel."

Fortunately, Roger Mason appeared at Molly's elbow. She turned to greet him and then started up a conversation on a different subject. She couldn't possibly discuss Jonah's departure and act cheerful. The very fact that he'd already informed Flora of his plans made them that much more depressingly certain.

Roger was still sticking close by when Casey and Jonah brought in the grilled steaks. Molly watched as Jonah's gaze searched the crowd until he found her. He glanced at Roger and frowned. Casey was announcing loudly, "Everybody grab a plate! Let's get supper over with so we can start the dancing!"

"Shall we get in line?" Roger asked, lightly taking her arm.

"You go ahead without me," Molly replied. She made her way toward Jonah. His grim expression changed to surprise and then to fierce gladness as he realized her intention.

Molly reached him and lost her breath as they looked

into each other's eyes. Among the emotions in his dark brown eyes, the simplest to read was his desire to kiss her.

"Are you hungry?" she inquired.

His wry smile alleviated some of the tension. "Now I am. I had just lost all my appetite."

She edged toward the buffet table, and he followed inches behind her, his hands clasping her at her waist. Molly's biggest challenge was resisting the instinct to lean against him. If she did, she knew his arms would come around her and hug her tight.

Restraint intensified a yawning hunger in Molly that eating couldn't possibly satisfy.

Eventually they arrived at the stack of plates and each took one and served themselves. Molly noticed that one of his selections among the bountiful array of food was the tamales she'd brought.

When they were ready to find a place to sit, Jonah guided her to a table. Molly accompanied him, not commenting on the fact that he'd chosen not to join Flora and Casey and the Pendergasts, who were all sitting together. He'd also bypassed Tim Perry.

They claimed two chairs side by side. Across from them were a couple in their twenties who seemed totally absorbed in each other.

"Be right back," Jonah said and was gone briefly. When he returned, he had a bottle of wine he'd uncorked and two glasses.

The candles in the centerpieces had been lit earlier, and the volume of the music had been toned down. A poignant love song by a female country-western singer was playing in the background. Molly hadn't bargained on quite this much romantic ambience with an illusion of privacy, and she sensed that he hadn't, either.

He sampled a tamale. "Hmm. The tamales are good. Did you buy them from Manuel's mother?"

"Yes. What an amazing memory you have."

"That can be a curse instead of an asset. I'll probably wish I didn't have total recall of every time you and I were together during the past two weeks."

Molly had sliced off a piece of steak, but instead of eating it, she forked up a biteful of salad. As always, the past shadowed the present. With his excellent memory, he'd still bought into her deception and believed her when she denied being the same woman he'd spent an hour with six years earlier in their hometown. Why had he? Because he didn't want Molly to be Karen Gulley's older sister.

"Where are you going next?" she asked in a hollow voice. "The Grand Canyon? You mentioned that it was on your itinerary."

"In other words, let's talk about something else besides how hung up on you I am?"

"You'll meet other women along the way and soon forget me." The prediction made her want to cry. If only...

"I keep telling myself that. When I'm not around you, I can almost convince myself."

"If we'd had a short affair, I guess it would have been easier for you to get me out of your system."

"Maybe."

Even the skeptical agreement hurt. Molly laid down her fork and took a sip of her wine. "Jonah, could we just enjoy tonight?" she implored.

"Sure. After all, a little friendly treatment is the nicest going-away present you could have given me. I guess you figure you're safe since I'm leaving. Sorry," he swiftly apologized. "You asked whether I was going directly to the Grand Canyon. No, I plan to stop off in New Mexico.

A college roommate of mine lives in Santa Fe. I'll look him up.''

"And Taos is nearby. You can visit it. The owner of Clementine's Closet also has a shop there.''

When everyone had finished eating, tablecloths and centerpieces were whisked off the tables in the middle of the room and the tables folded and stacked against the wall out of the way. The volunteer DJ, Charlie Pendergast, turned the music up loud again.

Casey came and grabbed Molly's hand. "Hope you don't mind my stealing your gal for this first fast dance, Jonah,'' he said and whirled her away.

Molly glimpsed Jonah standing on the sidelines watching her. Then she saw Flora leading him out onto the floor.

When the number came to an end, a slow song started up. "Where's your feller?'' Casey said.

"Right here,'' Jonah spoke up, slipping his arm possessively around her waist. Molly was slightly out of breath. When he drew her close, her heartbeat didn't slow down.

It was sheer heaven moving in slow rhythm to the music with him. Molly surrendered herself to the physical intimacy, to the mindless, drugging pleasure. Her breasts pressing against his chest, her thighs brushing his.

The song ended. Jonah loosened his hold slightly as they came to a standstill. Molly looked up into his face, somehow unable to care that her own expression must be as unguarded as his was. It must say, too, I could dance with you forever.

"They should write longer songs,'' he said.

"Definitely.''

They smiled at each other. Molly was only hazily aware of the crowded dance floor and voices and laughter.

"Hey, you two, the music started up again," Casey jeered as he sashayed past with a grinning Gloria.

"Shall we?" Molly asked.

"I might step on your feet. I don't know how to do that fast two-step like you native Texans."

She refused to allow the sharp stab of guilt to spoil the fun. "It's easy. I'll teach you."

He caught on fast and by the end of the number was leading her.

"I had a marvelous time." Molly said. "You're a good dancer."

"Not as good as you," Jonah replied. "You and Casey looked like a couple of professionals when you danced those fast numbers."

"He's such a show-off."

"I could tell he thrived on having an audience when everyone circled around and clapped. Of course, the men all had their eyes on you."

Especially me, his tone added.

He walked beside her, his arm around her waist, as they headed to her automobile. Molly couldn't seem to summon the willpower to pull away, which she knew she should do. The party was over for her. It was time for reality to set in.

"You can come back after I drop you off," she said. "You haven't had much to drink."

"I didn't think I would drink too much. That was the best excuse I could come up with to beg a ride with you. Wasn't I pretty transparent?" he chided.

"Yes, you were," Molly admitted. "But if I'd refused and you'd had an accident coming home, I would never have forgiven myself." The thought of any harm coming to him had pierced her heart with fear.

They reached her SUV.

"Dance with me," he urged, instead of opening the driver's door.

"What?"

"Dance with me. Right here in the parking lot. Your sitter can wait an extra five minutes, can't he?"

Music spilled from the building. A slow love song. Molly's wisdom and common sense lost the battle to her longing to experience a few more minutes of heaven, dancing close to him.

"I hope no one comes out and sees us," she said, sliding one arm around his shoulder and raising her right hand to clasp his."

"No, like this," he said and put both her arms up around his neck. Then he gathered her close with his arms around her waist, lifting her so that she stood on tiptoe, her hips welded tightly to his. "This is the old high school style. Remember? You stand in one spot and gyrate to the music and drive one another crazy."

Molly's blood was sizzling in her veins, and her skin was hot with the incredible intimacy. The only way to keep her sanity was to talk. "I remember seeing other couples dancing this way, but I didn't. I was too prim and shy in high school."

"You? Prim and shy? I find that hard to believe."

"It's true. I was a late bloomer."

"Boy, did you bloom. You have to be the sexiest woman in the world." He'd threaded his fingers through her hair, cupped her head and was tipping it back, his head lowering. "God, I've wanted to kiss you all night...."

"I know...."

His lips met hers. They were warm and firm. Molly returned the tender, hungry pressure, feeling her bones turn to liquid. It didn't matter that her knees sagged because his arms tightened. The fact that he had more than enough strength to hold her up added to her blissful pleasure.

The slow song ended. During a brief lull, she struggled with herself to heed the weak voice inside her that bade, Stop. Then another song began with a faster tempo that introduced urgency. Jonah kissed her harder with passion, and Molly kissed him back, opening to him, mating with his tongue.

Her heart wasn't pumping blood now. It was pumping hot desire through her arteries and veins. Kissing wasn't enough. Not nearly enough. To stave off the exploding need, Molly sent her hands on a glorious exploration of his broad shoulders. Through his shirt she could feel his taut skin and bunched muscles, feel the hot pulse of his desire.

Loud laughter and conversation penetrated her consciousness.

"Where does Larry come up with all those lawyer jokes, anyway?"

"On the Internet. Sure was a good party, wasn't it?"

"Yes, indeed. Good food, good folks, and ole Charlie did a bang-up job as DJ."

Other people were leaving the party.

"Jonah…"

He'd heard them, too. He was already setting her on her feet, releasing her slowly as he sucked in a deep breath.

Molly's legs were wobbly. She was grateful for Jonah's assistance when he boosted her up into the driver's seat.

"That was asking for frustration, wasn't it?" she said shakily after he'd climbed in on the passenger side. "A couple of adults making out like teenagers in the parking lot."

"I should be used to frustration," he replied, his voice husky with strain. He reached out his hand and brushed her cheek with his knuckles. "I've been wanting to make love to you since the first night I saw you."

Molly twisted the key and started the engine, choking back a correction. *You had seen me once before that, six years ago.*

The ride home was silent. Tension grew inside Molly. As she turned onto their street, she braced herself in case he asked her if they couldn't spend this one night together. Refusing would be the hardest thing she'd ever done. And yet she had to refuse. It was dishonest enough to let him kiss her when he was unaware of who she was. She couldn't make love with him.

"Here you are, safe and sound," she said, pulling into his driveway.

"I'm not sure about safe. Or sound."

Molly gave him a chance to expand on his quiet, cryptic reply while he was unbuckling his seat belt. He didn't, and she didn't dare probe into his meaning.

"Well, Manuel is waiting to be paid," she said.

Jonah leaned over and kissed her on the mouth, his hand framing her cheek. It wasn't a good-night kiss calling a conclusion to the evening, but a tender, possessive follow-up on the passionate kiss outside the community center. Even as Molly's lips clung to his, absorbing the sweetness and promise, she was rallying resistance to a proposition that would surely follow.

But he pulled away and, without a word, opened his door and got out.

"Tonight was wonderful," she said. "You put all the other men to shame in your southwest Texas duds."

Tonight doesn't have to be over. That was his line, she thought. Why didn't he speak it instead of giving her a look that more than returned the compliment. His eyes told her she was the most beautiful woman he'd ever seen, bar none.

"You'd better go pay Manuel," he said, and lifted a big hand in one of those versatile masculine gestures that could signal farewell or any number of other messages depending on the context, like *Okay, you win the argument* or *See you in an hour.* In this context with virtually no discussion of anything, it must signal, *Thanks. Good night.*

Stunned that the evening was ending like this, Molly couldn't muster an answering *Good night.*

He slammed the car door and strode toward the condo entrance, digging into his pocket for his keys. Her headlights spotlighted his tall, rugged physique. She'd caressed those broad shoulders while they kissed in the parking lot....

Molly shifted into reverse, almost overwhelmed by sharp longing and disappointment. The latter made absolutely no sense. She should be thankful he hadn't put her to the test of heeding her conscience. Obviously she'd rejected him often enough that he could read her mind. He must have sensed she would stand firm again, somehow. He'd decided to spare himself one final rejection before he left Big Bend country on Monday.

Tears of despair stung her eyes as she drove to her condo. She blinked them away. *I'll cry later.* As always, her self-assumed role of responsible parent imposed its discipline.

Manuel was wide awake, watching satellite TV. He gave his usual offhandedly upbeat report, assuring her that Joey hadn't given him any trouble. Then the teenage boy pocketed his money and left.

Molly locked the front door behind him and fought the despondent urge to lean on it and weep with her misery. Instead she made her way to Joey's room, turning out lights. He was sleeping peacefully, a smile on his dear little face. Evidently any dreams he was having were good

dreams. The much-treasured cowboy hat sat on the foot
of his bed. He'd been wearing it with his pajamas when
she departed earlier.

Maybe tomorrow she would tell him Jonah was leaving,
she reflected, kissing Joey on the cheek. If she felt composed enough to do so.

In a matter of weeks her nephew would have recovered
from whatever sadness and loss he experienced at Jonah's
disappearance from his life. Memory of Mr. Rhodes, a
kind man who'd paid him attention, would fade. Someday
when Joey was older, perhaps when he was ready to enter
college, Molly would tell him the whole story. At that
point Joey could look up Jonah, should he want to—and
he probably would want to. He could also meet his grandfather, if the elder Rhodes were still alive.

Molly could only hope that Joey understood her motives for secrecy.

In her bedroom she undressed and slipped on a nightgown, her movements slow with the dull depression
weighting her down. You've been depressed before, many
times, she reminded herself. You just have to keep going.
She'd taken a step toward the adjoining bathroom to re-
move her makeup when she heard a noise. Freezing like
a statue, she listened. After long seconds, she heard the
noise again.

Someone knocking lightly on the front door.

Reacting like a sleepwalker, Molly glided into the hallway. The faint glow of low-voltage night-lights in outlets
created a twilight in which furniture took on shape as she
moved through the main room. The Mexican tile was cool
under her bare feet in the foyer.

When she unlocked the dead bolt, it made a loud, rasp-
ing sound. With the door ajar, she said, "Jonah?" The
uncertainty in her voice was mixed with blatant hopeful-
ness.

"Yes."

That's all he said, the one word of confirmation, which Molly didn't need. She was gazing at him in wonderment, joy evaporating her despondency. Nothing seemed to have any relevance except the fact that he stood there.

But he wouldn't want to be here if he knew—

"Can I come in?" he asked.

Molly backed up, and he stepped over the threshold.

"This is wrong," she said, but he was already taking her into his arms, gathering her close in a powerful embrace. Her treacherous arms were winding around his neck. "You would hate me—"

He kissed her, cutting off her protest. Molly returned the hungry pressure of his lips and welcomed the invasion of his tongue. She would take on the extra burden of guilt for this one forbidden night of heaven.

Jonah released her just long enough to bend, slide one arm under her legs and pick her up. Molly tightened her hold while he carried her to her bedroom. Only one lamp was turned on, but it shed a soft, brighter light. He set her on her feet and looked at her, his hands caressing her back and rubbing the cream-colored silk of her nightgown against her skin. Molly shivered with the sensuous pleasure of his touch combined with the hot intimacy of his lover's inspection.

"I imagined you in a sexy nightgown, but the reality is mind-blowing," he said huskily. His gaze fell to her breasts. Molly didn't have to glance down to verify that her hard peaks were jutting against the silk-and-lace of the loosely fitted bodice.

"This isn't one of our really sexy see-through styles. It's rather modest…" Her voice drifted off, rational thought disintegrating. He'd cupped her breasts and was acquainting himself with their shape. Molly arched her back and tipped back her head with the ecstatic sensations he aroused when he rubbed her nipples with his thumbs.

He responded by lowering his head and planting warm kisses from the hollow of her neck down to her cleavage. She stroked his head and slid her fingers into his dark brown hair, feeling its texture. A delicious languor warred with urgency.

Now he was kissing her breasts, his breath warming the thin barrier of silk and lace. His hands—oh, his wonderful hands—were caressing her hips, her buttocks. They were dipping beneath the hem of her gown and sliding up the outsides of her thighs. Molly's languor melted in the heat of arousal when he stroked her stomach and rubbed lower, coming close—so close—

She flattened her palms on his shoulders and sucked in her breath with the helpless suspense. Finally he covered her mound and then used his fingertips to explore ever so delicately. Molly murmured his name as he discovered molten evidence of her desire.

He understood her real message and said, straightening up, "I want you, too, sweetheart. Every bit as much."

The endearment spoken with such caring as well as passion brought a sweet burst of happiness. Molly's love welled up, and she told him silently, Jonah, I love you.

The snaps on his shirt made popping sounds as he ripped them apart and made short work of removing his shirt. The sight of his naked upper torso opened up new realms of erotic pleasure to Molly. By the time he'd tossed the shirt aside, she was plunging her fingers into the dark curly hair furring his chest and exploring the powerful contours.

"I wondered whether—"

"Don't stop there," he demanded, his hands busy unfastening his belt buckle. "If you imagined me without my shirt, tell me."

She made the confession indirectly. "You look even more virile."

He kissed her, a hot, wet kiss, with their tongues making love. Molly could hear the rasp of his zipper sliding down. Without taking his mouth from hers, he captured one of her hands roaming his chest and carried it down lower, below his waist. She slipped inside his jeans and took full advantage of the intimate invitation to discover just how virile he was beneath constricting briefs.

"Sweetheart..." Jonah whispered against her lips when her hand closed around his hard, swollen sex. His voice held pain.

Their kissing took on urgency, but they soon pulled apart, driven by sharp need that frenzied coupling of tongues couldn't satisfy.

Jonah hurriedly removed his new boots and stripped off the rest of his clothes. Molly didn't even try to hide her feminine delight in his naked, aroused body. Only when he stepped closer and eased the straps of her nightgown off her shoulders did she realize that she'd stood there watching him, too entranced to disrobe.

"God, you're more beautiful than I imagined," he breathed, gazing at her breasts after he'd exposed them. It seemed impossible for hands as big as his to touch so delicately as he touched her.

"I love that..." Molly whispered, closing her eyes with the exquisite sensations.

"So do I, sweetheart."

His breath fanned her one hard peak, giving her a second's breathless warning before he nuzzled her sensitized flesh with his lips and then tasted her with his tongue. Molly grasped his head and knew he'd divined her wish somehow when she felt the suckling, wet warmth of his mouth.

He was tugging her gown down over her hips. Molly

helped him. The gown dropped down around her feet, a whisper of silk. The coolness of air on her skin added its own erotic stimulation. Then Jonah's hands began caressing her lower body. Molly held her breath with the sharp anticipation when he stroked up her inner thighs.

"Please," she said when he seemed about to bypass the most intimate caress.

"This?" Jonah asked, his voice husky and aroused.

"Yes...."

Still helpless with the shock waves of pleasure, she wasn't prepared for him to pick her up again as he'd done in the foyer. He laid her on the bed and knelt beside her, his gaze telling her what he'd already expressed in words, You're so beautiful.

Afraid of what he might be reading in her eyes, Molly drew his head down, bringing his lips to hers. Ever so briefly she relished the earlier delicious languor as she kissed him and slid her palms along his broad shoulders and down his back. Hard muscles tensed and quivered under her touch.

Soon his hands began to move over her body again, worshiping her curves, fondling her, exciting her, making her wild with desire.

"Now, Jonah!" Molly finally said.

He sheathed himself in readiness but delayed long enough to plant a trail of erotic kisses that made her open her thighs for him in shameless invitation. Molly clutched his shoulders, hurrying him as he reacted with his own sudden urgency, poising himself for entry. His thrust took him deep inside her, impossibly deep. She cried out helplessly with the ecstatic joy.

"You're incredible," he said, looking into her eyes.

The moment of completion was disrupted, regained, disrupted, regained with his masterful lovemaking, each thrust taking Molly with him to a higher, wilder plane of pleasure and a more intense level of emotion. I love you, Jonah! I love you! I love you! her heart chanted. Fortunately, when she reached climax with him, the welding of his body and hers proved too shattering, too beautiful for coherent language.

"I should have known lovemaking in Big Bend country would be bigger than life," Jonah said. His voice sounded deeply satisfied.

"I saw a burst of colors right there at the end," Molly recalled, suffused by wonderful contentment as she lay close to him, his arm around her. "A gorgeous kaleidoscope."

"Bright primary colors?"

"Yes, but also others that are more my favorites. Turquoise and deep pink and sapphire blue. It was my—" Just in time she caught herself before she said sister. "Lynette always liked reds and oranges and blues, the brighter the better."

He didn't make any reply right away. Molly sensed that he'd become more alert at her reference to Lynette, but his embrace didn't loosen.

"What time does Joey get up in the morning?" he asked.

She adjusted to the change of subject. "He normally wakes up by seven or seven-thirty, but tonight he stayed up later than usual. He'll probably sleep until eight tomorrow morning, at least."

"Good. I'll make it my business to be up before then."

He wanted to stay and sleep with her. Molly framed words to tell him he should return to his own condo, but she simply didn't have the moral strength to speak them. She wanted him to stay too much. How much more guilt would there be to have this one night, since she'd already let him make love to her?

"Excuse me. I'll be right back." He hugged her tighter and dropped a kiss on the top of her head before he got out of bed and walked to her bathroom. Molly had rolled over so that she could enjoy the sight of his rugged, manly physique.

On his return he asked, "Want me to turn off the light?"

"Please."

The direct route to the lamp, located on her dresser, took him past the chest of drawers. He paused and looked at the collection of framed photographs that no longer included the picture of Lynette. Molly thought about it, lying hidden in a drawer.

"I like this snapshot of you and Joey at the playground," he said. "Was it taken in Amarillo?"

"Yes. He was two. A nice older man who was there with his grandchildren snapped it."

"Tomorrow I'd like for us to do something fun with him." Jonah was on his way toward the dresser. He clicked off the lamp, plunging the room into darkness.

Either he hadn't found it odd that she didn't have photographs of her parents or her cousin out on display or else he just hadn't commented.

Chapter Twelve

Jonah could feel tension in Molly's body when he slipped under the sheet and drew her close to him again. Something was bothering her, but rather than ask questions and risk starting up a discussion he didn't want to have tonight, he stroked her back. His relaxation technique worked, but it also stirred fresh desire in him.

"Your skin is as silky as that pretty gown I took off," he murmured, sliding his hand lower and fondling her luscious bottom.

"I love having you touch me."

The pleasure in her voice and something else—a note of caring?—acted on him like an aphrodisiac. Jonah could feel himself going rock hard. Obviously she was just as aware of his arousal since they lay with their hips together.

"Again?" she said with mixed surprise and delight, easing away to create space for her hand.

"Yes, sweetheart," Jonah whispered when she laid claim to his manhood. "Like that." His entire supply of blood seemed to have zoomed back to his loins.

"Such a contrast of steel and velvet," she observed, her tone as well as the words themselves still another turn-on for him.

"The rest of me just turned to putty," he said.

"The rest of you is all gorgeous man, too."

Jonah posed no resistance to her gentle push on his shoulders, directing him to lie on his back. His eyes had adjusted to the darkness, and it wasn't pitch-black in the room. A low-voltage night-light in the bathroom shed a faint illumination through the open door. As she knelt beside him, he could just barely discern her naked, shapely figure.

He reached to capture her lush breasts. She deflected his hands and bent to plant warm, loving kisses on his face. His cheeks, his jaws, his chin, his forehead, even his nose. Jonah's chest swelled with the odd, but sweet sensation. Part of him wanted to bring her mouth to his for a wet, passionate kiss, but the part of him who won out couldn't bear to stop her from what she was doing.

Her hands measured the breadth of his shoulders, and she rained kisses all along them, too, her breath a warm trail on his skin. Then she nuzzled her lips in the hair on his chest, found first one pebbly nipple and then the other, licking with her tongue, gently nipping with her teeth.

Jonah groaned her name with the heavenly torture. He might have called a halt, but she was pleasuring herself, not just stimulating him with unnecessary foreplay.

His stomach muscles contracted into ropy knots when she moved lower, kissing, tasting, stroking, driving him out of his mind.

"Sweetheart, that's far enou—" Jonah couldn't finish

the sentence because she hadn't heeded him. He was exerting all his control to keep from exploding.

With a final intimate kiss, she raised up and reached for the packet he'd laid on her bedside table earlier. He needed the brief respite. After she'd attended to birth control, an arousing procedure in itself, she seemed to hesitate. In answer to her unstated question, Jonah brought her astride of him. Then he let her couple their bodies.

The penetration was slow and deep. Molly uttered the same helpless sound she'd made when he entered her before. Jonah grasped her hips, not so much holding her still as just hanging on to weather the surge of ecstasy himself.

"We're so damn good together," he said fervently.

"Yes, we are...." She leaned down and kissed him on the mouth.

Jonah was flooded with the odd, sweet emotion. Love? He tabled the question until later. Now was no time for analysis. Molly was moving her hips, riding him, and he wanted to caress her breasts, caress every inch of her. This fierce, but tender possessiveness he felt was entirely new. It went beyond merely wanting to give her physical satisfaction. He wanted to lay the world at her feet and give her anything she desired.

Scary. Very scary. But exhilarating as hell.

It didn't seem possible that a second round of lovemaking could be so rousing, so urgent. Molly's soft moans and gasps and murmured exclamations excited Jonah and inspired him to find the best ways to please her. He'd never been compelled to verbalize during lovemaking, but now he wanted intimate conversation. He needed to express himself, to share the mounting pleasure. Share was the key word. Jonah wanted her with him on that wild ascent to another climax.

When they were right there, cresting the final wave, and he couldn't hold out more than a few seconds longer, his

fingers found her sensitive nub. "Now, darling," he urged
her. They came within seconds of each other. Their climax—singular—totally destroyed body and mind. Just
like the first one had.

With the positions reversed this time, Molly collapsed
on top on him. Jonah hugged her tight, drowning in the
sweetness. "You probably don't want to hear this," he
said. "But I think I'm in love with you."

She raised up and looked at him in the face as though
she could read his expression in the darkness. He wished
he could read hers.

"Jonah you don't even know me!"

His heart sank at her note of despair.

"In other words, it's not a good idea."

"The chances of things working out for us are so
small." She kissed him tenderly on the mouth. Then she
laid her head on his shoulder again. He could feel the hot
wetness of her tears falling on his skin.

"God, I didn't mean to make you cry."

"I'm sorry."

"That's my line. I should have kept my mouth shut."

"I wish—"

She didn't finish the sentence, and Jonah was feeling
much too nakedly vulnerable to press her to finish it. He
was afraid of making her spell out her regret and say, I
wish you hadn't fallen in love with me.

"Don't feel bad on my account. Everything is large
scale down here in Big Bend country. I've probably blown
my feelings out of proportion. Notice I hedged and said
'I think I'm in love with you.'" His attempt at ruefulness
didn't quite come off.

Molly gave him another tender kiss before she eased
their bodies apart. Jonah made a second trip to the bathroom, finding his way without turning on a light. When
he came back and got into bed, she'd put her nightgown

back on. Jonah braced himself for her to say she'd changed her mind about letting him sleep with her, but she snuggled close in his arms.

"I wasn't sure whether you still wanted to stay," she said. "And if Joey should happen to wake up and call for me, I wouldn't have to fumble around for my gown."

"Does that happen often?" Jonah didn't respond to her first remark. It was pretty obvious he wanted to stay.

"Rarely. He seldom has nightmares."

"I wouldn't expect him to. He seems like a very secure, happy child. Let's take him horseback riding tomorrow."

"Oh, he would be thrilled."

Jonah relaxed at her answer. He hadn't blown spending the day with her and Joey tomorrow.

"I'm fairly sure I can make arrangements on short notice, but we'd better not clue him in on our plans prematurely."

"You're right. Children don't take disappointment well at all."

They talked a while longer until they both started yawning with drowsiness.

"I'm falling asleep on you, " Jonah finally said.

"My eyes keep closing, too. Good night."

"Good night."

They kissed.

I love you, Jonah told her silently as he nestled his jaw against her head again. In his half-asleep state, he could almost have sworn she was sending him the same message.

Light filtered into the bedroom when Jonah opened his eyes the next morning. He was lying on his back, and Molly was curled up beside him, her cheek pressed to his right shoulder. Her regular breathing warmed his skin. Only the fear of waking her kept him from pressing a kiss to her forehead and combing his fingers into her mussed golden hair.

His restraint caused an ache in his chest. So much for hoping that last night's revelation was a false alarm, Jonah reflected. At the age of thirty-five, after being married and divorced, he'd fallen in love. Suddenly all those love song lyrics and mushy valentines and romantic movies hit a real note instead of seeming exaggerated and rather ridiculous. Last night he'd experienced the difference between sex and lovemaking. And what a difference it was.

Now all the symbolism and poetry connected with marriage took on new meaning. The wedding rings, the vows that he'd spoken once without truly believing in them. There wouldn't be any sense of déjà vu in a second wedding ceremony with Molly as his bride. Jonah fantasized briefly and then gave himself a reality check.

A lot of those love songs were about unrequited love and broken hearts. Those lyrics hit home, too. Falling for Molly hadn't been a surefire road to happiness from the get-go.

She gave out such mixed signals. Go away, she'd said right from the start. But he'd read different, unspoken messages. I like you. I think you're interesting. I find you attractive. And last night either it was wishful thinking or she'd told him with her response to their lovemaking, I care about you. The fact that she'd allowed him to stay indicated she hadn't just consented to a one-night stand.

All those vague allusions to a checkered past obviously explained her conflicted behavior. What had she done that she figured would revolt him if he knew the details?

Or should he be asking, Who was she?

Jonah gazed soberly at the chest of drawers with the collection of photographs, including the snapshot of Molly and two-year-old Joey. If Betty Willie had shown it to him two weeks ago, he would have looked at it hard and said in a flat voice, "That's the older sister, Susan Gulley."

Would he have been making a correct identification? Was Molly Jones an assumed name?

A lot of the puzzle pieces fit to support that theory. They had all along. Lynette Jones sounded like a Karen Gulley type. The age was right.

He'd seen Karen a few times with Joel, seen her picture in Joel's room. If Molly had kept a picture of Lynette out on display, Jonah could have determined whether Lynette and Karen were one and the same. But there was no picture of Lynette, which he found very surprising considering Molly's avowed affection for her cousin, who was also Joey's biological mother.

Maybe the border patrol officer hadn't gotten confused when he'd remembered that Molly and Lynette were sisters. Then there was the business with Molly's buying silk flowers in the bright primary colors Lynette liked and the cross with the epitaph "Beloved Sister" having been adorned with a bouquet just as vivid before the sun had faded it.

Beside him Molly made a sound in her sleep and shifted her body, drawing up one knee and propping it on his hip and draping an arm across his chest. Now she really had him trapped.

And I wouldn't trade places with anybody in the whole world, Jonah thought, lightly covering her hand with his. He rolled his head sideways and looked at her. If anything the urge to plant a tender kiss was stronger than before. Whoever she was, whatever secrets she was hiding from him, he was in love with her.

Right now he could wake her up and question her and solve the mystery, once and for all. But he wanted her to trust him enough to take him into her confidence.

One thing Jonah was fairly sure about. Joey wasn't

Joel's son. If he were, it meant Molly had intended to let Jonah leave southwest Texas and be none the wiser. Surely she wouldn't have cheated him of the opportunity to know his own little nephew.

He would have trouble forgiving her for that.

Jonah put the thought out of his mind and focused instead on plans for the day ahead.

"How long have you been awake?" Molly asked, her voice muffled by his shoulder. She was regarding him with sleepy blue eyes.

"Thirty minutes or so, I guess."

"What time is it?"

"Quarter of seven." He kissed her on the nose. "I've been waiting patiently to do this. Now you can catch another nap. If you don't mind, I'll jump into your shower."

"Help yourself. I have disposable razors if you'd like to shave."

"Thanks. I would."

Jonah gave her another kiss, this one on the lips before he climbed out of bed. At the bathroom door, he glanced back and paused when he saw she was getting up, too. Fresh from bed and not fully alert, she looked not only sweet but alluring in the silk-and-lace nightgown.

"I'm going to check on Joey," she explained. "You haven't heard him, have you?"

"Not a peep. When you get back, why don't you join me in the shower? It's big enough for two, and I'll wash your back if you'll wash mine." Jonah didn't stick around for her to answer, but her intrigued expression didn't veto his invitation.

Joey was sound asleep, his covers barely rumpled.

Molly quietly closed his bedroom door and stood in the hallway, waging a battle with her conscience and judgment. Both told her she should go into the kitchen, brew coffee, let Jonah shower and dress in privacy.

There was no undoing last night with its glorious love-making. For all her guilt, Molly couldn't be sorry she'd been so weak. But today shouldn't be a continuation of last night.

With a sigh, Molly walked back into her bedroom to slip on her robe. She could hear the shower. Jonah would be standing under the spray, warm water coursing down his body. The image aroused a shiver of feminine plea-sure. Molly let herself imagine sliding a soapy washcloth over his broad shoulders and muscular back. Over his chest, his stomach...

A shower would be so refreshing. And this was a one-time temptation. There couldn't be any more nights like last night. Any more mornings like today. She had a whole lifetime ahead to content herself with memories of him as her lover.

Molly stripped off her nightgown.

"The little guy was still sacked out?" Jonah asked when he opened the glass door of the shower.

"Yes, I'll get him up after I'm dressed." She stepped in. Warm water cascaded down her body.

"Too hot? Too cold?" he inquired.

"Perfect."

"You use this pouffy net thing for a washcloth? And this body wash lotion for soap?" He was squirting creamy liquid onto the pouf.

"The body wash has a moisturizer that helps keep me from getting wrinkled like a prune in this dry climate."

"The manufacturers are missing a bet not using you for their ads. Your skin is beautiful. Here. Let me get your back first."

"That feels heavenly," she declared.

After he'd done a thorough job on her back and buttocks and even the backs of her thighs, he turned her around so that they faced each other. He smiled at her and she smiled back, her heart doing a flip-flop. He was rakishly handsome with his dark beard stubble and wet hair. And so dear to her.

"We sort of bypassed saying good morning, didn't we?" he said.

"I guess we did."

"Good morning." He kissed her on the mouth.

"Good morning." She raised up on tiptoes and kissed him.

"This thing is a little rough for here." He made a gentle circular swipe on her left breast. Molly's nipples jutted out into greater prominence. "See what I mean?" He touched both hard peaks with the pouf and then dropped it and squirted the soap wash lotion into his hand. "My hands won't be quite that abrasive."

Molly closed her eyes with the delicious pleasure of his palms massaging the silky foam on her breasts, her stomach, her hips. He squirted more lotion to work up a lather in her triangle of tawny curls. The strength went out of her legs when he slid a soapy hand between her thighs.

"I'm going to be squeaky clean everywhere," she gasped, clutching his shoulders for support.

"Now rinse."

She obeyed and then soaped up a washcloth and reversed roles.

"Rub harder," he told her when she was washing his shoulders and back and buttocks and enjoying the whole process thoroughly. "Like that. Great."

"Now you can turn around," she bade him at length.

He did, presenting her with a front view as gorgeous as the back. Neither of them had made mention of the fact that he'd been physically ready to make love since she joined him in the shower.

"Rub hard on your chest, too?"

"Yes, it's too much a turn-on when you're gentle."

She washed her way down past his stomach and paused to inquire playfully, "Hard down here?"

He grinned at her double entendre. "Take it easy down there."

Molly abandoned the washcloth and soaped up her hands to attend to the very intimate hygiene. Her pulse quickened with her own pleasure and excitement.

Jonah groaned and seized her wrists, stopping her ministrations. He pulled her under the spray with him. As soon as the soap had sluiced off his body, he gathered her close, hugging her. In addition to the rigid proof of his passion, she could feel tremors of need in his muscles. "Sweetheart, I want you right here. Now," he said, urgency in his voice. "But I'm not prepared."

"Yes, you are." She might have blushed with embarrassment over her own forethought—and felt sharper guilt, if she hadn't been so hotly aroused herself. "On the bath mat."

He wasted no time thrusting open the shower door to grab up the packet she'd brought from the bedroom.

Their mating was hurried and stripped to basics. It required his considerable strength because Jonah picked her up and held her entire weight. His deep penetration took her right to the brink of climax.

She gasped his name in ecstasy, and he understood her message.

"Me, too, darling—"

Her helpless cry mingled with his pained exclamation.

Afterward there was remarkably little awkwardness, and a great deal of sweetness. They kissed before they finished showering, with Jonah taking care not to scrape her with his growth of beard. He got out first and toweled off while Molly shampooed her hair. When she emerged, he was shaving.

This is so wrong of me, she thought as she dried her hair. But I can't be sorry. I'll always treasure the memory of last night and this morning.

More guilt attacked her when Molly and Jonah were getting dressed out in the bedroom. Opening a drawer in the chest of drawers for clean lingerie, she was reminded of her sister's picture hidden away in another drawer.

If there were only herself to consider, she would take it out and show it to him. But she had to think about the repercussions for Joey. And for Jonah himself. He was better off not knowing that he'd made love with Karen Gulley's sister. That he'd bought a cowboy hat for his own little nephew.

"I don't hear Joey stirring around," Jonah commented, pulling on his boots.

"We can have coffee before you leave, if you like. Then I'll wake him up."

He grinned. "You must have read my mind."

Out in the main room, he strolled over and studied the large studio portraits of Joey on the wall while she was making the coffee. "You can sure tell who's important around here," he said.

"I realize that decorators frown on using family photographs for artwork, but looking at Joey's pictures makes me happy."

"My mother took the same attitude. She turned our home into a photo gallery. All those pictures are packed away somewhere now, I suppose."

"You aren't certain what happened to them?"

"No. My father left a message on my answering ma-

chine a couple of months after he'd phoned to say he was
marrying Edna. He informed me in this message that he
was selling the house and I could have any pieces of furniture or mementos that I wanted. But I never responded
and didn't take anything."

"Weren't there things you would have liked to keep?"

"Yes, but between my anger and my grief, I really
couldn't bear to visit the house," he admitted. "It's probably just as well. I might have ended up having to rent a
moving truck. Mom was a real sentimentalist. She kept
every certificate and trophy. Even stuff like old toys and
books. All my trains I had as a kid were up in the attic."

"Maybe your father put all that in storage."

He shrugged. "I doubt it. And it doesn't matter. Is that
coffee ready?"

"Just about."

Her heart heavy, Molly took mugs down from a cabi-
net. The conversation had brought home once again the
futility of hoping she and Jonah could ever have a future
together. The past had left too many scars on his soul.

"Hey, I didn't mean to be gloomy," he said, accepting
one of the mugs from her.

At his suggestion they went outside on her patio.

"Jonah, we have to talk," she said after they'd sat in
chairs.

"Okay." He sipped his coffee.

"You made the comment last night at the community
center that I felt freer to be friendly because you were
leaving. Well, that's true."

"Now you're worrying about whether I'm still leaving
tomorrow."

"Are you?"

"Do you want me to?"

Molly couldn't get out a simple yes. "It would be best

for you to stick with your itinerary. Remember I suggested during that same conversation that you might have gotten over me more quickly if we'd gone ahead and had a brief affair? You agreed.''

"No, I didn't. I said something like maybe or perhaps. Are you telling me that you acted out of kindness when you opened your door to me last night?" His tone was gently chiding, not angry or baffled. Not even surprised.

"Of course not. But I'm not proud of myself in the least for not sticking to my principles."

"And if I'm debating about staying around longer, I shouldn't factor in having an affair with you. Right?"

Molly gazed at him in confusion. He still didn't seem offended. "Yes."

"Can I factor in friendship without sex? Or will I get the deep freeze treatment again?"

"Jonah, you don't want to be *friends!*"

"No, but I don't want to leave, either. I'll play by your rules, Molly." He glanced behind her, and a smile broke out on his face. "Well, look who finally tumbled out of the sack. Hi, partner."

Joey stood in the open doorway in his pajamas, regarding them with sleepy interest. He smiled in response to Jonah's greeting and walked over to stand between their chairs.

"Good morning, sweet boy." Molly hugged him, and Jonah ruffled his hair.

"We were beginning to wonder if you'd turned into ole Rip Van Winkle," Jonah declared.

"Who was he?"

"You don't know the story about Rip Van Winkle?" He patted his thigh and Joey responded by climbing up onto his lap.

Molly picked up her coffee again. Despite her anxieties,

she felt her heart lift with happiness in the moment. It was such a joy to listen to Jonah's voice, to observe man and child together. Both of them were so very dear to her.

After the story had been concluded, Jonah set Joey on his feet and stood up, announcing, "I need to go and make a phone call to a man who owns some horses. Then I'll be back."

"You will?" Joey said delightedly.

"Run and get dressed," Molly instructed her nephew. "I'll fix your breakfast."

"Can't I wait and have breakfast with Mr. Rhodes?"

"If he would like to have breakfast with us." She looked questioningly at Jonah.

He accepted with alacrity. "Sure thing."

Joey whooped with excitement and ran inside the condo.

Molly and Jonah followed at a more sedate pace. "You can change your mind about today," she said. "He won't be any the wiser."

"Why would I change my mind? I'm looking forward to today. See you in thirty minutes or less."

He bent his head, obviously with the intention of kissing her on the mouth. Anticipation rose up inside Molly. Then just before his lips met hers, he halted and changed course to give her a peck on the cheek instead. "Sorry. I have to reprogram," he said in gruff apology.

Molly tried to deal with her sharp dissatisfaction for the more platonic kiss. "This isn't going to work, Jonah."

"It's better than the alternative. Let's give it a chance, anyway." He squeezed her shoulder. "Everything's going to work out. Trust me."

With that earnest assurance, he departed, wearing last night's clothes and looking ruggedly handsome, the man who'd swept her off her feet quite unintentionally six years ago. The only man she wanted—and couldn't have—as her lover and her husband.

Trust me, he'd said, not having an inkling of the truth that would change his whole attitude toward her. With one blurted sentence of confession, Molly could wipe out any desire he would ever have to see her again.

Everything wouldn't—couldn't—work out.

Chapter Thirteen

"You did come back, Mr. Rhodes!"

From the kitchen Molly could hear Joey's words, with their artless revelation that he hadn't been entirely certain he could rely on Jonah's promise to return. At the sound of the door chimes, the little boy had run to open the front door.

"I said I was coming right back, " Jonah chided with an underlying serious note. "From now on, when I tell you something, you can depend on it."

From now on. The implication that he foresaw an ongoing relationship with Joey renewed Molly's multitude of regrets. How she wished that Jonah could be a permanent fixture in their nephew's life. But would Jonah want that himself once he'd associated Joey—and her—with the tragic death of his teenage brother and the subsequent deterioration of the Rhodes family?

"Did you talk on the phone to the man with horses?" Joey was asking.

"I sure did. And guess what? He's bringing three of his horses to a trailhead in the national park for you and Molly and me to ride."

"Oh, boy! Molly! Molly!" Shouting at the top of his lungs, Joey raced into the kitchen, reporting his exciting news that the three of them were going on a horseback excursion.

She managed to act enthusiastic for Joey's benefit. Jonah obviously wasn't fooled, but neither did he seem bothered about her lack of genuine enthusiasm.

"Hmm. Pancakes," he said, smiling at her. He'd changed into a clean shirt, but still wore his fancy belt with jeans and his Western boots.

"I hope my horse is gray like Smoky," Joey said during breakfast. He'd been chattering happily between hungry bites.

"Smoky?" Jonah said.

Molly explained, "He went horseback riding once on Chad Worthing's ranch, and the horse was named Smoky."

From Jonah's expression, his maple syrup had just turned sour in his mouth. "How many times did you go horseback riding on Worthing's ranch?" he asked.

"Just that one time. So I'm virtually a novice in the saddle." She could have disclosed that Chad had been more into piloting his airplane than into horsemanship, but she had no interest in glamorizing Chad or making Jonah jealous of him.

"You visited his ranch more than once, though," he stated tersely.

"Not all that frequently. Are you an experienced horseman?"

"Changing the subject?"

"Yes. To a much more relevant topic."

He sipped his orange juice, seeming to be mollified.

"In answer to your question, I did a lot of riding when I was a kid. One of my best buddies lived outside of town, and his father raised quarter horses. I'm hoping that riding a horse is like riding a bicycle, a skill you don't lose entirely."

"Today I'm gonna wear my cowboy hat." Joey, oblivious to the adult undercurrents, joined in the conversation.

"Maybe I'll wear mine," Jonah said. He looked endearingly sheepish as he met Molly's intrigued gaze. "I bought myself a hat at that same store in Presidio."

"We'll all three wear our cowboy hats," she declared, smiling at him.

Her mood lightened, and she felt the same buoyant happiness she'd felt earlier out on the patio. Nothing had changed to make the future any brighter, but why not make the most of the present? She resolved to put her conscience on hold and let herself enjoy the day with the child she adored and the man she loved.

After breakfast, they did a speedy cleanup, stacking the dishes in the dishwasher. Then they trooped outside and climbed into Jonah's truck. Joey was insistent that they use it as their mode of transportation, and Molly was completely agreeable. Jonah stopped by Flora's condo for his Western hat. He came out grinning and did an impersonation of a bowlegged cowhand that put Molly and Joey in stitches.

It was a beautiful, bright September day. The sky was a clear blue. A roadrunner dashed across the street in front of them as they set off on their adventure.

"I love this Big Bend country," Jonah said, glancing out his window toward the horizon, ringed with rugged mountains.

"So do I," she answered. "It has a stark beauty that never becomes monotonous."

"And such nice people live here. Real individuals. Life

is more low-key and down-to-earth than in urbanized areas, which suits me fine. So does the old-fashioned socializing that takes you back to pioneer days. Bingo games and potluck suppers.''

Molly wanted to ask whether he thought he might be happy living here in southwest Texas. Before she could phrase her question, Joey spoke up.

''The chili cook-off is fun.''

Molly and Jonah both cast indulgent smiles at the little boy, who'd evidently kept his silence long enough.

''I've been hearing about the chili cook-off and seeing the posters since I arrived,'' Jonah said.

''Oh, it's quite an event,'' she said. ''Gets bigger every year with more people participating and attending.''

''When is it?''

''The first weekend in November.'' More than a month away. By then he would surely have gone. But Molly wasn't going to think about that today.

''How far is the trailhead where the man's taking the horses?'' Joey asked. His child's attention had skipped on.

Jonah answered good-naturedly and didn't bring up the chili cook-off again or make any prediction about whether he would still be around for it.

They passed the road to the Mexican Village, and a few miles further on came to Study Butte. Jonah slowed down when they approached the RV park owned by the Hapsteads.

''According to Flora, no one has made an offer on this RV park,'' he remarked.

''That's what Sherrie Hapstead told me last night.''

''I might go and talk to them next week sometime and get a closer look at how well-maintained the place is.''

Molly didn't offer any response. Given the circumstances, how could she say anything positive about his investing in income property right here in Study Butte? It would be best for all three of them if he left with no ties of ownership connecting him to Big Bend country.

If only the circumstances were different....

"That lady has a sausage dog." Joey made another innocent intrusion. He was pointing toward a spry gray-haired matron walking a dachshund on a leash in the RV park. "I wish I could have a puppy."

"What kind of puppy would you pick out?" Jonah asked the little boy.

"A brown one."

Jonah chuckled with amusement, and Molly shoved aside poignant regrets that might spoil the day for her.

"I would name him Tramp," Joey said.

"My family had a dog named Tramp," Jonah recalled. "My little brother, who was about your age at the time, Joey, came up with the name. But it was appropriate, since Tramp was a stray who showed up at our house. My mother wanted him to call him Scraps because he had such an appetite for table scraps."

It was the first time he'd made any reference to his family and had sounded nostalgic rather than bitter, Molly reflected.

"Table scraps?" Joey was questioning.

"Leftover food after a meal."

They eventually arrived at the national park entrance, where Jonah paid a fee. It was still a forty-minute drive to their destination, but the time went by so pleasantly Joey didn't even get restless.

A guide was waiting for them at the trailhead with horses already saddled up. Jonah helped Molly mount after he'd boosted Joey up on a gentle mare. Then Jonah swung up into the saddle of his horse.

"All you need are chaps and spurs," Molly teased. He grinned with that engaging sheepishness.

She had brought her camera along. The guide obligingly snapped pictures before they set off at an ambling pace with him taking up the rear a little distance behind them.

"I'd forgotten it's a bumpy ride on horseback, even when they're just walking like this," Molly said laughingly.

"This is fun!" Joey exclaimed.

The rocky trail gradually climbed higher, affording them a magnificent view of vast desert plain dotted with scrubby trees and mountains forming a massive backdrop.

"Can't you just imagine a scene out of an old John Wayne movie?" Jonah said with a sweep of his arm indicating the scenery.

"Easily," Molly answered. "A sheriff with a star badge and his posse galloping after a band of bad guys dressed in black."

A short time later, Jonah drew her and Joey's attention to an eagle soaring above them majestically.

After a while they paused, and the guide handed out bottles of water for them to quench their thirst.

At noon they dismounted and sought the shade of a tree to enjoy a picnic lunch provided by the equestrian company. Molly was glad to stretch her legs. Joey took advantage of the opportunity to scamper about and release pent-up energy.

He was eager to climb back on his horse when the excursion got underway again. They continued along the trail another half hour or so before beginning the leisurely trip back to the trailhead.

Molly was quite certain that she'd never known this same serene happiness before.

"Time for bed, Joey," Molly said gently but firmly. "Tomorrow's a school morning."

The little boy yawned and got to his feet. He'd had his

bath earlier and come into the living room dressed in his pajamas. For the past thirty minutes he'd sat on the carpet, playing with miniature plastic figures of cowboys and horses while Molly and Jonah watched TV.

"Would you read me a bedtime story in my room, Mr. Rhodes?" he asked.

"Mr. Rhodes would probably like to sit here on the sofa and relax," Molly said.

"Why don't you sit here and relax, instead, while I go and read to him?" Jonah said, patting her knee. "Unless I'm overstepping boundaries."

"Don't be silly. You've just paid him a lot of attention already today."

"And thoroughly enjoyed myself. Okay, Joey, let's get you tucked into bed, partner."

He stood up, and the little boy slipped his small hand into Jonah's big hand.

"How about a good-night hug and kiss?" she said.

Joey sweetly obliged. Then he led Jonah toward the hallway.

"Oh, my aching thigh muscles," Molly groaned, stretching out on the sofa. She felt pleasantly lazy and drowsy after the day spent mostly outdoors.

Today was over and it was time to get a fresh grip on reality, but Molly's fears seemed to have been blunted by all the laughter and fun. Tomorrow she would wake up with a clear perspective and the false haze of well-being would be gone, she told herself, closing her eyes.

I won't fall asleep. I'll just rest for five minutes...

"Looks like I'd better tuck you in, too." Jonah's voice penetrated Molly's deep slumber. She forced her eyes open and saw him standing beside the sofa, gazing down at her. His expression was tender and indulgent.

"I must have taken a catnap," she said, sitting up. Her

body seemed as sluggish and uncoordinated as her mind was groggy. "Did Joey go to sleep?"

"He konked out in the middle of page three."

He sat down beside her and gathered her into his arms. Molly burrowed her cheek against his shoulder, mumbling in half-hearted protest, "This is against the rules, Jonah."

"I just want to hold you a few minutes before I go home." His hand gently stroked her hair. "I would massage your stiff thigh muscles, but that's probably not a good idea."

"No, a massage isn't a good idea. I mean, it sounds absolutely heavenly, but..." Her voice drifted off into a sigh.

"You wouldn't care to spell out your reservations about us, would you? I think I can deal with any dark secrets you tell me."

"I don't believe you can."

"Sorry. I didn't mean to pressure you." He rubbed the top of her head with his chin. "I'd better tell you goodnight, pretty cowgirl."

Reluctantly she pulled away when his arms loosened. Part of her wished he'd been more insistent that she confide in him. "Today was such fun, Jonah. Joey had a ball."

"He's a neat kid."

"You know you would make a wonderful father."

"File that thought away for future reference." He kissed her on the cheek and then rested his cheek against hers.

Molly ached to feel his mouth on hers. After tonight, she wouldn't allow herself to be placed in this vulnerable position. This was her only chance to taste his passion one last time. "You can kiss me good-night," she said.

"I just did, sweetheart," he answered in a husky voice.

"Remember those rules you mentioned a moment ago?" He sat back.

"I guess you were able to reprogram." Molly's words came out sounding like a complaint.

"Hey, be fair," he chided her. "I can't win if I kiss you and get turned on. Either I leave here frustrated as hell or else I take you to bed. Tomorrow morning, you would be showing me the door again, right? Sex obviously isn't the key to earning your trust."

Molly looked away, ashamed of her behavior. "I apologize. I must seem terribly inconsistent, running hot and cold."

He grazed his knuckles along her jawline. "Your hot stage is something to write home about," he said lightly and rose to his feet. "And that's my exit line."

Molly got up, too, and accompanied him to the door, where he gave her another chaste kiss.

"How about having lunch with me tomorrow?" he asked. "I'll come by the shop, say about noon?"

She couldn't form the word no and ended up nodding.

He bade her a cheery good-night and departed.

What a great day, Jonah reflected as he drove to Flora's condo. His memory flashed images of Molly and Joey that brought a smile to his face. Also a warm feeling to his chest.

He not only was crazy in love with her, but the little boy had claimed a big chunk of affection, too. No way was Molly getting rid of Jonah, not after the past twenty-four hours.

It was going to require iron self-control to be around her and play a platonic role, especially if she tempted him like she had tonight. Man, had he wanted to kiss her, really kiss her. But the next thing he knew he would have been caressing her body. She would have responded and gotten sexually aroused, too. Knowing that had made restraint fifty times more difficult.

The next time Jonah made love with her, he wanted to be in her confidence. When passion cooled, he didn't want her lying in his arms, thinking guilty thoughts she felt she couldn't share with him. To that end, he could wait a week. Maybe two. God, he hoped he didn't have to hang in there longer than two weeks to open up communication.

Those instincts he'd been heeding since the night he met her told him it would be free sailing once she unburdened her conscience. Molly didn't just have the hots for him. She cared about Jonah. Once she stopped trying to put on the brakes, she might fall as crazy in love with him as he was with her.

What a heady thought that was.

At Flora's condo, Jonah considered his two main options for filling the time before going to bed. He could watch TV or he could log on to the Internet, check his e-mail and do some research on the RV park business. It didn't take much deliberation for him to decide on the latter.

Minutes later he'd booted up his laptop computer and opened up the e-mail program. No new incoming messages, but the e-mail from his father sat there in his in box, unanswered. Jonah called the message up on the screen. A second reading stirred fresh turmoil, and once again he postponed sending a reply.

Instead he switched to an Internet browser and was soon engrossed in his research into the RV park business. When he turned off the computer a couple of hours later, he'd gathered a wealth of information and had a list of questions to ask the Hapsteads if he went to talk to them during the upcoming week.

''Time to wake up, sweet boy.''

Joey opened his eyes and smiled at her sleepily. He

looked around his room and then glanced toward the door before asking, "Is Mr. Rhodes here?"

"No, he went home to his condo last night."

"Is he coming for breakfast?"

At her negative reply, his face fell.

"Joey, yesterday was Sunday. Today's a weekday, and we're back to our normal routine," she explained gently. "It's okay for you and me to enjoy Mr. Rhodes's company while he's here on vacation, but he'll probably be leaving soon, going to other places."

"Will he come back?"

"This isn't where he lives," Molly pointed out, evading a yes or no answer. "Now hop up and get dressed for school. As a special treat, I'll fix you a blueberry waffle for breakfast. Won't that be yummy?"

He nodded glumly.

Molly didn't doubt that the little boy would have been more excited about a bowl of cereal served with Jonah seated at the breakfast bar with them. She completely empathized. She could barely manage to keep up a cheerful front herself with the burden of responsibility for the little boy's mood weighing heavier than her guilt.

What was done was done. Molly hadn't been strong enough to resist making love with Jonah. Now he'd changed his plans and wouldn't be leaving this morning. Consequently, she was still faced with the dilemma of whether to tell him the truth or keep him in the dark until he got discouraged and moved on.

What to do?

The answer was the same as it had been from the very beginning. Joey's welfare came first. Whether she kept her silence or not depended on what seemed wisest for him.

The key revelation wasn't *Jonah, I'm Karen Gulley's sister.* It was *Joey is your nephew.*

There was no point in making that revelation unless Jonah would want to be an uncle to his brother's little son. Molly had to make that judgment call.

Despite all Jonah's assurances that he could deal with her past, the truth would kill his romantic interest in her. Refusing to share that past with him would eventually have the same effect. Molly couldn't win, but maybe Joey could.

"How are the thigh muscles today?" Jonah asked. He'd shown up promptly at twelve for their lunch date.

"They've loosened up, but I walked stiff-legged when I first got up this morning." Molly's steps were unbelievably light as she walked along beside him toward the Cactus Café. For all her pessimism about their future together, it was such a joy to see him, to be in his company.

"I don't suppose Joey had any physical complaints."

"None. What about you?"

He admitted with a rueful grin, "I had a twinge or two."

Inside the café, he guided her to a table.

"By the way," he said after the waitress took their order, "Joey asked me last night if he and I could have another computer session with my laptop. I didn't give him a straight yes or no because I wanted to get your permission first."

"It's okay with me."

He looked both surprised and gratified that she hadn't acted reluctant. "Good. What about this afternoon?"

"If that's convenient for you. Any time after five-fifteen."

"I'll come about five-twenty then. Some of my friends in Atlanta have young children who're very computer literate. I thought it might be fun and educational for Joey to meet a couple of kids his age through e-mail. I'll help him do the typing, of course.''

"Jonah, what a neat idea. Speaking of e-mail, have you gotten any more messages from your father?" she asked hesitantly.

He shook his head. "I doubt I'll get any more unless I send a reply."

"So you haven't answered."

"I haven't figured out how to answer. Part of me wants to say, 'Take your olive branch and shove it, Dad. Don't bother me again.'"

Molly winced. "That's so harsh, Jonah."

"Yes, it is," he agreed soberly. "I haven't sent that message yet. Not so long ago I would have." He picked up her hand and squeezed it. "Maybe being around you and Joey is having a mellowing effect on me."

Their food was served and they talked of other subjects. After lunch Jonah walked with Molly back to the shop. He'd obviously put the troubling conversation about his father completely out of his mind, but Molly wasn't able to. She kept thinking about it all afternoon.

If he took such a hard line with his father, he certainly wouldn't adopt a more forgiving attitude with her. Right was right and wrong was wrong with Jonah. There was no gray territory, no mercy for weakness or human mistakes.

That kind of mind-set made Molly extremely doubtful that Jonah would welcome the discovery that Joey was his nephew. She doubted Jonah could look at the little boy, knowing his birth mother was Karen Gulley, without bitterness welling up and corroding any pleasure in the blood tie.

Jonah made a round of visits after leaving Molly. He dropped in on Flora at the real estate office and informed her of the change in his plans. She seemed genuinely delighted to hear he was staying longer.

Next he went by Casey's gas station and filled up his gas tank. He ended up chewing the fat, to use the station owner's expression, for nearly an hour. Then he dropped by Tim Perry's place of business and was greeted like a long-lost friend. Tim asked whether Jonah had given any more thought to buying the Hapsteads' RV park, and Jonah answered yes. Once again the other man offered to introduce him to the owners.

"I don't really have time this afternoon," Jonah said, looking at his watch.

Tim was tied up the next couple of days, so they settled on Thursday morning.

Jonah arrived back at his rented condo about four o'clock. That damn e-mail from his father was bugging him. He might as well go ahead and answer it, he decided.

At quarter of five, Jonah was gazing with frustration at the blank e-mail form on the screen. He'd read his father's message a dozen times, started his reply twice that many times and ended up deleting what he'd written. The conversation with Molly kept playing over in his mind and he kept seeing her wince and say, "That's so harsh, Jonah."

"Here goes again," he muttered and began typing.

Hi, Dad,
Needless to say, I was surprised to hear from you.
Yes, I've been divorced a year. No need to be sorry.
My marriage to Darleen was a mistake. So was my
career choice, over the long term. Again, no regrets.
I resigned from Dunton & Meyers to do some traveling. I'm down in Big Bend country in southwest
Texas. I met a very special woman here and like the

area so well there's a good chance I'll settle here permanently.

All in all, I'm fine. Hope you're in good health.

Jonah

After skimming his message and determining that it might not be warm and friendly, but neither was it "harsh," Jonah clicked on the Send button and then sat back. He felt drained but also surprisingly good.

His mood only improved when he drove to Molly's condo and saw her and Joey outside. She was watering the cape jasmine shrubs, and the little boy was plainly keeping an eye out for Jonah. His face lit up when he spotted Jonah's truck and he grinned a big, excited grin.

Now if only Molly would smile at me the same way, like I'd just made her day by showing up, I'd be the happiest man in the world, Jonah found himself musing as he got out.

Joey came dashing to the truck, shouting his hello. Jonah acted spontaneously, picking him up and tossing him into the air the way he'd done with Joel when he was that age. The small boy squealed his delight.

"That was fun!" he exclaimed.

Jonah took his cue and tossed him up again, but this time instead of setting him down, he held the little boy aloft and then maneuvered him onto his shoulders.

"Oh, wow!" Joey said. "Look, Molly! Look how high up I am!"

She was already looking. Jonah couldn't really read her expression, but she didn't seem alarmed for Joey's safety.

"How's the view from way up there?" she asked.

"I can see the roof of our condo!"

Jonah walked over to her. "Hi," he said, the one word conveying how glad he was to see her.

"Hi. Did you have a pleasant afternoon?"

"It just got more pleasant." He leaned down, carefully balancing Joey, and kissed her lightly on the mouth. Out here in public with Joey as an audience it didn't seem necessary to restrict himself to a peck on the cheek.

"You kissed Molly!" Joey observed from his perch, snickering.

"Do you mind?"

"No! You can kiss her again!"

"Thank you. I don't mind if I do."

Molly didn't avert her head, although she had ample warning. Jonah couldn't resist letting his mouth linger on hers slightly longer with the second kiss. His pulse was racing when he straightened up.

"No more of those," he said huskily. "Not under the present house rules, anyway."

Molly drew in her breath, making him suspect her pulse had speeded up, too.

They stayed outside awhile longer with Joey clearly enjoying the attention of both adults as he romped and played. Then Jonah retrieved his laptop from the truck, and the three of them went inside.

Joey was intrigued by the notion of sending messages to other children in a distant city over the computer. He dictated the e-mails. Jonah typed them, then let him peck out his signature and click on the Send button.

Molly moved about, busying herself with tasks like doing laundry. Jonah kept tabs on her and noticed that Joey did, too. No child could be more attuned to a birth mother than he was to her, Jonah reflected, mentally applauding when the little boy would summon her over to read the e-mail in progress.

"We're having hot dogs tonight for supper, Jonah," she said when she started meal preparations in the kitchen. "Shall I cook a couple for you?"

"That would be great," he said, quick to accept the casual invitation.

"I like hot dogs," Joey stated.

"I figured you did, since Molly was making them," Jonah told the little boy fondly. "I'll bet she cooks your favorite foods most of the time."

"Except when we eat at the Cactus Café or somewhere else. She can cook your favorite food tomorrow night," the little boy offered generously.

"Why don't I fix supper for the three of us instead and give Molly a break? After all, she works all day."

"Okay. Tomorrow night Mr. Rhodes is cooking supper, Molly."

"I heard," was all she said.

After supper the evening followed the same pattern as the previous evening with Joey having his bath and appearing in his pajamas, looking clean-scrubbed and boyishly sweet.

"I know a good program on TV," he said to Jonah. "It has these funny kids that are all different colors."

Molly dryly supplied the name of the well-known children's program on a cable network. "Mr. Rhodes is your company. You should let him pick out a TV program he wants to watch," she admonished the little boy in a mild tone.

"That sales pitch of his kind of sold me on Joey's program," Jonah said with amusement.

With a big smile of satisfaction, the five-year-old sprawled on his stomach in front of the TV and was immediately absorbed in the cartoon action. Occasionally he laughingly recapped the action for the adults. Jonah got a kick out of watching him watch the program. Plus, Molly had sat down on the sofa, not as close as Jonah would have liked but within touching distance if he stretched out his arm. He could turn his head and look at her, which he did often with pleasure.

No way did Jonah find it a boring situation.

When Joey's bedtime came, the little boy didn't put up an argument. "Who's going to read me a bedtime story?" he asked, looking torn.

"Molly is," Jonah said. He'd decided in advance not to usurp her maternal role tonight. "But I'll take a good-night hug."

Joey came over at once and wrapped his small arms around Jonah's neck while Jonah was hugging his sturdy body. The surge of affection was strong.

Molly handed him the TV remote before the two of them left the room. Jonah flipped through channels, hardly focusing on his choices for viewing. He was asking himself, Could I adapt to a family routine with Molly and Joey? The answer was a resounding, but qualified yes. He could be very happy with a family routine that allowed him full latitude as her lover and marriage partner and Joey's surrogate dad.

Maybe that knowledge should have made him patient, but it didn't. He wanted to hurry up the process of clearing away her anxieties about their future together.

"We had to read the same book you read last night," Molly reported on her return.

The fifteen minutes she'd been gone seemed more like an hour to Jonah.

"Did you get past page three?" he asked.

"All the way to page ten tonight. Would you like for me to make some coffee?"

"No, I'd like for you to sit on my lap and be friendly."

"Jonah, what are you *doing?*" she gasped in surprise when he reached and grasped her by the waist and brought her down on his lap.

"Giving us both a little incentive to come to an understanding. Kiss me, Molly.'' He cupped her neck with one hand, applying gentle forward pressure, which she didn't resist.

''But last night you said—''

''That was twenty-four long hours ago....''

Their lips met. Jonah groaned at the warm contact.

''You took me off guard. I wasn't expecting this,'' she murmured, drugged pleasure in her voice robbing the words of any emphasis.

''We'll just kiss, like this,'' he murmured back. They were both moving their heads to kiss at different angles. ''And touch. And hug.'' His hands caressed her back.

''You'll go home frustrated.''

''But happy. And optimistic.''

Her hands were stroking his shoulders, and now their mouths were parting and her tongue was flirting with his. Jonah was drowning in the sweet pleasure and ignoring the hardening of his body, which didn't understand that they weren't engaged in foreplay.

''Even kissing…is different,'' he said, carrying on the conversation punctuated by kisses, wet kisses now. Their tongues were coupling.

''Different?''

''When you're…in love.''

He could hear her silent protest. Jonah, don't say that. Don't bring up love and make me feel guilty. She turned her head and pressed her cheek against his, her arms hugging him tightly around the neck.

''It isn't all one-sided, is it, Molly?''

''Jonah, please—''

''Is it?''

''No.''

Exultation flushed away most of his disappointment that he'd had to drag the admission out of her.

"You know what?" he said lightly. "I'd like that cup of coffee after all."

Her body sagged with relief that he hadn't pursued the subject of their feelings for each other and what those feelings would or wouldn't lead to.

Chapter Fourteen

"Supper at my place tomorrow night, don't forget."

"Don't worry," Molly said. "Joey would remind me if I did happen to forget."

They stood in her foyer. She'd made coffee and they'd watched TV until he'd announced he'd better go home since tomorrow was a workday for her. There had been no more kissing. He'd shown that iron self-control of his.

"What about your laptop? Don't you want to take it?" she asked.

He shrugged. "You can just bring it when you come for supper, if that's not too much trouble. We'll check for e-mail for Joey."

"It's no trouble." Had he answered his father's e-mail yet? Molly had been plagued by that question during his and Joey's session at the computer.

Jonah's mind had moved on, as his next words indicated, "By the way, I'm making a run to Alpine tomorrow. Can I pick up anything for you or run any errands?"

"Nothing that I can think of. You're not going all the way to Alpine to buy groceries to cook a meal for us, are you?"

"I'll be buying some other things, too." From his expression, he was keenly anticipating making his purchases, whatever they were. "Good night. Dream some nice dreams and include me in them." He kissed her on the lips and then gave her a quick, hard hug.

Molly had been braced for him to say, I love you. She was grateful when he didn't and yet filled with longing to hear those words she wanted to speak herself.

After he'd gone, she rinsed the coffee cups before turning out the lights in the kitchen. In the hallway that led to the bedrooms, she paused to open Joey's door quietly. Normally she contented herself with glancing inside to make sure he was sleeping peacefully, but tonight she entered his room and eased over to sit on the edge of his bed and gaze at him lovingly.

Was she any closer to deciding whether to tell Jonah he was Joey's uncle? Yes, she was. Seeing them together this afternoon and evening had tipped the scales toward revealing the truth and hoping for the best outcome. Molly would give herself more time to be sure and give Jonah that additional time, too, to become even fonder of his little nephew.

She wasn't just buying a few more days as Molly Jones, the southwest Texas woman he'd fallen in love with.

"Can I do something?" Molly asked, watching Jonah place hamburger patties on the grill portion of the stove.

"No, just keep me company." He glanced into the living room where Joey had flopped down on the carpet to watch a program on a children's cable channel. "There's something I wanted to discuss with you."

She lowered her voice as he had done. "What?"

"I want the three of us to go camping this weekend."

"Camping? Joey and I don't even have sleeping bags."

"Yes, you do. I bought them today. And an extra tent, too. I already had everything else we need. Don't look so skeptical. It'll be fun," he added.

"Jonah, you shouldn't have spent all that money! Sleeping bags and tents aren't cheap."

"I can afford it. I may not be as loaded as your rancher, but some women might consider me well-heeled enough to be a good catch."

"You know darned well most women would consider you a good catch without a big bank account."

"I had to fish hard enough for that stroke to my ego," he said with a rueful grin. "The camping trip is on then?"

"Maybe in another couple of weeks you could take Joey by himself. I've had no camping experience whatever."

"That's all the better. I won't have to be wondering whether you're remembering sitting by a campfire with some other guy."

"When I'm with you, I never think about any other guy," she stated simply.

"Never?"

"Never."

He abandoned tending his hamburgers long enough to come over to where she stood and kiss her. "In case you're bothered by sleeping arrangements, you and Joey can share a tent and I'll bunk by myself," he said. "Okay?"

Molly gave in, despite her reservations. He'd gone to such expense and seemed so bent on taking them both camping with him. "Okay."

Her agreement earned her another kiss.

"How far apart will these two tents be?" she asked.

"Not very far apart at all. We'll pitch them side by side. You won't have any cause to feel nervous or afraid."

He hadn't exactly read her mind. Molly was imagining lying in a sleeping bag, with him just a few yards away. It would be about as relaxed for her as the two of them occupying separate beds in a motel room.

Jonah was flipping the hamburgers over. "We'll drive into the national park on Saturday morning and set up camp at a campsite. Stay overnight and come back on Sunday. That'll be long enough for our first camping trip."

It would almost certainly be their only camping trip as a threesome, because Molly would tell him the truth before the following weekend. There was virtually no doubt left that she had to reveal he was Joey's uncle. After that, he probably wouldn't want her along on any kind of excursion. She just prayed his interest in spending recreational time with his nephew wouldn't also die.

"Hey, don't look so anxious," he chided. "We'll only be an hour away from here. If you're miserable, we'll pack up and come home. I promise. Supper's on. These hamburgers are done."

Jonah waited until after they'd eaten to tell Joey about the weekend camping trip. The little boy reacted with such excitement that Molly was glad Jonah had been so insistent on including her and she wouldn't miss Joey's introduction to camping. She would join in the fun wholeheartedly. There would be time enough for feeling depressed later, when Jonah no longer gazed at her with love in his eyes.

Molly and Joey left shortly before the little boy's bedtime. Jonah walked them out to her automobile and gave each of them a hug and a kiss. When Molly's turn came, her lips clung to his. She wanted to pull his head down for another lingering kiss. And another. And another.

"Lunch tomorrow?" he asked while she was struggling with herself not to ask him to visit her later on.

"Only if I'm buying." He'd already invited them out to supper tomorrow night.

"Whatever."

He kissed her again, and she started up the engine, thinking about those two tents side by side.

He hoped she would confide in him soon. Maybe on the coming weekend, when they would be sitting out under the stars after Joey had gone to sleep.

Jonah watched the taillights of Molly's SUV disappear as she rounded a curve in the street. Since Saturday night when he'd first squarely confronted the possibility, he'd gotten more used to the idea that she might confess that she was Susan Gulley. But he still hoped there was another explanation of the physical resemblance between her and Susan.

Maybe she was a relative and knew the whereabouts of both Gulley sisters. Maybe that was the secret bothering her. If it was, Jonah was ready to swear that he wouldn't bother them. Not that he would ever want any contact with them. He couldn't imagine sitting down to the table with them at a holiday get-together, for example.

Maybe Molly wasn't a relative and had never heard of the Gulley sisters before he showed up. Maybe she just happened to be Susan's physical double. There were lots of instances of that sort of thing. Jonah remembered a newspaper story about a man who was Richard Nixon's spitting image.

He kept coming back to the fact that the only similarity between Molly and Susan was that superficial likeness in their facial features, coloring, height and figure. Could a woman undergo that big a personality transformation?

Unlikely. But if she turned out to be Susan, he could

deal with it. If she wasn't Susan, he couldn't believe she had done anything so terrible he couldn't deal with that, too.

Jonah just wanted her to confess and get the load off her chest so they could move on. And he didn't want to have to drag the confession out of her.

"Be patient," he told himself for the umpteenth time as he went back inside the condo.

Earlier when he'd checked his e-mail, there had been a couple for him in addition to those from several children in Atlanta replying to Joey's e-mails. Jonah hadn't taken the time to read his messages. He would do so now, he decided.

A new message had come in. Another e-mail from his father. Jonah braced himself and read it first. He hadn't gotten far before he realized it wasn't from his father, but from Edna Rhodes.

Dear Jonah,
Your father doesn't know I'm writing you. I wanted to tell you that it meant the world to him to hear back from you. Thank you for not saying anything to hurt him and make him feel even more a failure as a father than he already does.

He blames himself for what happened with Joel and for your mother's mental breakdown, too. He thinks he failed all three of you. I don't know whether you realize it, but he was close to a mental breakdown himself toward the end of your mother's illness. I ran into him in the supermarket one Saturday morning and inquired about his wife. He broke down into tears. I felt so sorry for him and asked him to come over to my house and talk. He did, and after that he came often. My husband had been dead several years, and I was lonely, too. As a Christian woman, I can say without shame that nothing wrong went on.

He's a good man, Jonah, and his family meant everything to him. Then one by one he lost his youngest son, his wife and then his oldest son. He's very proud of you. He never stopped bragging about you to other people.

I want to thank you again for writing him back.

God bless you.

Edna Rhodes

Jonah sat there, feeling like he'd been kicked in the groin. His composed, dignified father had started crying in a supermarket? "No way," he muttered. But his cynicism couldn't hold up to the down-to-earth honesty of Edna's e-mail. Every sentence rang with humble sincerity.

So why hadn't his father turned to Jonah if he was at the end of his rope? Because his elder son was away in Atlanta, busy with his own life. Too busy and self-absorbed to put himself in James Rhodes's shoes. His father had deserved that Jonah would give him the benefit of the doubt, but instead Jonah had been quick to criticize and judge.

As for Edna, she deserved a quick response to her e-mail and an apology in person one day. Jonah clicked on Reply and wrote:

Dear Edna,
Your e-mail really set me straight. In retrospect, I'm deeply sorry I wasn't there for my dad when he needed my support. Fortunately you were there for him.

Thanks for the insight.

Jonah

The next message was just as heartfelt and surprisingly easy to word.

Dear Dad,
I hope you'll forgive me for my lack of compassion and understanding during that difficult period in our family after Joel died. I had no right to stand in judgment of my own father. You deserved whatever peace and happiness you could find.
  Give my best to Edna.

Love, Jonah

Jonah hit Send and felt more at peace himself. Molly would thoroughly approve of both e-mails, he reflected.

Loving her really had changed him for the better and tempered a hard, judgmental streak in his character, whether or not Lynette and Karen were one and the same. Now he could even factor in Karen's background and cut her a little slack. It undoubtedly had been rough being raised in foster homes and not growing up with loving parents who were respected members of the community, like Jonah's parents. Rough on her and her older sister, who'd apparently never gotten in any trouble with the law before she'd fled her hometown with Karen after the pharmacy break-in.

Yes, he'd softened considerably and lost a lot of bitterness, being in love.

Jonah meant to tell Molly about the e-mail communication between him and his father and Edna, but the next day at lunch the subject didn't cross his mind. There were too many other things to talk about. Nor did he think about telling her that evening. Once again, the present was too immediate.

On Thursday morning he went with Tim Perry to meet the Hapsteads, who were, as everybody said, nice people.

They answered all of Jonah's questions about their RV park business to his satisfaction. He told them candidly he was an interested prospective buyer, but needed more time to decide whether to tie up a large amount of money in a business in southwest Texas.

Molly's reaction to learning that he'd met with the Hapsteads and toured the RV park disappointed Jonah terribly. Once again, she showed no enthusiasm for the idea of having him around permanently.

Love also made a guy awfully vulnerable when it softened him up, Jonah was discovering.

"Like this, Mr. Rhodes?" Using a small, child-size mallet, Joey hammered a tent peg that Jonah had already partially driven into the ground.

"That's perfect, Joey. Give a couple of taps to these other pegs, and we'll be all set."

"Okay." The little boy followed the instructions with an air of importance that made Molly's heart swell even larger with her love for him. And for Jonah.

He'd purchased the small mallet in Alpine, having obviously thought out this whole process of setting up camp with a five-year-old. It had taken him twice or maybe three times as long as necessary because he'd let Joey help. He'd praised the little boy, building up his confidence, and never showed the slightest impatience.

"Two sets of hands aren't always more efficient, are they?" she'd remarked with gentle irony earlier.

Jonah had flashed her a smile.

Molly had offered her assistance when they first arrived at the campsite, but he'd answered, "Joey and I can handle this, can't we, Joey."

"You just watch, Molly," the little boy had said.

Absolutely no doubt remained. She had to reveal to Jonah that Joey was his nephew. But not on this camping trip. Molly wanted today and tonight and tomorrow with both of them. Tomorrow night after they'd returned to the condos she would tell Jonah. That would be soon enough.

"I wish it was night!" Joey exclaimed when he and Jonah had finished. "Which tent am I gonna sleep in?"

Jonah indicated the tent on the right. "You and Molly can share that one."

The little boy wasted no time before ducking under the flap to explore. He soon stuck his head out. "It's big enough we could all sleep in here," he announced.

"Somehow I knew that was coming," Molly said, meeting Jonah's eyes.

"It would be close quarters for the adults, Joey," he said. "Anybody else ready for some lunch?"

"Me! I'm hungry!" Joey scrambled out.

Jonah's distraction technique had worked on his nephew, but not on Molly. She was still wrestling with the imagined temptation of crawling into Jonah's sleeping bag with him. Did he sleep in the nude when he was camping? Her curiosity quickened her pulse.

After they'd eaten, they climbed into Jonah's pickup and drove to the Rio Grande Village, another camping area with a store and visitor center. Nearby was an easy, but rewarding nature trail, which took them along the bank of the Rio Grande and eventually up to the crest of a hill.

"Wow!" Joey exclaimed as they caught their breath and gazed at the panoramic view.

Afterward Jonah bought them ice cream treats at the store before they headed back to their campsite. Joey had brought along some toys, including a miniature football. Jonah and Molly played catch with him. Then they relaxed in folding chairs while he entertained himself, spinning an adventure about cowboys and Indians and rustlers.

At suppertime Jonah lit his camp stove and cooked a

hearty skillet dish of pork chops and diced vegetables. Molly's contribution to the meal consisting of serving portions of green salad from a plastic bag and pouring a dollop of dressing. They ate at the picnic table. Jonah insisted on washing the few dishes himself. When he'd completed the chore, he and Joey visited the men's bathhouse to take showers while Molly visited the women's bathhouse.

By the time the three of them returned with fresh-scrubbed faces, dusk was fast giving way to darkness. Jonah lit a lantern that provided a soft glow.

"Now can we go to bed in our sleeping bags?" Joey asked, obviously intrigued with the novelty.

The little boy had had an active, exciting day. It didn't surprise Molly that he fell soundly asleep before she finished telling him a story from one of his storybooks that they both knew word for word from memory.

When she emerged from the tent, Jonah was standing a short distance away, close enough that she knew he'd been listening to her voice. He turned toward her, and Molly went straight into his arms. He hugged her close and she hugged him around his neck. The embrace seemed a culmination of the wonderful, companionable day.

"Tired?" he asked, caressing her back. Delicious sensations wrecked her contentment.

"No." Molly lifted her head and raised up on tiptoe to kiss him on the mouth.

He turned his head aside after their lips had parted and nuzzled his cheek against hers. She felt, as well as heard, his indrawn breath. "Sweetheart, I can't get up and go home tonight," he said. "If we start kissing, we'll end up making love."

"I assumed we would make love tonight." She had counted on it. "I thought the extra tent was for privacy."

"Maybe on our next camping trip. By then I hope we'll have things resolved between us." Slowly he released her. "Let's sit and talk. I'll turn out the lantern so we can get the full effect of the stars."

Molly bit her lip as he walked away from her toward the picnic table, but she couldn't keep back words that boiled up out of her sharp disappointment. "Isn't this a kind of blackmail? Either I tell all or we can't make love?" Appalled at herself, she said swiftly, "I'm sorry. Don't even answer. Actually I am rather tired. I think I'll call it a night. That sleeping bag felt awfully soft and comfortable just now. Good night."

She retreated inside her and Joey's tent, tears stinging her eyes. She'd so looked forward to making love with Jonah at least one more time. Looked forward to lying naked against him, touching him intimately, feeling him inside her.

"Molly, are you all right?" His voice came from immediately outside the tent. He sounded apologetic and concerned.

No, I'm not all right.

"I'm fine. And I'm not angry at you," she added. "I admire you for being strong."

"Won't you come out and talk to me awhile?"

"We can't really talk freely, Jonah, not yet." Her deception ruled out her entire past life. It formed a big wall between them. "I'll tell you what you want to know tomorrow night after we get back."

"Only if you're ready to confide in me. I'm not using sex to blackmail you. This has been pure hell—" He broke off. "If you need me, I'm right here close by."

I need you now, always....

"See you in the morning, Jonah."

His sigh was audible. "Good night. You have a flashlight in there, remember. You don't have to get ready for bed in the pitch dark.''

"Thank you for reminding me."

Good night. I love you.

Molly removed her shoes and got inside the sleeping bag fully dressed. She lay there wide awake and miserable. It was much too early to be going to bed.

Starlight filtered through the mesh flap. Joey's breathing was soft and regular. After what seemed an eternity, quiet rustling sounds from the adjacent tent told her Jonah must have retired for the night, too.

Would his love turn to contempt and dislike when he learned her full identity? She prayed that it wouldn't, but had to prepare for that heartbreaking outcome.

There was less doubt now about how he would react to the discovery that Joey was his nephew. Jonah wouldn't reject the little boy. His fondness would deepen into a lifelong bond.

Also gone was the fear of a custody battle. Molly didn't believe that Jonah would try to take Joey away from her. Nor would he join legal forces with his father for such an attempt.

Her back ached from lying so rigidly. Molly turned on her left side. The slow, heavy pumping of her heart marked the passage of seconds and minutes. What time was it? she wondered, turning over to her right side after she judged a whole hour must have gone by.

The suitcase she'd packed for her and Joey was there in the tent. Inside it was a satin nightshirt she'd brought along to sleep in. It was more modest than her silk-and-lace nightgowns. Maybe if she undressed and put it on and got more comfortable, she might eventually fall asleep.

Desperate enough to try almost anything, Molly sat up and shed her clothing in the darkness. Shivering with the coolness of the air against her bare skin, she groped for the flashlight and turned it on. Jonah was surely asleep by now, but she was careful not to direct the beam toward his tent as she searched in the suitcase and retrieved the nightshirt.

Before she could put it on, she heard Jonah's voice just outside, inquiring, "Is anything...wrong? God, Molly..."

He was looking through the mesh flap.

"No, nothing's wrong. I hope I didn't wake you up." She was slipping on the nightshirt while she answered him.

"I wasn't asleep."

Molly turned off the flashlight, plunging the tent into darkness again. "At this rate, Joey may be the only well-rested one among us tomorrow morning."

"Come and lie down with me."

The request held raw longing. Without a word Molly got up and went to him. Jonah didn't speak either until they were cocooned inside his sleeping bag, his arms holding her tightly against him.

"We can hear Joey if he makes a sound. I heard the click of your flashlight."

"He hasn't even turned over." She pressed a tender kiss to his shoulder. "You're covered with goose bumps." He was naked except for his briefs.

"That's not from the cold. You can't imagine how beautiful you looked just now. Like a vision." His tone was reverent. "Marry me, Molly."

"Ask me tomorrow night, and I'll say yes."

"Whatever you tell me isn't going to make any difference."

"I want to believe that so much," Molly whispered.

"Believe it."

Hope bloomed inside her, putting her terribly at risk.

They kissed, and the whispered conversation soon became intimate lovers' talk. By the time Jonah coupled their bodies in an urgent union, Molly almost did believe him.

Chapter Fifteen

"I'm not sleepy. I want to stay up and play," Joey complained.

"You'll be sleepy tomorrow. Now tell Mr. Rhodes good-night and come along to bed," Molly answered firmly, trying to be patient with him. He'd been uncharacteristically whiny on the drive back from the national park, and his behavior hadn't improved since they'd arrived at her condo.

Maybe he was picking up on undercurrents from the adults, she reflected. She'd gotten more tense by the hour as the day wore on, and Jonah wasn't his most relaxed, either.

"Good night, Mr. Rhodes."

"Good night, Joey. Do I get a hug and kiss?"

The little boy trudged over, his lip poked out. Molly watched, shaking her head. Of all times for him to show a bad mood, just when she was about to reveal to Jonah that he had a nephew.

True to his word, Joey didn't fall asleep quickly, like he usually did. Molly ended up reading him three storybooks before his eyelids got heavy and he finally kept his eyes closed.

Jonah had gotten up from the sofa and was gazing out at the darkened patio when she rejoined him. Something about his posture suggested that he'd been pacing the living room.

"Children can't always be angelic," she said. "He had such a stimulating weekend that coming home was a letdown."

"Kids have radar," Jonah said quietly. "He probably picked up vibes between us."

Molly took in a deep breath. "Well, I guess the hour of truth has come. Excuse me while I get something from my bedroom that will pretty much solve the mystery."

He was still on his feet when she returned. He walked over toward her, and she handed him the photograph she'd taken from its hiding place. "My sister."

Her nerves reached the snapping point while he studied the picture, gripping it so hard his knuckles showed white. "So Lynette Jones and Karen Gulley are the same person, after all," he said, handing it back to her. The possibility had obviously occurred to him.

"You were hoping they weren't," she said.

"Yes, I won't lie to you."

It did make a difference in his feelings for her that she was Karen's older sister. Molly could read the turmoil in his expression as he looked at her.

"I just saw you that once, but how could you have changed so much?" He shook his head in bafflement. "Susan was shy. She—you—blushed every time I looked directly at…" His voice drifted off as he struggled with the pronoun choice.

"I hadn't dated much, and you were so good-looking

you might have stepped straight out of my daydreams. Of course, in my daydreams I was the woman I am now. The woman I became when I changed my name to Molly Jones. The transition wasn't that difficult once we'd left Georgia and left our background behind. I knew we couldn't go back after Karen discovered she was pregnant with Joel's baby.'' She stopped her narrative. He was staring at her, obviously stunned. And, dear God, also obviously horrified.

"Joel was Joey's father?"

"Yes. I thought you would figure that out immediately.''

"But he was using birth control. I know it for a fact.''

"Then they slipped up. Karen wasn't dating anyone else. She was crazy about Joel.''

Jonah was shaking his head slowly. "You were going to let me drive away from here last Monday not knowing Joey was my brother's son?''

"You're so bitter about Joel's death, Jonah. I thought it was better for you not to know, if you couldn't take pleasure in having a nephew. You have so many wonderful qualities, but you can be very hard.''

Nothing she was saying was having any effect other than adding anger to his mix of strong emotions.

"If I hadn't hung around because I was so nuts about you, I never would have had an inkling, would I? Didn't it ever occur to you that Joel's family had a right to be a part of Joey's life?'' he demanded. "That Joey had a right to be a part of our lives?''

"Of course, it occurred to me! Try to look at things from my viewpoint, Jonah. I had no way of predicting what you and your parents would do if I notified you of Joey's existence. You might have sent the law to arrest my sister. You might have tried to get custody of Joey. I couldn't take those chances.''

"Your sister has been dead for three years. She was in no danger from the law when I showed up three weeks ago. And I was outspoken about admiring you as a parent from the very first. You had no legitimate reason to keep Joey's identity a secret this long."

"Maybe I was overly cautious. I hope you'll forgive me, but if you can't, please don't hold my actions against him," Molly implored. "He's a sweet child and he could be a joy to you."

From his reaction she might have slapped him hard in the face. "Whoever you slept with last night, it sure the hell wasn't me. You think you have to convince me that Joey could be a joy to me?" He turned on his heel and headed for the foyer.

"Jonah, don't go away angry. Let's talk."

"We'll talk tomorrow. I've had all the discussion I can handle tonight."

She followed after him. "Does that mean you'll still be here tomorrow?"

"Damn right, I'll be here. The two of us are going to tell Joey he can stop calling me Mr. Rhodes and call me Uncle Jonah."

Relief swept through Molly. He didn't intend to pack up and leave right away. She'd been so afraid he might, and they wouldn't hear from him for days or weeks while he went through an adjustment period and sorted out his feelings about Joey.

"We'll expect to see you sometime after we get home then," she said.

He acquiesced silently and didn't respond to her forlorn good-night.

Molly still clutched her sister's photograph. After the sound of Jonah's truck had died away, she carried the photograph back to her bedroom and placed it on the chest of drawers. She felt numb and empty.

It's done. It's over.

Jonah's anger would cool, and he would be civil toward her by tomorrow afternoon. But he would look at her with different eyes now. Maybe he might still desire her. In his own way he might still care for her, but he wouldn't want to marry her. He'd proposed to Molly Jones not Susan Gulley alias Molly Jones.

"Molly's on a coffee break," Delores told Jonah.

He thanked the saleswoman and walked to the Cactus Café. From the doorway he spotted Molly. She wasn't taking her break alone. Roger Mason, the park ranger, sat at a table with her, drinking in the sight of her along with his coffee. Jealousy twisted inside Jonah like a sharp two-edged knife.

He strode over toward the table, galled at himself because he was drinking in the sight of her, too, realizing how much he missed her. Molly turned her head and saw him. Surprise flashed across her beautiful face. Then she forced a smile, that same regretful, resigned expression in her blue eyes. It was the way she'd greeted him the next afternoon after their big blowout a month ago. In less than twenty-four hours she'd written off their relationship as a lost cause.

That had hurt more than anything else. More than her low opinion of him as a man and a human being. She'd actually thought she had to beg him to give himself a chance to love Joel's little boy, whom he already loved. "So you'll be here tomorrow?" she'd asked, revealing that she hadn't expected him to hang around. God, he'd asked her to marry him the night before.

"Hi, Jonah," she said.

"Molly. Mason." He nodded at the park ranger.

"Hey, Jonah. Pull up a chair." Roger gestured half-heartedly at one of the empty chairs at the table.

"I hate to interrupt, but I need to talk to Molly," Jonah said tersely.

"Roger, would you mind?" she asked.

"No, I have to get back to the park, anyway." The ranger rose and reached for the bill that had been torn from a tablet.

Molly covered it with her hand. "Please. The coffee's on me today." Both her tone and her smile conveyed apology.

Jonah jerked out the chair across from her and sat down while Roger was objecting. Molly stood her ground pleasantly, and the ranger departed.

"So the coffee's on you *today?*" Jonah's attempt at irony fell flat when his emphasis came out sounding grim.

"Roger has bought me coffee on a number of occasions. We didn't have a coffee date today," she added.

"Are you dating him?"

"No, I'm not dating anybody. Would you like coffee?" When he answered in the affirmative, she signaled a waitress, who brought over a coffeepot and a mug. After the woman had served them and modified the bill, as instructed by Molly, she left. "You don't seem to have a problem with letting a woman pay," Molly said. "I really like that about you. It's not a big thing, but I always get annoyed when a man can't just say thank you, like we women do."

Jonah was stirring sugar into the dark brew. "You didn't seem annoyed with Roger." It bothered him that he hadn't picked up on her reaction.

"I was, though. I guess I haven't shed all of my phony Southern politeness."

"You struck me as the least phony woman I'd ever met, which is one of the things I liked so much about you."

"When you met me the second time, you mean. At the fund-raiser."

"At the fund-raiser," he said, conceding her clarification of his statement. "You were even up-front about the fact that you had something to hide. Another thing I like a lot is that you don't play one guy against the other. In my experience, that's damn rare." Jonah realized he'd switched to present tense—*like*. "Just now, for example, you didn't make me sit here and wonder whether you've got something going with Mason."

"Being honest is second nature to me. I hated lying to you. And I felt horribly guilty when we made love. I don't blame you for being angry and resentful, but couldn't we bury the hatchet and be friendly, for Joey's sake? He's very confused. One day he sees us hugging and kissing and then suddenly we go for weeks avoiding each other and barely speaking."

"You expect me to be friendly toward you?" Jonah repeated incredulously.

She sighed. "I guess it's asking a lot. You said you needed to talk to me."

He ignored the reminder. "Damn right it's asking a lot. You don't even know what's eating at me, do you?" Her bewildered expression egged him on. "It's the fact that you could live with the two of us being friendly after what we had together."

"What choice do I have but to live with it? What do you expect me to do? Jump off a cliff? If my background has taught me anything, it's that the world doesn't come to a stop because I'm depressed and unhappy. I still have a child to raise, a job to do."

"I expected you to hang in there with me, to fight for us. I crawled way out on a limb, Molly, and you only edged out far enough that you could retreat when the tree started to shake." She still looked only faintly comprehending. "Forget it," Jonah said. "It's a stupid analogy. The reason I needed to see you was to ask if I could take Joey to Georgia to meet his grandfather. How about the Thanksgiving holiday?"

Her body language rejected his proposal even before she answered him, a note of alarm in her voice. "If his grandfather wants to meet him, let him come here. No, Jonah, I don't want you taking Joey out of state."

"For God's sake, you're not afraid I won't bring him back? I own a business down here now and a house." He'd not only bought the Hapsteads' RV park, but he'd purchased their stucco home built up on a bluff with a view of the Rio Grande.

"I'm just not comfortable with the idea. Are you and your father even on good terms?"

"We're on very good terms. We e-mail back and forth and talk occasionally on the phone."

"I'm so glad to hear that."

"Didn't Joey tell you he'd spoken with Dad a couple of times?"

"Yes, he always gives a report on his visits, but I didn't question him about whether you seemed friendly with his grandfather. Joey's main conversation is about the puppy you got him. He adores Tramp. Maybe when he's older, you can take him to Georgia."

Jonah clamped his jaw but he couldn't keep back the alternative plan that had popped into his head. "You could take some vacation time and come, too. After all, Columbus is your hometown as well as mine."

"Sure, I could drive Joey around and point out the foster homes I lived in. Columbus has very few nostalgic memories for me to share with him, Jonah."

"That's the first hint of bitterness I've ever detected in you," he remarked.

"Bitterness is pointless. I decided that early on, probably before I was old enough to define the word."

"Was that about the same time you decided you were better off not trusting anyone?" he asked.

"Don't pity me, because I don't pity myself. I didn't have an ideal upbringing, but I wasn't a little match girl, either. Karen and I were never abused. We had the essentials, and we had each other. We were never split up except for a brief period when I turned eighteen."

"At that age you were on your own?"

"Yes, I got a job and found an apartment I could afford. Karen wasn't allowed to live with me at first, but she kept running away, and eventually the foster care people consented." She glanced at her watch. "I have to get back to work. I'm sorry, Jonah, but the trip to Georgia at Thanksgiving is out."

"Okay. I had some doubts anyway about separating him from you for five or six days," he admitted.

"If your father and his wife decide to come here, Joey can spend Thanksgiving day with you and them and spend some additional time, too. Just let me know."

"You've been very flexible and cooperative about giving me time with him."

"I'm so pleased for him that you're settling here and the two of you can be close." She put money on the table and rose.

Jonah got up, too, and accompanied her outside, where she said goodbye and walked away from him along the boardwalk with her sexy, purposeful Texas Woman stride she'd developed along with her air of independence that was never an in-your-face brand of feminism. He liked both of those things about her, too, along with a thousand other things.

All she would have had to say was, "I'd like to see you," and he would have said, "When? Tonight?" If she cared enough at some point to ask him, "Do you still love me?" he would answer, "Yes, of course, I still love you."

Dammit, if it wasn't important enough for her to find out, what was the point in volunteering the obvious?

"Why don't you come, too, Molly? We had fun the last time. Remember?"

"Joey, I'm not invited this time. Uncle Jonah wants to take you camping by yourself."

"You're invited. I asked Uncle Jonah if you could come, and he said you could if you wanted to."

"It's not right to tell fibs," she admonished.

"I'm not telling a fib. He said that."

Molly paused in the act of folding a pair of jeans to pack in the duffel bag Jonah had bought for his nephew, just one of numerous gifts. She was hearing her own voice from a few days ago. He always gives a report on his visits. He referring to Joey. "Could you repeat Uncle Jonah's exact words?" she asked.

"He said 'Molly can come if she wants to.'"

"That's not the same as an invitation, and Uncle Jonah will be here to pick you up in thirty minutes. Next time I'll ask him ahead of time myself. Okay?"

"You promise?"

"I promise."

"Okay." His voice was glum.

"Which pair of pj's did you want to bring?"

"My old ones with the cowboys and Indians. Or my new ones with race cars that Uncle Jonah bought me."

As she'd intended, the ever-important decision of choosing his night wear served as a distraction. His excitement built up, and when the doorbell chimed, he raced to open the door. Molly picked up the duffel bag off his bed and followed less hurriedly, although she was no less

244 CHILD MOST WANTED

eager herself to see Jonah. She could hear the greetings between uncle and nephew.

"Hi, Uncle Jonah!"

"Hi, Joey. All ready to go?"

"Uh-huh. Molly's not coming on this camping trip, but next time she will. She's gonna ask you ahead of time."

Molly stopped in her tracks, waiting for Jonah's response.

"Is that right?" he said noncommittally.

"Joey, don't forget your clothes," she called out, her voice hollow.

In the foyer she handed the duffel bag to Jonah, then knelt to give Joey a hug.

"We could wait while you pack your stuff," he said wistfully.

Jonah had gone on outside, but was easily within earshot. He said nothing.

"Run along and have fun," she urged. "Remember to show Uncle Jonah your packet of school pictures so that he can pick out several."

He brightened and trotted after Jonah, who was striding toward the pickup.

Molly closed the door, took a deep breath and went directly to her bedroom, where she got out a small suitcase. There wasn't any great hurry. It would take them at least an hour to set up camp once they arrived in the park, giving her plenty of time to stage a surprise appearance before they went off hiking. But her courage might fail her if she dawdled.

The drive seemed interminable. It was nerve-racking to obey the forty-five-mile-an-hour speed limit after she'd entered the national park and the two-lane highway stretched on mile after mile after mile through desert plain. Molly's palms felt sticky on the steering wheel, and yet her mouth was bone dry. She kept sucking in deep breaths.

The closer she got to the campground the more anxious she became. Jonah had told her he planned to choose a site in the same area reserved for tent camping where the three of them had camped five weeks ago. However, there might not have been an available site. What if he had gone elsewhere? The park was huge. She could spend all day tracking them down.

That fear dissipated shortly after she'd turned off on the narrower road that wove its way through the wooded campground. She soon spotted Jonah's silver pickup. Enormous relief washed through her, but it lasted only seconds before panic hit her.

What if she was making a total fool of herself by just showing up like this? What if Jonah's coolness wasn't just a cover-up for hurt? Sure, he'd acted jealous of Roger this past week, and today his eyes had given her figure a hungry once-over, but he might not be happy to see her at all.

You'll find out.

Molly pulled up behind his pickup, taking in the scene. Jonah was crouched down, driving a tent peg into the ground. Joey stood by, holding his small mallet. He glanced and saw her getting out. A big smile broke across his face.

"Molly!" he shouted, and came running toward her. "Molly! You came!"

Jonah looked over his shoulder, then slowly got to his feet. His larger mallet dropped out of his hand. Aside from surprise, she couldn't read his reaction other than to rule out hostility.

Her heart was knocking against her ribs. She gave Joey a hug before getting her suitcase out. He pranced beside her, clapping joyfully. "Oh, boy! You're spending the night! Molly's spending the night, Uncle Jonah!"

Not a word from Jonah. Nor had he taken so much as a half step toward her. Molly walked to him, carrying her suitcase. She set it down and held her arms wide in a theatrical gesture. Her voice, though, held no bravado, as she said, "Here I am, way out on a limb."

Suddenly his expression wasn't impassive anymore.

"I figured the apron strings pulled too tight."

He'd thought her mother's instincts had motivated her.

"No, the heartstrings. I'm not expecting to just kiss and make up. I realize it can't be that simple and easy."

"Why not give it a try?"

Molly didn't need any more encouragement. She moved up close to him and framed his face with her hands, holding his gaze. He let her draw his head down. Their lips met, and instantly his arms came around her, crushing her against him.

"I love you," she whispered.

"I love you," came his low, fervent answer.

Joey giggled and acted as boyish commentator, exclaiming with delight, "Molly kissed you, Uncle Jonah, and you're hugging her!"

Jonah loosened his embrace and held out a hand to him. "Come here and let's make this a three-way hug." Joey promptly responded, and his uncle bent and lifted him up. Grinning broadly, the little boy hooked one small arm around Molly's neck and the other around Jonah's.

Her heart overflowed with love for both of them, man and child.

"Are we a family, like that song says on my TV show I watch?" Joey asked.

"I'd sure like for us to be," Jonah said, looking into Molly's eyes.

"I can't think of anything that would make me happier," she said.

Her world was complete in a way she'd never dared to dream it would ever actually be.

It was later when Jonah and Joey had resumed setting up camp that the little boy brought up practical considerations. "Molly doesn't have a sleeping bag," he commented. "You didn't bring hers, Uncle Jonah. And we just have one tent."

"I guess all three of us will have to sleep in the same tent, won't we?" Jonah said. "And Molly can share my sleeping bag, if she doesn't mind having me as a bed partner."

Her pulse quickened as she met his gaze. "Molly definitely doesn't mind having you as a bed partner."

Joey appeared perfectly satisfied with that solution. "You can both tell me a bedtime story."

After lunch they hiked the Lost Mine Trail, which had markers along the way identifying distinctive Chihuahua Desert vegetation like the agave or century plant that spent years storing up nutrients to produce a single stalk topped by a splendid flower. Rustic benches at intervals provided ideal spots to appreciate the increasingly spectacular views as they ascended higher and higher. Joey rode Jonah's back the last quarter mile when the trail grew steep and more challenging.

There was no question about whether the effort expended was worthwhile when they emerged onto a rocky summit with an elevation of almost eight thousand feet and the whole universe seemed spread out before them, awesome and pristine. Jonah and Molly sat side by side on an immense boulder, her arm around his waist and Joey anchored safely on his lap.

This moment is absolutely perfect, she thought. Then

Jonah turned his head and kissed her tenderly, creating another moment just as perfect.

Molly still had much that she wanted to say to him, but there was no sense of an urgent need to tie up the threads of understanding. They'd already established the basic communication with very few words. They loved each other and were committed to having a future together and being parents to the nephew they both loved.

"You remember asking me that day we drove to Alpine if there had been a special man in my life?" Molly asked.

She and Jonah were at the picnic table, their legs extending outward. Joey was sound asleep in the tent. Molly wouldn't have traded the hard bench for the most luxurious sofa, not with Jonah's arms around her.

"I don't think I want to hear about him tonight," he said. "Let's just talk about us."

"I am talking about us. When I said yes that day, I was referring to you. It was love at first sight for me when we met. No man during the past six years measured up to you."

"Yet you kept trying to chase me away after I turned up here."

"My first priority was protecting Joey. I made a judgment call that was wrong when I decided that you wouldn't ever be able to put the tragedy of Joel's death behind you."

"I can see how you concluded that. I came across as being bitter and unforgiving in some of our conversations."

"Also, it became apparent to me that you turned a blind eye to all the clues to my identity because you didn't *want* me to be Karen Gulley's sister."

"For about the last week before you finally confided in me, I had faced up to the possibility."

"You had? You mean you proposed to me thinking I might be Susan Gulley?"

"Yes. But still holding out hope that you weren't," he admitted honestly.

"If only I'd known—"

He completed her sentence. "We wouldn't have spent these past five miserable weeks apart."

"You'll have to be patient with me, Jonah. There probably is just a remnant of a little match girl inside me."

"I finally began to grasp that, once you opened up and gave me some insight into your background. I want to know more. And one of these days I would like a tour of our hometown from your perspective."

"How about Thanksgiving? We can take Joey to meet his grandfather."

"I'm assuming they will already have met before then. I figure Dad and Edna will make a trip here to attend our wedding. We are getting married before Thanksgiving, right?" He kissed her lingeringly on the lips as though persuasion were actually needed.

"You want us to have a bona fide wedding, not just a marriage ceremony?"

"Sure. Don't you?"

"Yes, but you've been through it all before."

"Believe me, nothing about this wedding will be old hat." He gave her another kiss that threatened to distract them both from further discussion. "I'll leave the details up to you," he went on, "but I vote for a Texas-style reception. We'll invite Flora and Casey and Tim and all our other friends. Maybe Gloria can cater it."

"You read my mind." Molly brought his lips back to hers before she said, "I thought I would keep my assumed name. I've been happier as Molly Jones."

"Okay," he said after a split pause. "More and more women are doing that these days."

His reply momentarily baffled her until she realized he'd misunderstood. "I meant keep my first name, Molly," she clarified. "I definitely want to be Mrs. Jonah Rhodes."

He brought her onto his lap. "Good. That has a nice ring to it. Speaking of rings…"

They postponed the subject for the time being in favor of more kisses that quickly became passionate, and caresses that aroused hot desire. Suddenly Jonah stopped.

"What is it?" Molly asked.

"Something just occurred to me. I didn't come prepared to make love."

"How do you feel about a pregnant bride?"

"I'm all for it," he said without taking even a few seconds to reflect.

"Me, too."

They picked up where they'd left off.

Much later, when they were snugly zipped into his sleeping bag and had told each other good-night, Jonah murmured drowsily, "It just hit me that I never sent a check to Betty Willie. I need to do that Monday."

"Betty Willie?"

"The woman in Amarillo who put me on your trail. I owe her ten thousand dollars."

"That's very honest of you, Jonah. Though I'm not surprised."

He sighed a deep, contented sigh. "Worth every penny and more…."

*   *   *   *   *

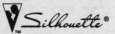

Available July 1999 from Silhouette Books...

AGENT OF THE BLACK WATCH
by BJ JAMES

The World's Most Eligible Bachelor:
Secret-agent lover Kieran O'Hara was on a desperate mission.
His objective: Anything but marriage!

Kieran's mission pitted him against a crafty killer...and
the prime suspect's beautiful sister. For the first time in his
career, Kieran's instincts as a man overwhelmed his lawman's
control...and he claimed Beau Anna Cahill as his lover. But
would this innocent remain in his bed once she learned his
secret agenda?

Each month, Silhouette Books brings you an
irresistible bachelor in these all-new, original
stories. Find out how the sexiest, most-sought-after men
are finally caught....

Available at your favorite retail outlet.

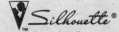

*This June 1999, the legend
continues in Jacobsville*

Diana Palmer

LONG, TALL TEXANS
EMMETT, REGAN & BURKE

This June 1999, Silhouette brings readers
an extra-special trade-size collection
for Diana Palmer's legion of fans.
These three favorite Long, Tall Texans
stories have been brought back in
one collectible trade-size edition.

*Emmett, Regan & Burke are about to be led
down the bridal path by three irresistible women.
Get ready for the fireworks!*

**Don't miss this collection of favorite
Long, Tall Texans stories…
available in June 1999
at your favorite retail outlet.**

**Then in August 1999 watch for
LOVE WITH A LONG, TALL TEXAN
a trio of brand-new short stories featuring
three irresistible Long, Tall Texans.**

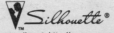